T0247555

God's Kettledrum

A Novel

Kenneth Kuenster

God's Kettledrum

A Novel

Addison & Highsmith

Addison & Highsmith Publishers

Las Vegas ◊ Chicago ◊ Palm Beach

Published in the United States of America by
Histria Books, a division of Histria LLC
7181 N. Hualapai Way, Ste. 130-86
Las Vegas, NV 89166 USA
HistriaBooks.com

Addison & Highsmith is an imprint of Histria Books. Titles published under the imprints of Histria Books are distributed worldwide.

All rights reserved. No part of this book may be reprinted or reproduced or utilized in any form or by any electronic, mechanical or other means, now known or hereafter invented, including photocopying and recording, or in any information storage or retrieval system, without the permission in writing from the Publisher.

Library of Congress Control Number: 2022941229

ISBN 978-1-59211-177-0 (hardcover)
ISBN 978-1-59211-241-8 (eBook)

Copyright © 2022 by Kenneth Kuenster

Part One

If Ada had not arabesqued (my appropriate word) into my life I wouldn't have known her twin. That's what was to ultimately draw me from my usual role of detached narrator.

Ada and Blain, twin A and twin B. Two redheads.

I first met Ada when she arrived at the studio to audition for a new piece our dance company was developing. We had run an ad in the city's free weekly paper, and this being Portland there was an outpouring of very young candidates. Ada was fifteen and not shy.

"I'll dance with your company and I don't care whether you pay me or not but I have one condition, I'm into movement, not body shows so don't put me in anything skimpy." She said this before her audition. When I said I hadn't seen her dance yet, she shrugged. She'd brought a CD and I was surprised to see it was Eric Satie's spare piano nocturnes. I expected something current, confrontational, with an attitude to match her own. When the music began, note by note picking precise sounds out of the cube of space we inhabit, she absorbed these sounds and released them in movements as light as a Matisse drawing. Her face which moments before held a pink defiant stare was now a porcelain pale sky powdered with a small constellation of freckles across her nose. Her movements were quick and light as though it were she striking the keys. She left the floor on one note and descended on the next. It was as though Satie had watched her dance and had written the music in celebration. Her speed ranged from the futile gestures of a drowning swimmer to an Olympic sprinter turning in circles as she crossed the floor with dazzling speed. She finished with a surprisingly sensual descent to the floor as though the wood was her lover and it was essential to have every surface of her squirming body caress the boards. When the music ended she lay on her side, her deep red hair splayed out in a circle around her head and her hands out, fingers spread. We waited for her to stand but she didn't. After a few moments, I knelt down close to her face. Her eyes were closed. "Well?" she said softly.

"I won't ask you to wear anything skimpy," Ada nodded.

Within seconds of the start of her audition, all the dancers in the company were watching her intensely, each of us knowing that this was a display of raw talent not likely to appear often out of the blue.

Afterwards, I watched her moving around the studio talking with various people. Even at fifteen, Ada who obviously thought of herself as outside the realm of expected behavior was now meeting people who were more outside than she, and I couldn't tell if she was pleased or intimidated. We're a diverse crew and it would be more accurate to characterize us as a theater company than a dance company since we are even on occasion referred to as a circus or less kindly more as a zoo. Everyone received Ada with open-ended interest except Rasputin who only wanted to see some of her body because after watching her audition he had some compelling ideas about how to tattoo her. Rasputin is rich in visual skills and poverty-stricken in social skills. When he got too close to her Ada shoved him in the chest with enough force to take his breath away. It was more like a boxer's body blow and Rasputin was leaning over with his hands on his knees glowering at her. People smiled at her fiery red spirit and were quick to draw her into rehearsals of various movements we'd been working on. She was a fast learner and there was an immediate and spreading feeling of appreciation at having her in our midst.

I'm the director of this theater troupe, and I'm the narrator of this tale. I have a name, Stephen Dunken III, but I refer to myself as Narrator, as do the members of our company. I personally fund this avant garde performance group. I was the final descendant of the Chicago Stock Yard Dunken Meat Packing family. My only connection to the company was the required rite of passage when I was sixteen and had to spend that summer working at doing one week of horrible smelly scary chores for each of the workers on their vacation. As a result, I did virtually all the jobs in the company. The only exception was the work of Adam the sticker. All day he stood by as hogs went past him, hung upside down on a conveyer belt and stuck them in the neck with his long-pointed knife. His workstation was a scene of screams and blood. At the end of the day, he leaned his raincoat, stiff with coagulated blood against the wall.

I offer this information so I won't be perceived as a typical inheritor of wealth. However, I was able to study dance, music, choreography, painting, theater art, and more. I was pretty good at everything but not exceptional at anything.

Here is my philosophy of creativity, or more to the point, the art of working with live performance. Then you may draw your own conclusions about me and the veil I choose to place between myself and those around me.

Let's say my art is like a cauldron, and my performers, or more accurately, my participants, are like found natural ingredients meant to complement and provoke each other, and I am the alchemist, or at my best, the sorcerer. The magic that results is the theater piece of the moment. I don't have an end 'soup' in mind in the beginning, I let the colliding of personalities determine the direction of each piece and often too, its conclusion. Let's say, I'm a choreographer of accident. And by accident I mean everything from just oops! to epiphany, to calamity, and anything else juicy and ready to happen.

Everyone in my company, and you'll meet them all soon enough, are found people, each with an extreme talent of a kind, combined with an element of mystery I don't want to solve, just want to use. And there's usually a fairly serious flaw, which always comes in handy. You may say I'm the ultimate opportunist, and to that, I can only agree.

So, considering all the above you'll soon see why Ada was such a gift from the gods of provocation.

For the next week, Ada appeared each morning barely able to contain the explosion of dance energy she would release during the day. She was responsible for a pandemic edge of rejuvenation infecting the whole company. Even the toughest of our people could not help but smile at the effect of her presence. Prior to her arrival, we had reached a stubborn plateau in our current piece, with equal parts negating equal parts. I found myself watching her carefully, studying her, looking

for ways that this unpredictable bright red spice could agitate the mix in the cauldron.

The piece we were working on was evolving intuitively. I had begun with an
arbitrary passage of music and movement and let that provoke what followed. It is
my method and my style and is how I see life unfolding, always a response to
something, rarely an initiation of anything, a reluctance to give answers but a need
to ask questions. It's a peculiar contradiction that I am unable to remove myself
from and at the same time is a perpetual threat to my need to stay just out of reach
of life.

The home of our troupe is a discontinued brewery with crumbling brickwork
and two huge copper vats long since retired from the creation of an Oregon mi-
crobrew. I purchased it and had it whitewashed and converted into a perfect rehearsal and performance space. It had an interim life as a church/convent but that's
another story, although that was the source of two of our company's players, Father
Joseph and Sister Agnes.

The opening passage of our new piece began with the copper vats being struck
by a six-foot pole bound with a tight clump of padding at the end. The sound has
no equivalent in an orchestra. Someone said if God had an orchestra, this would
be his kettledrum. It is an outsize sound, and because each of the vats has a different pitch our percussionist went back and forth between the two. This obsessive
drummer was Father Joseph, a fallen-away Catholic priest/aimless Buddhist. As
always he wore a black suit with a clerical collar of fluorescent orange, the color
deer hunters wear. After a few introductory moments of pounding on the vats (he
calls this his Vatican sonata, but usually, he's totally humorless), a female voice
entered the arena with a note matching the note of the last vat strike and coming
in softly just as the vat note was fading. It then increased in volume and richness
until every eye in the room was glistening. This is a fact, not a figure of speech.
The only person who ever remained consistently dry-eyed was asked to leave the
company. We all thought he was a bad omen.

Our contralto is Mojobe, from a Wodaabe tribe in Niger. Her voice is part
Maria Callas and part primal moan. She is well over six feet in height and has shiny

black skin, shiny black hair, and a face so sculpted it's like black marble. Her hair is a complex configuration of thin dangling dread locks interwoven with chains of silver. Her dress is white with purple piping along cuffs and hems and has clusters of horizontal stripes of bright hues here and there. The dress is fashioned with an opening to reveal her bare abdomen, which is a maze of hard raised scars in elegant geometric patterns.

I watched Ada as she stood listening to Mojobe and biting her lower lip to keep control. When Mojobe ended on an extended high howl, a spotlight came on shining onto the thirty-foot high ceiling, illuminating a corner of the upper space where a platform held a figure wearing a silver leotard with a crimson cross spanning her chest. She stood on her toes and released herself holding a rope, swooping down in an arc into the brewery like Archangel Gabriel as a comic book character. On her third traverse of the brewery she was caught by Father Joseph, or to be accurate she collided with Father Joseph even though he was running below her in the same direction. They slid across the floor with her on top and before they came to a halt Sister Agnes (our trapeze artist) released what seemed a shriek of pain, but which all of us knew was quite the opposite.

Agnes was still catching her breath when Ada asked her if she could learn to rope swing. I had told Ada that she should speak up when she saw some aspect of performance that particularly appealed to her because I wanted her to be understudy to some players in case they couldn't go on, and also to see what appealed to her and to see what she could do.

"How did you first get interested in trapeze, this is like trapeze isn't it? and why are you called Sister Agnes?"

Sister Agnes studied Ada for a moment before she began, "I saw my first circus performance when I was twelve. There was a trapeze artist whom I fell in love with. She was so daring that I felt if I could do what she did I could escape from my life which was miserable. She was fearless in leaping. I was sitting with my parents and I had my legs crossed tightly while I watched her because I was so excited I was afraid I was going to pee when she released her grip and flew through the air. I didn't pee but I felt acute pleasure and I shrieked so loud my parents thought there was something wrong with me. I'm called Sister Agnes because I was later put in a convent for a while because after that circus show I began doing anything I could that involved high speed and high risk, because the thrill excited me so much it became a kind of addiction."

As Ada stood by Sister Agnes she noticed curlicues of color like flags creeping up out of the low neck of her leotard and looking down in she saw a girl flying through the air tattooed over her chest. In fact there was a whole circus scene spreading in all directions.

Sister Agnes saw Ada staring at her tattoos and said, "Rasputin. Stay away from that man"

"But didn't you want him to do that?"

"Yes and no. Stay away from him."

"But..."

"It's a long story, just stay away from him. And, don't be swayed by what Aimee has to say."

"Aimee...? Who's Aimee?"

"Aimee is a sculptor and is part of our company, that is, her sculptures are part of our company."

"Her sculptures are part..."

"Look Ada, there are people you haven't met yet, and lots that is peculiar about us, everything in due time, so calm down and try to grow up a little my dear."

Before Ada could register her response Sister Agnes had turned to walk away. Ada turned to me when she saw that I had overheard everything.

"What the...?"

I looked at Ada with a neutral expression and said, "So calm down and try to grow up a little, my dear."

She stared at me with irritation, but when I raised my eyebrows in an exaggerated way, a previously unrevealed lightness and levity emerged and she laughed and said, "Yeah, grow up and be old and ordinary like you?"

"No, grow up and be maybe extraordinary like with some luck you might be."

"I'm a minor, don't flirt with me."

"All right, I'll wait a few years and see how you turn out."

"Then you'll love me to death...yours, that is."

Chronicle of a Death Foretold, my favorite Garcia Marquez title, slipped into my mind as I watched Ada prance off.

As the day progressed, I found myself reluctantly speculating on the provenance of this girl, not only as a dancer which would be my preference, but as a total young being with her own history.

Two weeks later, when she was leaving for the day, I offered to give her a ride home, with the explanation that I had errands to do with the brewery van. This invitation came out of my mouth like someone else said the words. She was as surprised as I but accepted. She gave me general directions and we drove in silence. At a corner she said, "Let me out here." We were in a pricey part of downtown. "Where I live is my business" and got out. I waited till she turned a corner and then followed her. I saw a parking space, and abandoned the car to continue on foot some distance behind her and on the opposite side of the street. She entered the lobby door of a high-end converted warehouse filled with huge lofts which was already a declared architectural landmark in the city. As I reached the front door an au pair girl was coming out with a stroller. I held open the door for her. She thanked me with a Swedish accent, and went on her way and I went on my way through the high-security front door. The center of the building consisted of an open atrium planted with tall bamboo surrounding several fountains. I left the building and crossed the street. As I compulsively studied her corner of the build-ing from below, I saw that it was a double height loft with tall windows. Through these windows, I could see various levels of balconies and stairways. The magazine also reported that the owners of this huge corner loft were a family of enormous wealth whose source was unknown. As I studied this architecture of opulence I noticed movement on one of the stairways. It was Ada and she was looking down at me.

"You were standing outside the corner of my building," Ada said while the company was taking a break from work the next day. Her tone was neutral and that surprised and relieved me.

"That's true."

"Well, I knew you would follow me, even before I saw you park your car. I expected it."

"Oh, and why did you expect it?"

"Because you know how important I'm becoming to the company and you can't contain your curiosity."

I was on the verge of asking her about her family's loft but instead I refrained. "OK people, I said, let's get back to work." I knew the less I asked her, the more she'd offer up on her own. But the troubling question was, why should I care what goes on in her life outside of the brewery? For the first time I acknowledged to myself a growing sense of shift in the destiny of our theater company and my own with it.

Rasputin was a harp maker and a harpist and sometimes contributed music to our productions. He had long hair, long fingernails, and longs for Aimee obsessively, whom he has virtually covered with tattoos, a jungle of tattoos, with vines and leaves and flowers everywhere. Aimee makes ceramic nude figures, life-size. They are self-portraits and covered with the same jungle of flora as her body. No one knows which came first, Aimee's tattoos to inspire her sculpture or her sculpture's flora to inspire Rasputin's tattooing of Aimee. It all started before they came to the Brewery and they came together. When Rasputin played his harp, he crouched behind the strings, looking like a primate trapped in too small a cage. Actually, his music was what was too small for him and that's why his creativity is always fugitive, seeking some new medium.

Rasputin's other obsession was butterflies, which we learned when he insisted we accompany him on an excursion to a remote redwood grove on the coast. He had gotten word that there were tens of thousands of a rare species called Arctic Alizarins arriving at this forest to breed.

"Rasputin, where did you hear about these Alizarins? And what do they have to do with me? If you don't mind my asking for the tenth time."

This was Sister Agnes. Rasputin had told her these butterflies would be an important link between them, but he wouldn't tell her why. She was the most tolerant of Rasputin of any of us. I think it had to do with the menacing nature of the man, which appealed to her addiction to danger. She was wearing her silver leotard, complete with a crimson cross and a pair of hiking boots. Aimee, was always with Rasputin, despite the fact that over time she has told everyone that she hates him and wished him dead. Father Joseph was at the head of the line as we hiked single file down the forest path, because someone said we might encounter deer poachers and his fluorescent orange clerical collar might save a life. Mojobe was in front of me in one of her long white dresses. She was barefoot and walking over every kind of flesh-piercing plant one finds on the forest floor. The soles of her feet are beautiful and pink but hard as shoe leather. I know because I asked her once if I could feel them. I just wanted to feel some part of her body other than her hand which she once slipped into mine as an expression of gratitude for my suggestions on how she moved in one of our pieces. Ada said to me, "I wanted to see you outside of your role as detached master of all of us, see if you're a breathing person, not just an observer and director of movement and theater. What's your name anyway. No one ever refers to you by name, just Maestro, which I happen to think is pretty pretentious. What can I call you that doesn't begin with 'M'?"

"Narrator."

"Narrator?"

"Yes, that's who I am. Without me, no one would know about any of this."

"About any of what?"

"This butterfly outing, this dance company, you."

"Me? You don't know anything about me."

"I will."

"Well, I'll know plenty about you too, won't I?"

"As a matter of fact, no."

"Why?, why will you know about me and I won't know about you?"

"Because you're in life, and I'm an observer of life, I'm the Narrator."

Ada had become increasingly agitated as we spoke. Her pale skin had flushed red, approaching her hair color, and I was again feeling a sense of being far more than only a reporter of life around me.

Rasputin was leading the way on this high trail through some of the largest redwoods in the world, over three hundred feet tall and a thousand years old. The Alizarins were on the endangered list, and entrance to these breeding grounds was restricted, limited to scientists with official permission and papers. This of course meant nothing to Rasputin and he told us only later. By mid-morning, we were exhausted and hungry. We had started out before dawn and Rasputin had set a fast pace through this wilderness, loping along like some species more native to the Amazon than here. We stopped at a large limestone ledge projecting out over a swift moving spring. Rasputin had told us that this was where the Alizarins were to be found. The rock was dry and everyone lay back eating sandwiches and listening to the silence. One by one we drifted off first to private thoughts and then to sleep. There was only the bubbling murmur of the spring beneath us and the soft wafts of foggy breeze moving up through the trees like giant exhales from the ocean below. Sister Agnes was the first to waken and through half-opened eyes saw brief flashes of crimson appearing and disappearing like giant fireflies emitting blinking color rather than blinking light.

She heard a low growl from Rasputin, "Don't anyone move, we're surrounded by them."

There were hundreds of Alizarins, having come down to rest on the rock and the warm immobile bodies lying crisscrossed over the ledge. Everyone was in awe and Sister Agnes whispered, "Now I'm really curious what they have to do with me."

Rasputin said, "You'll learn soon enough once I..."

But Rasputin was interrupted by a stern voice, "What are you people doing here? Let me see your papers!"

These words, delivered with a Russian accent, came from below the ledge, where the Arctic Alizarins could not be seen. At the sound of the voice, the startled movements of those on the ledge caused a riot of winged color as the Alizarins lifted up in a shimmering cluster and moved off on the breeze into the redwoods behind. There were moans all around, not the least of which came from the man standing below, who was holding a long-handled butterfly net. He started up the slope to the ledge, again demanding, "Show me your papers please."

When he reached the ledge he stood with his legs apart and the handle of his net planted on the rock and held upright with the net flapping in the breeze like a medieval battle banner. He was a large man in his sixties wearing a khaki shirt and shorts and green knee socks. His head was mostly bald and he was wearing glasses so thick his eyes seemed twice the size they should. His face was flushed from exertion.

Rasputin was the first to speak, "Let's see *your* papers."

The man opened his mouth as though to speak, but instead took a folded paper from his breast pocket and handed it to Rasputin. Rasputin studied it a minute. "Vladimir Nabokov? Vladimir Nabokov is dead."

The man stood straighter. "He was an impostor."

The puffing lepidopterist was now encircled by a tall African diva, a blond trapeze artist in silver leotard, a long-haired, long finger-nailed malcontent, a black-suited priest with a fluorescent collar, a small young woman whose tattooed flora is creeping out from under her skimpy skirt, a red-haired fifteen-year-old in a challenging mood, and a cool passive observer. He was silent as he considered this bit of theater staged on stone, surrounded by an audience of enormous trees patiently drinking in the fog as they had for millennia.

Aimee sat down, pulling her skirt up to cross her legs, revealing perfect round thighs adorned with vines and flowers. She pointed to a crimson butterfly tattooed among the leaves on her. "See, all is not lost. Now sit down and have some juice and a sandwich. You're all worked up."

The man looked carefully at Aimee's thigh and softened his warrior's stance. He smiled slightly looking around at the people before him, each in a role he'd never experienced before, and felt a fleeting taunt at who he said he was. But that passed and he sat down next to Aimee with all the authority of émigré intellectual, novelist, and lepidopterist, discoverer of Nabokov's Blues.

Everyone dug around for anything left from lunch to hand to this large man who had forgotten that he hadn't eaten since breakfast. He gratefully consumed everything handed to him. When he finally finished swallowing he gave a smile all around and said, "Actually I'm here illegally too. My papers are forged." He hesitated a moment and added, "I'm not always Vladimir Nabokov. I am Russian though and I do write fiction, and I do love butterflies. Two decades ago, I became aware that everything in literary fiction that intrigued me had been done by Nabokov. A devastating discovery. To further complicate matters I look like him. There have been fewer lucid moments when looking in the mirror I believed I was him. So, on occasion when I feel his presence the most, I allow myself to be him and it becomes an exorcism...but never a total one, unfortunately."

"Or, fortunately", I was compelled to say, because this Vladimir was so charming in the role of narrator of his own fictitious life.

He smiled at me appreciatively. "How gracious, thank you."

Mojobe had been watching Vladimir. She was standing and swaying from side to side slowly. She began to sing softly in a range uncannily like the voice of Vladimir, like a nonverbal playback in interpreted sounds. Sister Agnes was stepping back and forth and as Mojobe's voice increased in volume she ran across the stone ledge and leaped into the air. She grasped a low tree branch with her strong hands and swung back and forth trapeze style. As though the branch was a lever to open a flood gate of crimson, thousands of Arctic Alizarins poured out of the woods past Agnes and toward Mojobe, seemingly drawn by her voice. They swirled around her in a giant spiral as the sun broke through, heating the air enough to suck them skyward. If sound could be seen Mojobe's voice would be the tail on a red swirling kite lifting up among the redwoods to disappear from sight. When our eyes returned to ledge level we studied each other to see if everyone's expression was as stunned as our own. Sister Agnes had returned and stood with her chest heaving from exertion, her breasts infusing her cross with raw sensuality. Vladimir studied her and the circle around him, one by one as though we were examples of a new species he had discovered and should pin in a box labeled with names.

"What are your names?", He asked.

He listened to our nomenclature unfold, "Aimee," "Mojobe," "Sister Agnes," "Father Joseph," "Rasputin," "Ada." I didn't say my name of course because I'm the narrator. But Vladimir watched me expectantly, and so as not to slight him, I said "Narrator."

He replied, "How wonderful."

Ada scowled at me.

Father Joseph said, "I should bless this profound experience."

Vladimir looked uncomfortable, but Father Joseph only joined his hands Buddha style and nodded three times.

"What do all of you do? Is Lepidoptera your interest?"

Ada answered, surprising everyone, "No, we're just following this weirdo around today. She nods toward Rasputin. We're actually all theater people."

Vladimir was delighted, "Really? And what do you do my dear?"

"Right now I'm waiting for these people to realize that I'm the new principal dancer for this company."

Everyone stared at Ada, and Ada stared at me with eyebrows raised. Then she added, "Of course, the decision is up to the Maestro here."

Everyone stared at me.

Ada added, "Oh, I forgot, he doesn't decide things, he just narrates what goes on." At this, Ada began a fast circle of amazingly precise steps of her own design around the edge of the stone outcropping. She did a series of false approaches to the others each time appearing to be about to leave the ground to be caught by them, finally choosing me as her target. Fortunately, I anticipated the velocity with which she would strike me and could get a leg behind to shore up my balance. Even so, she hit hard enough to almost drive us both off the ledge for a five-foot drop below. When she reached me she wrapped her legs around me and held her hands out, arm's length on my shoulders, and looked into my eyes. Her face was flushed and her hair was wild. Her eyes were wild. She knew we were on the outer edge of danger.

"Risk nothing, and make no art." She stared hard into my eyes.

A low moan turned us all toward Sister Agnes. She was standing wide-eyed with her hands clenched high between her thighs. Only Vladimir didn't know what she had just experienced.

"Narrate that Maestro." Ada said softly.

"I will."

And I did.

Single-file, our party of intruders hiked back out of the ancient forest. In the center, Vladimir Nabokov lumbered along like a great bear we had captured in the wild and were bringing home to train.

Ada had been rehearsing with us now every day for three months. When I asked her about school she said it was none of my business. So I've made it none of my business. Her attitude of flinty independence was essential to the content of her dance. She had chosen to work with Rasputin when I gave her a choice. I deliberately pair up people who are disparate in their skills because we all have contempt for anything smacking of "beauty" in performance. The beauty must come from the observers' response to the performance. And that must always be open to interpretation. But Ada's insistence on working with Rasputin was in direct proportion to our insistence in warning her away from him. For his part, Rasputin watched Ada like a viper in a cage eyeing a mouse for dinner. But good. Ada could take care of herself. I'm not her guardian. The menace in the air between them fed their art, and it fed Ada's obsession to be our prima donna, for which I could only respect her. She was the single most gifted young dancer I'd ever encountered, and she knew it. She also knew she needed me to achieve what she wanted. My problem was that I didn't know what she wanted, besides being the star. I didn't know that she knew, either. I was convinced she had the capacity for important art, perhaps great art and it seemed to be the only thing that really mattered to her. And, she was only fifteen. It was unnerving to watch.

The performance of Ada and Rasputin was based on improvisation. Either she moved first and he responded with harp fingering to complement her or he played first and she responded with movement and they continued, going back and forth. There is a tradition in Indian music where a violinist plays sounds and a singer literally matches the sound with her voice or vice versa. The sound of the violin is closest of all instruments to the sound of the human voice. With Ada and Rasputin, again the observer must provide the transformation and the result is that movement and sound are equivalent but not equal and complement each other eerily.

I had seen Ada go off with Rasputin after rehearsals to who knows where for who knows what. The first time I saw it, I pulled her aside and reminded her of all of our warnings. She said, "Are you jealous, old man?" I have since come to this theory about Rasputin. I believe the repulsion/attraction equation is circular. As Rasputin appeared more and more repulsive he moved backwards in a circle so far that he began to enter the other side, the side of attraction. Especially for someone as contemptuous of romantic beauty as Ada was.

Vladimir had taken to visiting the brewery. On his first visit, he said, "Ah the brewery, where you brew your art." Then he greeted everyone with an old-world handshake and a slight bow. When he saw Ada again, he said, "I'd written a book about you, you know." Which turned out to be true, that is the original novel Nabokov did indeed write titled Ada, which was written in Europe before he immigrated to the U.S., and was a precursor to Lolita. Ada was standing next to Rasputin. Vladimir looked back and forth between them like Ada was a Faberge egg and Rasputin a badly botched omelet. Having already gotten a taste of our group in the form of Mojobe's butterfly aria and Sister Agnes's trapeze accompaniment, Vladimir was intrigued by the spirit of what happens in the brewery.

When he saw Ada and Rasputin at work, he said to me, "This gives entirely new meaning to the theme of beauty and the beast." At the end of his third visit, he said quietly, "This is such an inspiration, it makes me want to write again, which I haven't felt in a long while."

I had the feeling that it was no accident that we had encountered Vladimir in the woods and immediately urged him on.

"Really?" he said, "Would you like to see what this experience inspires in me in the form of words?"

"Yes, and even more so if the words can be integrated into our theater."

"I take that as a pleasing challenge."

And so it began. Vladimir sewing together bits of nonverbal drama with his sublime spools of words.

One evening, Vladimir and I were sipping Russian vodka and eating caviar on odd small green crackers, all of which he had brought as a token of appreciation because his days and nights were now happily filled with writing for the brewery (none of which I'd read yet). We were sitting way up on Sister Agnes's trapeze platform in a corner by the ceiling. It was a logistical challenge getting him up here but he insisted because he had had a dream in which he observed all our work from above... "Like God" he said with no trace of modesty.

After discussing various of the people below I asked him, "Do you have family?"

"Yes, an extremely small family" He answered, and laughed, partly from the vodka and partly because what he had said was funny, funny, and terrifying, as it turned out.

"I have an Italian wife. Her name is Lucrezia. She is a successful theater impresario. We have been married for fifteen years. She is just under one meter in height. Yes, a midget, literally. A perfect small-scale model of an exquisite beauty. She was as drawn to my fame as novelist as I was drawn to her exotic presence. Because she so thoroughly believed me when I told her who I was, I could never bring myself to tell her the truth. For eleven years she thought she was married to Vladimir

Nabokov. She is not a literary person and never read anything to contradict what I had told her. But alas, she did discover the truth one day quite by accident, and she said to me, 'I will get even with you, and in a manner quite in proportion to the outrage of your lie.' The fact that she came from a Sicilian clan with a long history of brutal revenge helped me decide to leave Italy the next day and I haven't been back since. Legally and in the eyes of the Church we are still married, she being too much a Catholic to initiate divorce. In the end, she will have her revenge, and it won't be pretty."

Three days later he said, as he handed me a scenario, "My epiphany, sir. It is for a performance piece to feature Ada, Sister Agnes, and Father Joseph." He gave me a brief outline, "This stems from the Annunciation. Our players are to be: Sister Agnes as Virgin, androgynous Ada as Archangel Gabriel, and Father Joseph as, well, Joseph. As with all triangles, there will be competition for the prize. What is the prize? I don't know yet. However, appropriately, it will all take place both here on terra firma and in the heavens above."

At the final two words, Vladimir looked up and swept his hand from left to right, indicating the arena of Sister Agnes's daring feats.

"There will be spoken exchanges, mostly between the players and the audience, but they will be concise, precise, and of course richly spoken treasures. Now as is true with all effective art, it must be developed inductively, that is, we will not be following a strict script, only improvised movements which will suggest what comes next. Now if you are in agreement, let's confer with our players and see what kind of response we get."

We met that evening with the proposed cast. Vladimir was standing before the three, who were seated on the floor before him. I was standing slightly off to the side. Vladimir was pacing back and forth before them silently. He stopped in front of Agnes, "The Virgin Mary." He said this looking at her intensely. She looked back, raising her eyebrows, waiting for more. Vladimir resumed pacing and stopped in front of Joseph, "Joseph, husband of the Virgin Mary." Joseph said nothing. Vladimir walked over in front of Ada. "Archangel Gabriel, with wings, descending from above, in a display of flying virtuosity, to deliver the word of

God!" He spoke with ever-increasing emphasis, and Ada was up in the air flying into the arms of Vladimir, beaming with ambition. I saw Rasputin watching from a dark doorway across the room. As narrator I can tell you that an Annunciation does occur at another time and in another country and in terms of consequences, this one is benign by comparison. In fact it's safe to say that our theater was in many ways a rehearsal for life.

In a complete contradiction of my expectations, Ada, after six months of work with our company invited us all to her family loft to a party for reasons I'm to understand only later. It was a party purportedly to celebrate Ada's success as a performer. We had recently given an informal pre-performance rehearsal in the brewery for a select group of theater people including a visiting critic from New York, who was so taken with Ada's flying grace as Archangel Gabriel, that she wrote an article in *The New York Times* about our company but mostly about Ada. Her 'parents' learned from the article for the first time just what Ada had been up to for the past several months and went through three stages of reaction, any of which or none of which may have been ingenuous. First, there was outrage or feigned that she had not also been in school during that time. Then there was pride in her achievement. And finally, there was interest in our theater company. Also, there was suspicion. Since I am the artistic director of the company they wanted to know my name. It's so difficult for people to understand that it's possible to be part of life and part of a story at the same time. It's the story part that causes trouble. But what is life if it's not transcended?

We arrived in ones and twos the evening of the party. If we had arrived all at once it would have been impossible to integrate us into this gathering of wealth and influence inhabiting various levels of the labyrinthine loft space. It was a curious contradiction that this group of people, by temperament so outside the world of theater, by being arrayed on various levels and in various costumes representing the gloss of affluence, and lighted by constellations of discrete but dazzling halogen lights, were more theater than theater (but not I would hasten to say, good theater).

Ada greeted me with her usual caustic whimsy, "I'm surprised that you would lower yourself to this level of bourgeois self-congratulation."

"Actually I took the elevator *up*. You've got your levels wrong. And I think you do better, non-verbally, on a trapeze."

Ada was wearing a one-of-a-kind designer gown, a world of creativity I don't follow closely, but I was impressed. There were layers of flimsy fabric starting and stopping at various points showing other colors underneath in thin slices of surprise. The palette was of rich earth colors each making constant reference back to her shiny red hair. The shape of the dress was elegant but predictably gave no hint of the shape of the wearer.

A tall carefully groomed woman appeared at Ada's side. My quick assessment was that she was some high-end plastic surgeon's specimen (I would say work of art but she's not), and to further my lack of generosity, I would say species rather than specimen because in the end, regardless of how much fee was involved she looked like any other moneyed matron gravely combating gravity. We took an instant dislike to each other.

"Do you do something else in life besides direct teenagers on stage?"

"I don't discriminate on the basis of age."

"Well then, would you direct me?"

"What can you do?"

"I can express myself forthrightly."

"Go ahead."

"I think your theater work is arbitrary self-indulgent mediocrity with no reference to classical stage."

"That is forthright."

"Correct. So would you direct me, in spite of my age?"

"You would like me to direct you?"

"Yes."

"Turn around and exit forthrightly."

Surprisingly, with an unpleasant smile, she did, turning on a Manolo heel and striding away.

I turned to Ada, "Who was that?"

"Penelope, Khalid's new wife."

"Khalid? Who is that?"

"You'll find out very soon."

"Well as Narrator", I said, "Since I have the privilege of control over casting, I don't think she'll appear again in my story."

Ada gave me her first genuine smile.

As the other players arrived there were ripples of attention turned in their direction. Mojobe drew the most response as she strode in, a head above everyone in all her supreme regality. There were world-class paintings and sculptures dispersed throughout the loft and Mojobe seemed more one of them than one of us. She saw Ada and me and headed in our direction smiling. On her way she was intercepted by Penelope and she leaned over to hear what was being said to her over the din of conversation. She reacted with a frown and continued toward us. She greeted us each and said, "Who is that dreadful woman?"

Ada laughed mirthfully and said, "The newest member of my family"

Mojobe said, "I'm sorry."

We both knew that Mojobe meant she was sorry that Penelope was in any way a member of Ada's family.

I saw Rasputin moving through the crowd toward the bar. People parted for him like discreet guests not wishing to embarrass their hosts by acknowledging a rodent in the room. He was followed by Father Joseph and Sister Agnes. Joseph was dressed as usual but Agnes had on a short stylish black dress with a low-cut back that revealed an ornate and very erotic female nude in the form of a scarlet cross. On another side of the loft from a balcony came a resonating Russian voice, causing people to stop their conversation. It was of course Vladimir, who later told me he was improvising on the nature of the people below. "If I'd said it in English, I would have been asked to leave, and I didn't want that until I'd sampled the hors d'oeuvres table." Only Aimee was missing and later we learned that she'd gone to the emergency room because Rasputin's most recent tattoo had become nastily infected.

In a lull in the conversation, Ada took my hand. It was so out of character I turned to look at her. She smiled and said, "Someone wants to meet you." She led me up a flight of stairs and across an open ramp to a closed door. She knocked and a voice called out, "Come." She opened the door and delivered me into the room. She closed the door behind me and was gone. The room was glass on two sides with dramatic views of the city, the river, and its bridges. There were competing spectacles in the room: A handsomely dressed Arabic man seated in a Mies Barcelona chair with a portfolio of drawings in his lap, framed by a wall displaying a Modigliani, and a Bonnard. I looked from him to the paintings and back to him. He watched me eye his priceless paintings with satisfaction, then stood to walk to an antique carved cabinet where he poured two brandies. He came to my side and handed me a glass.

"I'm Khalid, Ada's father"

I turned to him for a closer look. "I'm..."

"I know who you are"

He watched me while waiting for my response to the fact that he couldn't possibly be Ada's natural father. He struck me as a man for whom niceties were an annoyance.

"Yes, well I guess I don't see much similarity between you two."

"I'm not related to her."

"She's adopted?"

"I acquired her."

"Acquired her?"

"Both of them."

"Both of them?"

"Ada and Blain."

"I see, and who is Blain?"

"Ada's twin."

I looked at him for a moment and then walked to the windows to look out at the night light show. I refused to be baited by his desire to startle me.

With my back to him I asked, "And what is your interest in me?"

"I have no interest in you."

I turned. "Then why did you have your red-headed chattel bring me here?"

"Blain has been abducted. No one knows this except me, and now you. Some-one connected to you knows the people who have her. It's one of your theater people. Mojobe by name. But she knows nothing about this. Sources of mine have traced Blain's abductors and find a connection with Mojobe."

"Is this about money? Or does someone have a score to settle with you?"

"Both and more."

"Why are you telling me all this?"

"I have a photograph that I'd like you to show to this Mojobe."

He handed me a photo of two tall black men in native African dress. In between them was Ada, or could be Ada if she were not downstairs. She had red hair and was wearing a school uniform, a gray blazer with an emblem on the pocket, dark skirt, and white knee socks. She was smiling stiffly.

"If she's been abducted, why is she smiling?" I asked.

"It's a smile forced upon her, I assure you."

He walked over to stand next to me. He looked out at the cityscape. My guess was he was deciding how much to tell me. If I'm to be only a messenger to Mojobe, I don't need much information. If he's going to ask me to help in some way that he thinks I'm in a position to do he'll tell me a lot. The question is how much of it will be true. My instinct is to not trust this man. After a few moments of silence, he told me more than I expected.

"Blain has none of Ada's pragmatism. Ada will always take from any situation all she can to serve her own needs. She has no more fondness for me than Blain, but she has no interest in making moral judgments. Ada can have edge as I'm certain you've learned by now, but Blain can be dangerous."

"Is that a school uniform she's wearing?"

"Yes, she's in, or was in, a private school in Zurich."

"How did *these* men get her from the school?"

"They obviously had an intermediary."

"What kind of information do you expect to get from Mojobe when she sees this photo? Do you think she knows these Africans?"

"She knows them and more."

"Then why don't you show her the photo? She's downstairs."

"It's my understanding that Mojobe trusts you, has respect for you, and would want to help you."

"Help me what? Why should I get involved?"

He handed me a note.

"This came with the photo, and the postmark was Rome."

I unfolded the note and read, *Two are more than twice as valuable as one.*

"What does this mean?" I asked.

"It means that they can up the ante by taking Ada also."

"What do you mean by 'taking Ada'? She's told me you have people watching over her. How are they going to take Ada?"

He sighed with resignation, "Ada can elude the security people whenever she wishes and she does it frequently, partly because she's strong-willed and partly to show me that she can."

"Well explain the situation. Tell her that if she ditches her bodyguards her life's in danger."

"Unfortunately Ada has taken a liking to danger, due to her admiration for her mentor, that trapeze artist who has flying orgasms in the name of God. And her peculiar tie to this Rasputin. Who knows what influence he's having on her."

I realized that this man had taken great pains to learn a lot about us. But where is he getting his information? I'd never seen him at the brewery, and I was sure Ada told him nothing. Do we have a mole in our company? I was silent for a full minute while I considered the option of just refusing to involve myself in his dark dealings.

He broke the silence, "If you're thinking about refusing to cooperate, consider the prospect of your current theater production without Ada."

I did consider that prospect and I didn't like it. Ada brought something as a performer and a presence to my life right now that I didn't want to lose.

"All right, give me the photo and I'll talk to Mojobe."

As I walked to the door I could feel him watching me. The man had a manner of menace about him that made me uneasy. Why was I doing this? It's the kind of thing I usually avoided like the plague because it required personal involvement when all I really desired was to passively observe life and direct my theater group. When I came down the stairway Ada was across the room surrounded by groupies of all ages and genders absorbing in advance some of her glory to come. She was watching me and I was reminded of exactly why I'm doing this. Her talent was too exciting to let slip through my fingers. She left the others to hear about what I'd just experienced.

"What did he want?"

"I thought you already knew."

"I don't know anything. Khalid guards information carefully."

"Well, he just gave me a lot, including the fact that he's not your father."

"Well, you could have figured that out for yourself just by looking at him."

"And he told me about Blain."

For once, I'd said something to affect Ada.

"What about Blain?" Her cheeky teen facade had totally collapsed.

"She's been abducted."

Her face was pale. "Who's got her? And why?"

I showed her the photo. She studied it with a puzzled look.

"Who are these Africans?

"That's precisely what I asked Khalid."

"And?"

I was fascinated by the Ada who was suddenly revealed. More dimension to her had appeared in the past few seconds than in all the previous months I'd known her.

"And, the answer to your question is that I don't know, although Khalid claimed that Mojobe does know. Khalid also told me about Blain's nature as opposed to your nature."

"Such as?"

"Such as the fact that Blain hates him and enjoys provoking him."

"And me? What did he say about me?"

"That you're more pragmatic, more willing to set aside your principles in order to benefit from what Khalid has to offer you. By that, I assumed he meant all this affluence."

"That fucker, he said that?"

"Not in so many words but it was clearly what he meant."

Ada was angry. "Or maybe that was just your interpretation because you resent me."

"What reason have I to resent you?"

"You resent me because I'm so valuable to your dance company and I don't fawn all over you with admiration like everyone else in the company."

"No one fawns over me, and you know it. We all respect each other equally."

Ada was reaching for something, something that had been bothering her right along but she didn't understand.

"Well, you don't respect me."

"That's the opposite of what you just said which was that you're so valuable to the company."

"That's different. You think I'm very talented and that's valuable to you, as director. But you don't respect me. You see me as just a combination of artistic skills. You don't respect me as a person."

"Then maybe you should start acting like a person and not just a collection of artistic skills looking for admiration."

Ada stared at me, white with fury. She turned and marched off into the maze of Khalid's powerful party guests and the show of his massive wealth, his multi-level penthouse interior filled with masterpieces. I walked over to Mojobe to ask that she accompany me back to the brewery for an important conversation.

"Ohhhh, this is very bad."

Mojobe released this melodic exclamation as soon as I had shown her the photo, with no forewarning on my part.

"But I don't understand when Ada was with these men."

She looked at me with a truly stricken expression. We were alone in my study in a quiet corner of the brewery.

"It's not Ada, Mojobe, it's her twin Blain."

"I didn't know Ada had a twin. Ohhhh, that makes it even more serious. Where did you get this photograph?"

"I got it from Ada's so-called father. He asked me to show it to you. He claimed you know these two men."

"Ohhhh, Ohhhh, Ohhhh."

I had never seen Mojobe like this before. She was always the epitome of calm grace. Her lips were trembling. She was taking short breaths and looking into the pink palms of her hands as though they were an open book and she was looking at a pictograph of a tribal tale of horror.

"In my country, Niger, there is a courtship/marriage tradition that you would find odd. It involves two male cousins, called Waldeebe, who have between them a special intimacy. You would call it homosexuality, but it is beyond that, more complicated. One of these Waldeebe courts a young woman and in their marriage, both Waldeebe share her from then on. The woman readily agrees to this or it does not happen. I was bequeathed to a Waldeebe and his cousin, both of whom I was strongly drawn to. However, I was more drawn to myself, to my possibilities as an artist in the world. So I left my country and my Waldeebe with the assistance of an Italian theater impresario, who promised me the Waldeebe would never be able to find me, and that she would protect me if they did. You see, my family is tribal royalty and very wealthy, from a source I find despicable and choose not to discuss. So I am a highly prized bride. The men in this photograph are the Waldeebe I'm betrothed to. This twin of Ada is being held hostage because of me. They are very important men, my defection was a large insult to them, and given our tribal culture, anything can happen. This girl could become more than a hostage, she could become a surrogate for me. These two men have high status in our tribe and they also have wealth. They do not have my education and that makes them more dangerous. They are very intelligent, and fearless. In a tribal custom, as adolescents, they each had faced down fierce predators and they believe they have been granted by our gods lifetime supremacy in facing any predators to come. Anyone pursuing them in a quest for this girl would be considered by them a predator. And I would add, if they know this girl has a twin the situation becomes even more serious."

"They already know she has a twin. Why does that make it more serious?" I asked.

"Because twins are rare in our tribe, but there's more to it than that. Right now I'm wondering about other things. If this girl is a hostage held against my returning to the Waldeebe, they are mistaken. I will not return. If she is a hostage against something someone wants from Ada's father, that is his affair and has nothing to do with me. Also, you know there has to be another collaborator. The Waldeebe could not have arranged her abduction. They are being used for a fear factor, and to involve me. But who is the common denominator in all this? Who would know

of the connection between the Waldeebe and me? Who would know of the connection between this girl and her twin and her father and our theater company?
Where did this come from? Was there an envelope with a postmark?"

"Yes, Rome."

"Rome?" Mojobe stared into space for a moment. "Now I have a suspicion."

After my conversation with Mojobe, I needed to talk to Ada again. Mojobe's
characterization of the situation concerned me for Ada's safety. The two Waldeebe
in the photo sent shivers down my spine.

I told Ada I'd talked to Mojobe.

"What did she say?" Ada's attitude toward me had softened a little since last
night.

"She said that she is engaged to these two men holding Blain and they want
Mojobe back and that Blain is apparently their collateral."

"Mojobe is engaged to *two* men? That wicked girl! I'll bet she was doubly jealous when she saw the photo. I've been thinking about all that Khalid told you last
night. He has plans for you, you'd better watch out."

"Watch out? Why?"

"His family comes from a district in Iran where it is believed that the more
information a person has about you the more that person is obligated to you.
That's the opposite of the usual Middle Eastern secrecy where it is believed that
you become more vulnerable the more others know about your personal matters.
His people believe that when you share secrets, the other person owns the secret
and must not only guard it but must also guard the teller of the secret. It is an
honor to receive a secret. Especially in this case where the secret is so outrageous.
It is outrageous for an Arab to buy two beautiful pale redheaded little girls don't
you think?"

Ada was smiling while she awaited my answer.

"I think it's outrageous for anyone to buy anyone."

"Yeah, yeah I know, but an Arab buying little white girls, doesn't that have a special appeal to one's prejudices? Especially since it's so titillating."

"Whose prejudices? Yours or mine? And is it titillating?"

"Doesn't it titillate you?"

"Not particularly. Does it titillate you?"

"Sometimes."

"Are you saying Khalid acquired you and your sister as sex objects?"

"Partly."

"Did you have sex with him?"

"The answer to that question could be yes, or it could be, if he had ever touched either of us, we would have killed him."

"I see. You're not going to share secrets with me to obligate me to you."

"I'm not an Arab. Anyway, why would I want you obligated to me?"

"So that I would continue to help you develop as a dancer and performer, in spite of the fact that you're a pain in the ass."

Ada was quiet. I was surprised to see her eyes glisten. She walked over to me and facing three quarters away leaned into my chest. It's the closest Ada had ever come to an embrace.

"I'm scared of how important dance is to me. It seems to be the only thing I have in life. You were right last night. I do long for admiration. Because I feel like without my dancing, I'm nothing."

I realized that in the many months I'd known her, this was the first exchange we'd had that wasn't coated with her self-protecting sarcasm.

"I know who's behind this."

This was Mojobe speaking in a very somber tone. She was standing in the doorway of my study. Behind her was Vladimir, looking equally somber. I watched them both as I waited for Mojobe's explanation. But it was Vladimir who spoke first.

"It's Lucrezia."

"Lucrezia?" The name is familiar but I can't remember where I'd heard it.

"My wife Lucrezia, who had promised to settle her score with me."

"Oh yes, now I remember. But what could she actually do, and what is her motive in terms of the twins and Khalid?"

"Lucrezia is an ambitious impresario," Mojobe says. "She loves combining different elements of drama on the stage. She is creating a stage here, and we are her players, all of us. She helped me to leave Africa expecting that she could present me to an Italian audience in some grand manner. When I chose to come here instead, I was astounded at how much fury could be contained in so small a body. She told me I'd be sorry for my decision. I thought it was a figure of speech, but after talking to Vladimir I realized she was threatening me as she did him."

"But what is her connection to Khalid and the twins?" I asked again.

Vladimir responded, "I'm beginning to remember that right before Lucrezia and I parted ways, she had an elaborate theater production in need of financing and there was a hugely wealthy Arab who was going to front the money, not because he thought it was a good investment but because he wanted the prestige of being associated with an important theater production. I had the impression at the time that he was also intrigued by Lucrezia, drawn to her. She is an exceptionally beautiful woman, or I should say she's a scale model of an exceptionally beautiful woman. For reasons I don't remember, at the last minute he pulled out of the arrangement. Lucrezia has it in her to use her unique beauty to manipulate men, and as I remember, rather than lose the financial backing, knowing he was fascinated by her, she offered him some exotic experience of an erotic nature, the details of which I never knew, but Lucrezia has an extraordinary imagination so I can imagine what it might have been. Well, this Arab (and I'm now quite certain it was Khalid, remembering the photos of him then and having seen him recently) rejected her offer, insulting enough for Lucrezia, but he made the fatal error of referring to her size in his rejection."

"So Lucrezia has three interconnected targets for her wrath," I said.

Mojobe spoke with a quiet dread, "Three so far and more to come, because anyone becoming involved in this will immediately be counted as an adversary of hers. She has uncanny ways of acquiring information, and I would say, you (Mojobe looked at me) will soon be an enemy of hers because Khalid has involved you."

"But how could she know Khalid has involved me? She's in Rome and we are here."

Sister Agnes had been listening from the doorway, "We are not *all* here. Aimee was released from the hospital last evening, and I was told this morning that a man whose description could only be that of Rasputin had picked her up and there was talk of Italy. Neither of them is to be found at the brewery today."

There was silence as we all absorbed this bizarre information.

"Why don't you go to the Italian police?"

I was in Khalid's office and I said this to him after he had absurdly suggested that I coordinate efforts to get Blain released by the Waldeebe, or more to the point released by Lucrezia.

"Have you ever dealt with the Italian police? The Rome police?"

"No, but I've never had any reason to, and you do."

Khalid sighed with impatience before saying, "Of all the people involved in this, I'm the one least concerned. Blain has been a disappointment to me from the beginning, as has Ada for that matter. Blain could just vanish into the mountains of Sicily, or the back streets of Palermo which is where she'll be delivered if she's not handed over to one of you in Rome, and it wouldn't change my life at all."

"Why don't you just make Lucrezia an offer?"

"Because I don't know what she wants. It's not money. It's never a matter of money with Lucrezia."

"Then ask her what she wants."

"You ask her."

I realized that Khalid was telling the truth when he said he didn't care what happened to Blain, and I also realized that bizarrely I was now the one coordinating her release.

"Do you have contact information for Lucrezia?"

He shook his head and shrugged his shoulders.

"Are you interested in anything besides money?" I said, before turning to leave.

He offered no response to my question.

Mojobe, Vladimir, Ada, and I were sitting at an outdoor café table drinking wine and trying to formulate a plan to deal with the kidnapping of Blain. When the term was first used, Vladimir was amused. "It's true isn't it? She is a kid who's been napped!" Then he said, "But what can Lucrezia do to us? We are here and she is there. She can't harm Mojobe, she can't harm me, she can't harm you." He said this to Ada.

Ada looked at him coldly, "So the only thing she can do is let those two Africans fuck my sister? and that's nothing to worry about?"

"Oh my, I'm so sorry my dear."

I then brought up the subject of Rasputin and Aimee supposedly now in Rome and possibly with Lucrezia.

"I know something about this." Ada responded, "You know Rasputin has been obsessively pursuing me, wanting to tattoo me, and when I refused, wanting to see my body, any part of my body, following me like a madman. One night I said to him, 'You should be chasing my twin, not me. Blain's a real body show-off and has even talked about being tattooed.' Rasputin was mesmerized by the idea."

"We must find out how to contact Lucrezia and just ask what she wants." Mojobe said, "We must get Blain away from the Waldeebe, who my dear" (she looked at Ada) "are not, ordinary Africans but intensely determined and intelligent men with true nobility in their blood."

Ada raised her eyebrows comically and said, *"Excuse me!"*

Mojobe laughed, and we all laughed, realizing how much this whole situation had infused us with tension and dread.

Vladimir said, "I have a lawyer friend in Rome who told me some time ago that he'd keep track of Lucrezia to protect me in case of trouble with her. I can ask him to deliver a message to her. What shall we say?"

We all answered practically in unison, "We said, 'What do you want?'"

Thinking that we'd done all we could for the moment, we were relieved to have some brief respite from the dark aura of Lucrezia while Vladimir's lawyer friend did his work. It was a short-lived respite however, within two weeks we received word from Rome.

Lucrezia's message was short and to the point.

"I want the other twin and I want the Narrator."

Mojobe and Vladimir were each relieved but said they felt guilty for not being designated ransom by Lucrezia. I, of course, was puzzled as to why Lucrezia wanted me, but I found out soon enough.

Ada said, but not with her usual bravado, "This appeals to my sense of adventure. I think." She looked scared.

"I wish to apologize for my insensitivity to this matter the other night."

This was Khalid, who had asked me to meet with him at his office downtown. We were high up in a corner of a steel and glass high rise. The room was minimally furnished with elegant chrome and black leather chairs and a low black granite table. Near a window was a tall Brancusi sculpture, a black marble version of his Bird in Flight series. Khalid stroked the marble as he spoke as though by association he was as beyond judgment as Constantin Brâncuşi.

"I have two things to offer you if you will be our negotiator with Lucrezia. I will of course cover all travel expenses and provide security in Rome. In addition, I will grant your theater company funding of a large amount of money."

My disdain for this man showed in my tone of voice. I ignored his offer to buy me.

"*Our* negotiator?"

"Yes, I'll be honest with you. Lucrezia has revealed to me that she has certain information about activities of mine which I wish to remain confidential. So for personal reasons, I'm willing to involve myself in dealing with her."

"She's blackmailing you?"

"Yes."

"I don't like you Khalid, and I don't trust you. Why should I involve myself in this?"

"To save a near sixteen-year-old from a possible gruesome fate. To acquire some funding for your theater company. To ingratiate yourself to Ada, and maybe then you'd have better luck with her than I've had."

"Better luck in what sense?"

My contempt for him was increasing by the second and I could see from his expression that it showed.

"I didn't mean sexual luck, if that's what Ada's been inaccurately telling you as seems to be her habit. I'm talking about connecting with her as a human being, something no one else has succeeded in doing."

He said this in such a way that I was tempted to believe him, and it is true that no one seemed to have connected with Ada. I decided that even if he was an un-savory character, that didn't necessarily make him an exploiter of minors. Espe-cially since Ada seemed to be open in reporting the facts of life, at least her life.

"What did you mean by saying you'd provide me with security in Rome?" Se-curity against whom?"

"Not against Lucrezia. She's not a violent person, even though she has a vol-canic temper, which comes I think from growing up near a volcano in Sicily. It's the two Africans I'm concerned about. I don't know how much control Lucrezia has over them. And of course, there's her family, her brothers. You can ask Vladimir about them."

"Lucrezia wants Ada to accompany me, or more accurately, me to accompany Ada. Why should Ada be put at risk?"

"Ada is more than willing to go. She does not want Blain harmed. They are closer than you could imagine. I have talked to Mojobe and Vladimir and from what I know of Lucrezia, she does not want violence, and she does not want money. She is a world-class impresario and she has in mind some kind of grand scheme to serve her own unique desires. In the end, she places art above everything, performance art, which she does not see as separate from life in the sense that we think of life."

"Well, at least she and I have that in common."

He studied me for a moment.

"Yes, I believe you do."

"OK, if I do this how do I know who my security is?"

"It's best you don't know. Just trust me."

Seeing my incredulous expression at the word 'trust' he had to laugh, as did I. I left fighting some perverse inclination to begin liking this man. Maybe it was his role as classic theater villain.

"You know, I cannot guarantee your safety. And I can't believe your father is encouraging this."

I said this to Ada in hopes of getting some idea of her orientation not just to the immediate situation but to her life in general."

"I've told you, he's not my father."

"I know, who is your father?"

"I'll tell you on the plane."

"Why wait till then?"

"Because it's information that is above everything, above national borders, above the mundane details of life, above all other kinds of connections."

"It's that important?"

"Very, very, very important."

We sat in silence for a few minutes before I said, "What about Rasputin, and Aimee? What is their role in all this?"

"Rasputin is an amazing artist, have you seen Aimee's body?"

"No"

"Well, I have. He wanted to show off his virtuosity to me in hopes that I'd agree to be his next canvas."

"And?"

"She's covered with vines, leaves, and blossoms with a few butterflies thrown in."

"But why are Aimee and Rasputin in Rome?"

"You've seen Mojobe's body decorations, done with deep scars. She said that one of her two fiancées is the most renowned body marker in their tribe. I think Rasputin has become obsessed with including incising and scars in his repertoire with Aimee and I think she too wants it."

"But it must hurt like hell."

"Aimee is into pain. And she hates Rasputin. You figure it out."

"How do you know all this?"

"I hung out with them a little. I saw some things."

"Like what?"

"You sir, have a morbid curiosity."

"Yes, it's a source of some of my art."

"How come I've never seen any of that when you create dance for me and direct me?"

"Because you're fifteen years old."

"Ah, you feel protective of me."

"Yes."

"As you should."

"Yes."

"But not because I'm fifteen."

"Then why?"

"For a much more important reason."

"Such as?"

"You'll see."

I say "OK, let's get back to why Aimee and Rasputin are in Rome. Do you think Lucrezia has some interest in them too?"

"I was just starting to get some idea of who this nasty little midget is, but my guess is that for who knows what reason Lucrezia has an interest in all of us separately and all of us together, at least that's what I've been hearing."

Part Two

"This is cushy. Khalid really splurged on our tickets."

Ada and I were at 35,000 feet on our way to Rome and she'd been lounging around in her plush first-class seat in a kind of perpetual semi-horizontal dance motion while browsing magazines. I'd been perusing the dinner menu. She sat still for a minute while we discussed our food choices. When the flight attendant asked if we'd made up our minds, Ada responded.

"I will have the pasta and my father will have the salmon."

The flight attendant seemed to melt at the sweetness of Ada's tone of voice. She was probably thinking, what a wonderful unjaded teenager.

I laughed and said to Ada, "That was pretty convincing. Maybe we should give you some speaking parts."

Ada answered, "I said I'd tell you on the plane who my father is."

"We were talking about your biological father."

"I'll never know who my biological father is."

I was waiting for Ada to break into a mischievous grin. But none came.

"Khalid acquired me, and Blain" She continued, "We had nothing to say about it. We were small children. We knew nothing about him. There is no connection between us."

This was information I couldn't even begin to process.

"So?"

"So, I'm acquiring you as my father because there is a connection between us."

"There's a connection between me and everyone in our company."

"Not like the connection between us."

She stared at me intensely while I'd been staring out the window. I turned to face her. Her eyes seemed to be changing color. What was usually hazel was shifting to violet. Finally, I lifted my eyebrows in a kind of a last appeal for Ada to just start laughing in her mirthful way. But no, she put her hand on mine just as dinner arrived, served by two smiling flight attendants.

Eating our surprisingly flavorful Alitalia dinner, Ada and I talked about the food and about the people around us. While attacking her spectacular chocolate dessert, she said,

"Well, what do you think?"

"Think about what?"

"Our new family."

"What will Khalid think about our *new family*?" I laughed.

"Why are you laughing?"

"Because you can't have two adoptive fathers and because I haven't agreed to anything."

"Of course, I can't have two adoptive fathers. Khalid is very pleased by my decision. I've been a big pain in the ass to him."

"You've told him about this?"

"Of course, why do you think he's giving you a huge bunch of money?"

"He's giving the company money because that's the deal I negotiated with him."

"What deal? I haven't agreed to anything."

"Well, I never agreed to be acquired by Khalid."

"So what do we do, proceed with you believing I'm your father and me knowing I'm not?"

"Of course not, if I believe you're my father, you are my father."

Ada was pouting and had tears in her eyes and looked not fifteen, but about eleven.

She spoke in a very quiet voice, "You should be pleased."

"And why is that?"

"Because I'm going to be the best dancer you've ever had and your whole artistic life and the reputation of your company will be altered because of me."

I stared out the window thinking what she had just said was probably true.

"Speaking of your dancing, you've obviously been trained, when and where was that?", I asked, sensing that Ada would not give me a flippant answer as usual because she wanted to keep our conversation serious.

She was quiet for a moment then, "OK, here's what you've been trying to find out from the beginning, and I've always changed the subject, right?"

"Right."

"Well, since you're going to be my father, you should have knowledge of my history, right?"

Smart girl. It's the best my tired brain could come up with.

"Right?" She repeats, then "Right Dad?"

"Yes, Ada."

"OK, This will be a broad outline of my life before you!" She smiled brightly. "The details I will fill in, as best as I can remember them, over time. Blain and I were never separated until very recently so this is our joint story: We never had a father or mother, and we never thought that was odd. We had nannies and we had tutors, all of them sweet and sensitive and usually very intelligent. We did go to excellent schools, and we both studied dance from a very early age. All of this in Switzerland. The one person in our lives who seemed to have authority over all of this we called 'Auntie.' She was elegant and kind and lived in the same house we did, but we rarely spent time with her. That's it for now. You'll learn everything in time. Right now I'm too sleepy to tell you more."

We both nodded off, after a period of drowsy silence.

"Dad, I want hot chocolate for breakfast."

Ada was looking up at me with her head on my shoulder where she'd been sleeping for the past three hours and where her sleepy drool had formed a slow stream down the front of my shirt. She was smiling like an agent of Lucifer in the form of an innocent girl. She stretched and rolled over on her back so that her head was in my lap and her bare feet were crossed against the window that was revealing the first streaks of dawn over Italy.

"We need to have a breakfast party to celebrate our first full day together as a family."

While she was grinning at me, I was having selfish thoughts, such as, how will this new status she's assigned to herself affect her brilliance as a dancer.

As though clairvoyant, she said, "You have no idea how inspired I am to start dancing again."

After asking to get up so she could pee, she leaped the eight paces to the bathroom with a lightness bordering on levitation. She passed a businessman whose barely opened eyes revealed a dreamer in lechers' heaven.

Leaving the airport, after an annoying delay by Italian customs because of a debate over who is related to whom and how, and heading in a taxi to our hotel, Ada lectured me.

"Let that be a lesson. When we get to the hotel, just accept the family suite that Khalid has reserved for us without a big fuss. Look, there's the Colosseum!"

I decided Ada was right, the sooner and smoother we conducted our business in Rome the sooner we could return and get back to work. Our current performance piece was in total suspension until we resolved this business, and I was feeling edgy and impatient, even though beneath the edge it was inspiring to be in Rome again.

"Oh, hey!"

That was Ada's response as we were shown into our suite at the Excelsior, an indulgence of marble floors, silk curtains, and rich antiques. We had a parlor and two bedrooms, each with a bath. I was beginning to soften, and consider that this was not so bad. Anyway, how demonic can this Lucrezia be?

In the hotel lobby and later in the restaurant Ada persisted in referring to me as her father and though everybody treated us with the respect the rich expect, nobody believed it for a second. It's not a question of age. It's a question of personalities. Put two strong artists together with all their creative quirks and any notion of traditional family goes out the window.

Walking back from dinner and looking in the shop windows of via Veneto, Ada said, "You know, we could be anything to each other, given our rich combination of imaginations."

I didn't know where she was heading with this, but I saw one ray of light that I immediately pounced on.

"Exactly, that's why you shouldn't be in such a rush to label our relationship as you have. Over the years our working relationship could take on all different dimensions of friendship."

Ada turned to me and opened her mouth to deliver a spirited rebuttal, but to her credit, she just studied me for a moment and said nothing. I felt hopeful. Another source of hope had been watching Ada's response to the spirit of Rome around her. She missed nothing and often she would move quietly in a way that showed she was converting her encounters with Italy into a kind of shorthand of dance movement to be drawn on later. I saw this as something that could replace her obsession with replacing Khalid with me.

In the course of dressing for dinner and preparing for bed, Ada had been a little careless about having her body not totally covered as was her rule at the brewery, where there is casual nudity among artists in the course of changing into and out of costume. It was nothing approaching nudity but rather a reveal of a bit of underwear here and there and surprised me. And when I was in bed reading she came in wearing her plush Excelsior robe. She wanted to talk about meeting Lucrezia the next day. She sat on the edge of the bed and her robe relaxed, emitting heady fragrances of luxurious soaps, shampoo, and oils. A thigh, pink from the heat of her bath was revealed as was a pale collar bone. I was alarmed. It was too sensual. She's a fifteen-year-old girl. All of which caused me to say, "Is this any way to appear in front of your father?"

Ada stood up with a mirage of smile, and pulled her robe carefully around her. "No. Of course, it wasn't. I'm sorry. Good night Daddy." She leaned down to kiss me on the cheek and exited the stage in triumph.

On our way to Lucrezia's apartment the next afternoon I asked Ada about her relationship with Blain.

"In recent years, we haven't seen a lot of each other, with her being in school in Switzerland and all. We're close because we're twins and we have had some of those experiences researchers talk about where separated twins have the same physical or mental sensations without the other knowing. Also, we were in school classes and dance classes together all the time we previously lived in Zurich. But when you see Blain and me together, you'll see a difference. You'll see it because you're the most perceptive person I've ever known, and I'm so proud to be your little girl." Ada looked at me with widely opened eyes, comically conveying childlike innocence.

I had to laugh. "Seriously Ada, why me?"

"Because you're the Narrator, you decide what happens, right?"

The taxi delivered us to an elegant sixteenth-century stone building on Via dei Coronari. We went up to the second floor and knocked on a richly varnished door. We were both nervous, not knowing what to expect. After some delay, the door was opened by a child with light olive skin and delicate features below a cascade of black curls. She was wearing a soft violet ankle-length dress. There were several silver bracelets on each wrist. Her feet were in red leather sandals and her toenails were painted silver. She glanced at me, then stared at Ada.

"We've come to see Lucrezia. She's expecting us," I said.

The girl remained silent as she studied Ada. Almost as an afterthought, she said, "I'm Lucrezia." Then added, "I suppose you were expecting someone as old and ugly as Vladimir, yes? Come in."

She turned and started down a hallway, calling out in rapid Italian until a maid appeared who was given instructions about drinks. Lucrezia led us into a large sitting room. The ceiling was high, with ornate plaster molding. The windows were tall and looked out onto a garden and then a park in the distance. The room was filled with small furniture and normal furniture, that is, furniture for Lucrezia and furniture for everyone else. There were many framed photographs of Lucrezia with dancers, actors, musicians, and celebrities of all kinds, all towering over her. Lucrezia sat back on a miniature gray velvet couch and lit a cigarette. Ada and I sat on a matching larger gray velvet couch opposite. The maid brought in a tray of glasses (one small, two large), ice cubes, a bottle of Campari, and a pitcher of fruit juice and set it on a square marble table between us. Lucrezia asked me to pour drinks and when I gave her the small glass she took it in her tiny perfect hand and said, "I'm older than I look but of course younger than you expected. Vladimir married me when I was sixteen, fifteen years ago. Before that, he courted me secretly, chastely, and dangerously for three years, the old pervert. He kept saying it had literary significance. All part of his pathetic charade. He took advantage of my fascination with him, and of course as I'm sure he's told you I thought he was someone else entirely. Secretly, he gloated over his deception and that's why I detest him. It was my brothers who sent word to Vladimir to get out of Italy and he did immediately. He's lucky to be alive, and in fact, should I decide I don't want him alive..." Lucrezia snapped her little fingers, and the look of vengeance on her face made up for the tiny sound her fingers made.

While Lucrezia was talking she'd been looking more at Ada than at me. She was obviously fascinated with her. She said, "You're a dancer?"

"Yes."

"Walk across the room please."

Ada did, and as always when she walked, the grace and energy of her dancing brilliance were barely contained.

"Lovely."

Lucrezia turned to me. "And you are Ada's...?"

Ada immediately said, "Father."

"Father? So Khalid has lied to me once again, which is not surprising. It's the only thing he's good at besides making money."

She looked at me again and asked, "And Blain? You're her father too of course."

Again, Ada quickly said, "Yes."

Lucrezia, having seen two frowns in a row from me said, "Surely you can speak for yourself."

Ada was staring at me with her hands on her knees and her eyes large with expectation.

"It's all a bit complicated..."

Ada's eyes become even larger...

"But yes, I'm Ada's father."

Ada sunk down in the couch with a lovely smirk and her eyes darted around the room happily. I needed Ada as an ally in dealing with this elf out of Brothers Grimm, who is scaring me more by the minute, and who is not to be distracted from the information she wants:

"And Blain?"

"Yes, Blain."

"Good, this is important information for me, because I make deals and it's important for us to all want something from the other in order to make our deal, yes?"

"Our deal?" I said.

"You're the negotiator. There are lots of players in this drama, but who can I trust? Not Vladimir, not Khalid, not Mojobe after she abandoned me professionally. Can I trust Ada? Can I trust Blain? Perhaps, but it's too early to tell."

She turned to Ada, "Can I trust you?"

Ada was caught by surprise. "Trust me? Trust me for what? I don't even know what you want from me."

Lucrezia looked at Ada with approval. "I like your forthrightness. Same with Blain. When I say trust, I'm making a distinction between truth and deception, between words and actions. Yes?"

Ada glanced at me, confused, and answered, "I guess so."

Lucrezia was quiet for a moment while she looked out the window toward the park far in the distance as though looking back into her life. She turned back to us.

"I'm going to ask you to do something in a minute that will involve your making a decision, a choice, on a moment's notice, but first I'll tell you a story."

She again looked out over the park to her history, and said, "When I was a thirteen-year-old girl in Palermo and even smaller than I am now, but perfectly formed, a man who had done business with my father caught me in a hallway and picked me up saying how perfect and doll-like I was. I yelled at him to put me down but he only laughed and began squeezing me. I pulled a three-inch pin from my hair and jammed it into his neck. I hit an artery and he wailed like a stuck pig which was what he was. He was taken to a hospital quickly enough so that his life was saved. However, I'd told my brothers what he'd done and when the man was released from the hospital, my brothers broke both his knee caps."

Lucrezia was quiet for a moment, then went on, "At the same time that I detest being picked up like some perfect little toy, some novelty, which is more of a temptation for people than you might imagine, I also savor physical contact with people who are drawn to my intelligence, my expertise in producing beautiful performance art, and my spirit. And believe me when I'm touched I always know why. Now here's what we're going to do and you have just seconds to make a critical choice."

Lucrezia got up from her couch and walked some ten feet away.

"Now stand up. We're going to walk toward each other and you must decide to either look past me when we meet, or stop to pick me up. You must do one or the other."

At this, Lucrezia started toward us, and we toward her. Ada gave me a true teenager's rolling of the eyes. She was looking to me for a decision and eying me for clues. When Lucrezia, looking straight ahead was about to walk between us, I knelt down and Ada quickly followed suit, and we enveloped her in our arms, holding her gently between us, and stood. There was a brief moment of immobility during which I wondered if I was about to get a hairpin in my neck. She began to move slowly, a kind of soft squirming turning movement, stretching out an arm then a leg to encircle the bodies pressed against her. Then with arms out and a hand on the chest of each of us, she leaned back smiling, a real smile, her perfect white teeth contrasting with her olive skin.

"OK, put me down."

She said this in the tone of a confident impresario closing a deal. Going back to recline on her little velvet couch, she took a sip of Campari and said, "Now you wish to discuss Mojobe, Khalid, Vladimir, the Waldeebe, Blain, yourself Ada, and *yourself* Mr. negotiator/narrator, yes?"

Ada and I spontaneously laughed, partly out of relief at having been accepted by this dangerous creature, and partly because we could now get down to working out how we can get back home as soon as possible. Lucrezia joined in, her laugh high and bell-like, totally belying the power of this tiny Sicilian beauty.

We were invited to stay for dinner and as we approached the table, Lucrezia climbed a couple of small steps to a chair that matched the others only was smaller and higher. When she was seated the maid moved to push her chair toward the table.

"No Maria, let the gentleman do that."

She said this smiling and nodding toward me. The maid stepped back and I obliged.

Then she said, "I never let anyone help me who I don't trust."

Still smiling, she added, "You'd better never betray me or you'd have my brothers to deal with."

How much of a joke this was I didn't know, and Lucrezia left it that way.

The food was excellent. We started with a small first course of pasta and moved on to lamb and various vegetables. Lucrezia had before her a miniature version of the tableware that matched our full-size set. As she ate she dispensed with conversation and I imagined a tough Palermo kid having just come in from the streets, packing away fuel surrounded by a large family doing the same. Between courses, she talked about the food, certain seasonings, and methods of cooking she had taught the maid. It was one more example of this small woman's large will to control everything in her life from the minutiae of herbs in a sauce to the precise casting of a theatrical event.

Over cheese and fruit and espresso, Lucrezia brought the conversation back to why she had brought us here.

"As you know, in Spoleto, Italy, every summer there is the famous Festival dei Due Mondi, the festival of two worlds. For the benefit of Ada, I will explain. You of course (Lucrezia looked at me) are totally familiar with it, but Ada is probably not and this is very important to her. The festival brings together the best in performance art from your country and mine. The originator of the festival is Gian-Carlo Menotti and he wields great power over it. Unfortunately, Maestro Menotti some years ago developed a dislike for me, and said I was dictatorial and difficult to work with (all hearsay. I'd never worked with the man but he had friends who resented my success). As a result, I have never been invited to participate, even though the work I produce is world-class. Gian-Carlo has total control over who participates from Italy, but the American participants are chosen by a separate group, one of whom I know and who is supportive of me."

Lucrezia paused to take a bite out of a grape like it was a small plum. She chewed for a moment, then noisily spit a seed onto her plate with her head down. She lifted her eyes to look mischievously at us and said, "You can take the kid out of the street but you can't take the street out of the kid. Old Sicilian proverb, yes? No, your own Jimmy Cagney."

The maid cleared the table and returned with cognac and cigars. I poured a glass for Lucrezia and myself. Ada held out a glass and said, "Dad?" I was about to pour but instead I said, "I don't think so, you're fifteen years old." She glared at me.

Lucrezia lit a cigar and as cigars go it was not a large one but was just right as the power instrument to manipulate as she planned to manipulate us.

Lucrezia looked into her brandy for a moment as though she was reading a scenario, then looked at Ada.

"Does the idea of dancing at Spoleto appeal to you?"

"Oh yeah! And I know the Festival. I've seen clips from it."

Lucrezia smiled and looked at me.

"And you, proud father of this virtuoso dancer, would you like to have Ada dance at Spoleto?, and choreograph her?"

"Possibly. You seem to have a plan in mind, Lucrezia. Would you mind telling me what it is?"

"Ah, good, I like directness. We will be good partners."

"Partners?"

Lucrezia blew three perfect smoke rings. Remarkably, the first was moving at a slower speed than the second, which was slower than the third, so the second floated through the first and the third floated through the second. Lucrezia beamed.

"In theater, everything is precise teamwork, yes?"

I said, "Partners?"

Lucrezia looked at me steadily and seriously.

"I plan to produce a major performance event for Spoleto. You will be the co-producer. You will be the director. I will be the co-director. The performers will be Ada, Blain, Mojobe, the Waldeebe (who are remarkable dancers), Sister Agnes and Father Joseph (yes, I know all about your company), Aimee, Rasputin, and Vladimir too will perform, he, specifically under my direction. We will be an

American company. My participation will remain confidential until everything is settled with Gian-Carlo, then I will be billed as co-director and co-producer."

I sat silently studying Lucrezia as I processed all she'd said.

"And if I don't agree?"

"Then Blain goes back to Africa with the Waldeebe."

"Where *is* Blain?" Ada said.

"Rome."

"Where are the Waldeebe?" I said.

"Rome."

"You could go to prison Lucrezia."

"Do you think I'm stupid? Intermediaries, *trusted* intermediaries, have arranged everything. I've never laid eyes on Blain or the Waldeebe. And I would add, you are not so outside of all this as you so smugly think you are. My brothers are already involved because they have taken it as a major family insult that Gian-Carlo Menotti has spurned my Festival efforts every year."

"And why do you say *I* am not outside all of this?"

"Because my brothers will consider you the obstacle."

"So I should agree to put my creativity into your theater piece because I've been threatened with broken knees or a bullet through the head?"

"*Our* theater piece."

"I don't know anything about your theater work."

"I know a lot about your theater work and I think you're brilliant."

"What are we playing here, good Italian mobster / bad Italian mobster?"

Ada laughed loudly. I glared at her.

"I'm sorry Dad, that was really funny."

"It was really funny. It could be the name of our piece," Lucrezia said.

Lucrezia and Ada were ahead of me. There was no way I could refuse to do this and they knew it. But I needed to hold out for as much leverage as possible. Lucrezia must feel that she'd be luckier to have me than I would to have her in spite of her brothers.

I took a chance on a power grab.

"I will think about it overnight. We can meet tomorrow, but when we meet I want Blain and the Waldeebe to be here."

"Why?" Lucrezia asked.

"Because I want to be sure that you actually have control over them."

"But by doing that, I'd be giving up my anonymity in this."

"Precisely, then you would have to trust me. After all, you're asking that I trust you."

"I'll think about it tonight.," Lucrezia said in a reasonable tone, "Come in the morning and they will either be here or not."

"And we will either have a deal or not," I said, refusing to let her have the last word.

Lucrezia walked us to the door. There was a moment of hesitation as I considered the various forms of good night gesture; a leaning little handshake, a squatting embrace, just some words? Finally, I bent down with my hand out.

"No, up," Lucrezia said.

I bent over and reached down, putting my hands under her arms, feeling the moisture there as evidence of her effort at making her deal. As I lifted her, she hiked up her skirt so she could wrap her legs around my torso and her arms around my neck like a small wiry monkey climbing a palm tree. A cacophony of scents was released; delicate cologne, Sicilian sweat, cigar, brandy, garlic, and just Lucrezia scent that came from her skin and was Lucrezia and no one else. She turned to Ada, did the same thing, and I was given a glimpse of a perfectly proportioned small leg complete with delicate black hairs rising from her ankle.

As Ada and I walked across Piazza Navona to a taxi stand, Ada said, "Boy she scares me." After a moment of silence she added, "But won't it be exciting, to perform at Spoleto?"

"Whether we perform at Spoleto is an open question."

"What do you mean?, there's no way we can let those Africans take Blain home with them."

"We have to protect ourselves, in complex ways."

"Ways? What ways? I don't understand, Dad"

"That's because it's beyond your life experience, daughter."

"Whoa! I'm beginning to think I liked you better before we became family."

"Well, we could go back to that status anytime you'd like."

I'm feeling like I've had enough manipulation by small provocative females for one night.

"You're mean," Ada said.

"Maybe, but right now I'm thinking how calm my life was before you sauntered into it."

"Sauntered?, I don't saunter. I either move or I don't. Sauntering is for losers."

After a moment, she added, "If I wasn't in your life your theater world would be pretty mediocre."

"Who do you think you are, Martha Graham?"

"As a matter of fact maybe I am Martha Graham, reincarnated."

At that, Ada launched into a series of incredibly Graham-like, very exaggerated dance movements. We were approaching a group of Italians getting into a cab, and being Italians, they burst into enthusiastic applause. Ada bowed dramatically, then turned and thumbed her nose at me. In seconds she had gone from sexy siren to saucy brat. She was grinning wildly.

When we got up to our suite, we were both exhausted but also wound up from our time with Lucrezia.

"Can I sleep in your bed, Dad? It's huge and it is for two people. I'm too excited and it'll take me forever to get to sleep if I'm by myself. We can talk about this whole thing with Lucrezia."

"Talking about Lucrezia is the last thing I want to do."

"OK, then we can talk about anything you want."

"I'd rather just let my mind calm down silently."

"Then we can be silent."

"No Ada."

"Why not? What are you afraid of? We can't have sex, because we're father and daughter."

"I wasn't thinking about sex."

Ada was silent for a moment, then said, "You know when we left Lucrezia's and she climbed up me like a monkey, that was sexual."

I remained silent.

"Was it sexual for you, too?"

"Yes, it was sexual."

"I mean she's so small and perfect. Her face is so beautiful and she's got those classic little breasts and that cute little ass, and there's something about her smell."

We were both silent. Then she said, "And when she went from climbing up you to climbing up me I felt like she was connecting you to me and us to her."

"Well that is her plan, you were there."

"I didn't mean theatrically."

"How did you mean?"

"I'm not sure."

In the morning there was a knock on the door. "Room service."

I turned to look at the window to see if it really was morning, and there was a small bare foot, inches from my face. I got out of bed and there was another bare foot sticking out of the covers. At the foot of the bed was Ada's riot of red hair. I went out to the sitting room to open the door.

"Buon Giorno, Seniore"

An elderly waiter pushed in a cart of food ennobled to the level of art. He silently set our antique round table with breakfast. When he turned to leave we both heard, "Hey, where'd you go?"

The waiter looked discretely straight ahead and left.

I returned to the bedroom and looking at Ada, said, "So?"

"Well I thought it'd be less, you know, personal, if we were head to foot. I just couldn't get to sleep, I was so excited about dancing at Spoleto, and I looked in your room and you were out cold. I was planning to be back in my room when you woke up. So we slept in the same bed and it was no great disaster, right, so we don't have to worry that one anymore, Yes?"

When Ada delivered the last word, her expression was a ringer for Lucrezia's as was her voice. I had to laugh even though I had the feeling I was sinking into the quicksand of a bad chapter in my life.

Then Ada stunned me into a blank stare.

"Here's a bit of nice family news Dad, next Friday, we will be sixteen, Blain and I."

In the morning, Maria opened the door to Lucrezia's apartment, and with a subdued "Buon Giorno" motioned for us to follow her. There was a feeling in the air that what was being played out in the household this morning was beyond her capacity to acknowledge. We walked past the living room and the dining room to a spacious solarium that extended out onto a balcony. It was flooded with bright morning light diffused by gauzy white curtains billowing gently in a breeze from open windows. There was a variety of flora, tall sweeping ferns, tropical palms, and exotic orchids. In addition to an array of rattan furniture (small and large), there was a tall bird cage housing several parrots and bright-hued birds with long tail feathers. One of the parrots was squawking, "Grazie Lucrezia" as she put out seeds on a dish. Lucrezia was wearing silver silk pajamas, and in bare feet seemed smaller than ever. Her hair was still damp from washing and some curls adhered to her forehead as if drawn by a Renaissance master. She was as entrancing as the orchids and the birds and I would have stared longer if not for strained mumbling behind us. We turned to see three more exotic creatures in this bell jar of paradise.

The Waldeebes were half reclining on a chaise lounge covered with floral print pillows. Between them was Blain (easily recognizable because her carbon copy was standing next to me). She had on a white sleeveless knee-length dress from which her legs reached for some purchase on the floor for space from the smiling Waldeebe.

The Waldeebes were wearing long finely made white robes with amulets of various materials and colors hanging around their necks. They stood for the introductions and were even taller than Mojobe and their blackness in their white robes and turbans was total.

I had expected an outburst of joyous greeting between Ada and Blain, but Blain just nodded at Ada. She was silent and frightened. The Waldeebe were clearly fascinated by Ada, the other half of this matching pair of striking specimens. I remember Mojobe saying that twins were a rarity in their tribe. And the likes of these twins with their pale skin, hazel eyes, and flaming hair clearly were not to be seen in the heart of darkness that's home to these Waldeebe.

When I was introduced to Blain she shook my hand firmly and nodded but didn't smile. Her hair was shorter than Ada's, a boy's cut really, and was very attractive on her. The Waldeebe were very gracious in greeting me. They each kept my hand in theirs for a long time as though either to extract something from me or to impart something to me. It was unnerving because they were so exotic. No other word would do.

Blain was the first to speak, "The cousins were telling me how much I will entice the Waldeebe I will meet when I return to Africa with them."

I thought that this was something Lucrezia had coached Blain to come out with in order to emphasize the terms of our deal, or no deal. But no, Lucrezia was stunned by what Blain had said, and made no attempt to hide it. The Waldeebe spoke some English (they were tutored by Mojobe) and Waldeebe One spoke in response to a wild glare from Lucrezia, of whom it was obvious he was terrified, in spite of being three times her size.

"Please Maestro Lucrezia, all we wish for is a reunion with our Mojobe. We do not wish to take this young lady Blain anywhere against her will."

Waldeebe One had panic in his eyes because of Lucrezia's stare, but he said, "Only if we cannot have Mojobe, then will we take this one."

"You will not have or take anyone unless I say so," Lucrezia said forcefully.

Waldeebe Two stepped forward and said in more limited English, "Mr. Khalid say what will be, or his boss say so."

Ada and I said simultaneously, "Khalid? His boss?"

Lucrezia was frustrated, "Yes, there is more to this than I said last night, but I didn't expect it to surface."

She turned to the Waldeebe. "I cannot agree to anything right now, I have to make some phone calls. Leave Blain here and we will talk again tonight."

Waldeebe One pulled a cell phone from his robes, and poked at it with what seemed a seven-inch-long index finger. He said into the phone, "We are coming."

Waldeebe Two pulled a short spear from within his robes, a real spear with a sharp hand-hewn point.

Waldeebe One took Blain's arm and said, "We are leaving. Don't interfere."

The cousins and Blain walked through the apartment and out the front door. Blain was ashen with fear. We all went to the window to see them climb into a black Mercedes down below.

We sat down and stared at each other.

Ada looked at me with a scowl, "Why didn't you do something? You're her father!"

"I didn't do anything because I didn't have my spear with me," I said with lame frustration.

Ada gave me a blank stare.

"This is no joke, believe me," Lucrezia said.

"Good, Lucrezia, now are you going to share the information we should have had before we showed up here this morning? Like what does Khalid have to do with this and who is Khalid's mysterious boss?" I said.

Surprisingly, Lucrezia was contrite. "I'm sorry. I thought things were going to go smoothly. I didn't expect any of what just happened."

I asked, "Who is Khalid's boss?"

Lucrezia sighed, and spoke softly. "Khalid's boss is the person from whom Khalid originally acquired Ada and Blain, some time ago, when they were small children. And now he wants them back. I was assured (falsely) that he was out of the loop on our Spoleto deal, and I thought that by achieving our Spoleto deal we'd all be in the US and out of reach of these people, and we would all have what we wanted."

Ada was now serious. "But who is Khalid's boss? Blain and I knew nothing about any of this. We were too young."

Lucrezia said, "I don't want to be over dramatic, but this is Italy, which in some ways has changed less than you probably think. His identity is not clear, and the name most associated with him is one that is just not spoken."

Ada said, "Do you know his name?"

Lucrezia just stared out the window and I knew she was not going to answer.

I took a different tack. "Why does he want the twins back? And what claim does he have to them, was he a legal guardian?"

"I would rather not have this conversation in the presence of Ada."

Ada sat upright in her chair and yelled, "Who the fuck do you think you are, jerking us around like this? Blain and I are not your goddamn property! Everything about you is sneaky."

I was amazed that Lucrezia barely registered any of this. She just got up and left the room. Because of her non-response to Ada, I knew that the situation was even more serious than I thought.

"I just want to get out of Rome and go home but now I can't because they've got Blain," Ada said.

I didn't say it but I thought, they have us too.

Ada and I returned to the hotel. We were followed by a different black luxury car. Once in our suite, I walked to the window to look out over Rome. I was thinking, given what has unfolded in this city, our situation is but a comma in the history books. But that doesn't make it any less real or less terrifying for Ada who stood next to me.

"If you abandon me, I'm lost to these monsters," she said.

"Why would I abandon you?"

"Because they don't want you, they want me. You could go back home and pick up with the company where you were before I showed up."

"But I can't do that."

"Why not?"

"Because I love you, and because I'm the narrator and without me no one would know how the story ends."

"Do you mean that?"

"Of course, I mean that, who else could tell this story?"

"No, I mean about loving me."

"Because I'm your father, I love you, yes?" I give a lame imitation of Lucrezia.

"Don't joke, I'm scared."

"Of what?"

"The only reason you say I'm your daughter is because I tricked you into it."

"That's true."

'See, so when you say you love me because I'm your daughter it doesn't prove anything."

"That's true, it doesn't prove anything, but how do you prove love?"

"Even though I think she's a creep, I think Lucrezia knows something about how to tell how someone feels about you by holding onto them."

"Maybe."

Ada thought for a minute, then asked, "Will you hold onto me and tell me you love me and not because I'm your daughter, and you won't dump me?"

I put my arms around her and pulled her to me and she put her arms around my neck and pressed against me and I said, "I love you Ada, and not just because you're my daughter, and I won't dump you."

"Can I trust you?"

"You can trust me."

I was about to suggest that we have some ice cream brought up but my thoughts were interrupted by a bullet smashing through the window high above our heads.

When the Polizia arrived, I was unsure how much to tell them. If I said anything about Khalid, the Waldeebe, Blain, Khalid's mysterious boss, or anything connected to Lucrezia, I would be jeopardizing Blain, and Ada too for that matter. So I said it must have been some nut randomly shooting at Americans in Luxury hotels. The inspector, when he looked at the bullet picked out of the wall by an officer, said, "This is from a very high powered, very sophisticated rifle, surely with a scope, and that means if they wanted you dead, you'd be dead. Could someone be warning you off?"

My gallows humor kicked in since I couldn't tell him the truth. "Well, yes, I'm a famous theater director and you know how jealous theater people can be."

He looked at me with contempt, either because he thought that what I'd said I believed was true, or that I know someone was after me and this being Italy, I was afraid to say anything, and he had more pressing matters than to stand around a $900 a night hotel suite talking to an American jerk.

Before leaving he said, "Here's my card, call me if you're willing to cooperate."

Ada was devastated. She said, "Anything could happen to us at any time."

"That's true but one thing that won't happen is that we'll be killed."

"How can you say that after what just happened?"

"As the inspector said, if they wanted us dead, we'd be dead. We're of no use to them dead. They wanted to scare us."

"Well, I'm scared."

"Yes, well, I'm a little uneasy myself, but we're going to outsmart them."

Ada turned to see if I was serious or just trying to cheer her up.

"You're serious aren't you?"

"Yes."

"And how are we going to outsmart them?"

"Through hot tribal lust."

"Please don't joke, you're the only hope I have."

"I'm not joking."

"Then please explain, Mr. Wise Ass Dad."

I was pleased to see Ada returning to normal.

"Let's review what happened in Lucrezia's solarium: Thinking back, what is the most striking image that comes to mind?"

"Those big black scary guys."

"Good, and why were they so scary?"

"Because they were like dangerous animals, beautiful dangerous animals."

"Why dangerous?"

"Jesus, they had a fucking spear!"

"No, that was at the end. Why were they dangerous before that?"

Ada thought for a moment. "Well, because they were obsessed."

"Excellent. What was the object of their obsession?"

"Well, they had all this raw sexual energy filling the room. And they kept eying Blain and when she accidentally backed into one of them, he got wild-eyed."

"That's all accurate, but do you think they're obsessed with just any female around? Is it only physiological lust?"

"Well, they did say they really wanted their Mojobe back."

"Excellent, Ada."

"What's so excellent?"

"The Waldeebe are being driven mad by the absence of Mojobe, the loss of Mojobe. They had her in the village and she was going to marry them both, and the three of them had sex together as is the custom of their tribe and the cousins cannot forget that. They are wild-eyed with the memory of it. Every primal ounce of energy and thought in those two virile guys is now focused on Mojobe, and ravaging Mojobe in every conceivable combination they can fantasize."

"Wow, you're a guy, so I suppose you know."

She eyed me impishly, "So now are you fantasizing about ravaging me in every possible combination?"

"Not till after gelato riso"

"What in the world is that?"

"Rice ice cream, the best thing you'll ever taste."

She smiled, and sat back on the couch. "OK, so now we have these two tall white-robed black sex maniacs obsessed with reclaiming their hot babe Mojobe, how do we cash in on that?"

"We bring them back to Portland, to Mojobe."

"But what about Mojobe?"

"That's for Mojobe to work out, we're not the gods of love. She did say she missed them."

"And Blain?"

"The Waldeebe bring Blain with them."

"Once they're all back everyone will know everything and there'll be total pandemonium."

"Yes! And we'll make art out of it."

Ada thought for a moment and I had the feeling everything I'd said was swirling around in her artist head into some positive pattern.

"Is it going to work, Dad?"

"It is."

"How do you know?"

"Because it has to, we have no other viable scenario, plus we know everyone's weaknesses."

"What about Lucrezia?"

"We know her weaknesses too."

'Yeah? like what?"

"I'll tell you in the morning. I have to think about her role more."

"Can I sleep in your bed tonight? We almost got killed today but didn't, so we could almost have sex but not."

"What kind of logic is that?"

"It isn't logic."

"OK."

"OK, really?"

"OK."

The hotel management moved us into an even more luxurious room.

When Ada squirmed happily into bed next to me I couldn't tell her that the reason I'd agreed to this was that I was far less sanguine than I seemed and in fact believed we could easily be dead at any moment in the days to come as this drama unfolded.

"Do we have to sleep head to toe?" Ada said.

"No."

"Really?"

"Really."

"So there are no restrictions?"

"Just don't drool on me."

"I drool?"

She seemed genuinely embarrassed.

"You did last night, and you did on the plane."

"So I'm a kid, yes?" (With her Lucrezia accent)

"Good night, Lucrezia."

"Don't even think of being in bed with her."

I was beginning to relax, so remained silent.

After a few minutes, she said, "I mean it, Dad."

Then, "I mean it. Are you asleep? I really mean it."

As I drift off, I think how convoluted is the sexuality of our species.

In the morning, I woke with the weight of what was ahead with the mobsters of all countries, colors, motives, etc. I was not optimistic. Then I heard voices.

"The flowers should go here, yes?"

"Si, signorina."

"And the fruit here!"

"Si, signorina."

I walked out into the sitting room and Ada was directing the same elder room service man as they set the table for breakfast. He had a cluster of flowers jammed into his lapel, obviously the work of Ada, who was beaming brightly. She had on a pink T-shirt and my white boxer shorts. The server's face wore a conflict of pleasure and embarrassment, more of the latter when he saw me.

"Ah, Buon Giorno, Signore" He looked at Ada and the table and held both hands up as though to say, what could I do?

I put my hand on his shoulder and said, "It's OK, Grazie! bene!" I found a $20 bill of Khalid's money and gave it to him. He pushed his cart toward the door, turning and smiling, turning and smiling. When he had left, I said, "I think that man just had the most exciting morning of his life."

"He's sweet. Have some mango Dad, *it's* really sweet!"

She pushed a slice of mango into her mouth.

"Watch!"

Ada started loping and turning and leaping in her style of levitating grace that always brought tears to my eyes because it was so fresh and so Ada. The idea of her dead and never doing that again, or me dead and never seeing it again was beginning to fill me with determination to pull off my grand scheme with the array of wild card players I had to begin to manipulate, and soon, today.

Ada came to a stop, panting slightly.

"So, did I drool?"

"I don't know."

"Let's go check."

Ada took my hand and led me to the bed. She pulled back the covers. All was dry.

"See? I've already outgrown it."

Then we both saw a generous riverbed of moisture on a pillow, my pillow.

Ada muttered, "Oh oh."

Then she brightened, "I guess you caught droolyitis from me, yes?"

"No, I think you were sharing my pillow."

Ada was barely concealing a smile.

"Mea culpa. I was listening to your brain while you slept. It's amazing what goes on in there while you look so calm and peaceful on the outside."

I turned to Ada. Her cheeks were flushed pink from her dance movements. Her red hair was wildly awry, her eyes were clear, almost mauve in color and bright with being alive. Her pink T-shirt was wrinkled from sleep, and her shorts (my shorts) were slightly twisted from her loping and leaping. We were close enough so I felt her body heat from dancing, and I inhaled her myriad scents, a combination too complex to decipher. I knew I'd never again so poignantly experience the essence of another human being, because, at her age and stage, nothing was concealed.

"Let's go indulge in that culinary art out on the table."

I walked from the room.

Ada waited, then followed.

As we quietly indulged in our glorious breakfast, Ada said, with pastry flecks on her mouth, "My birthday is today."

When we knocked on Lucrezia's front door, it opened but a crack so that Maria could safely look out. She opened the door for us and led us to the solarium. Lucrezia looked over at us as she talked on the phone. Her face was filled with unease.

She was about to hang up. "I don't know when... you'll have to wait to hear from me." She listened a moment longer, frowning, then hung up the phone.

She motioned for us to sit and asked Maria to bring coffee.

"This is dangerous, and so complicated, too many conflicting interests. At least so far, you two are safe." She said this with an edge of resentment.

"We were shot at last night through our hotel room window, with a high-powered rifle."

"Oh my God."

"Yes, well, Lucrezia, your God is not doing us much good right now."

"Were you hurt? What did you tell the police?"

"We're unhurt, and I told the police that I had no idea who would have done it or why."

Lucrezia said, "I was just on the phone with..."

"With...?"

"Better not to say, but the last thing said was, "You know what he wants.""

"Well, whatever *he* wants, what's more important is what *we* want, and by that I mean Ada, me, and you."

Lucrezia looked skeptical.

I took a swallow of coffee. "One of the things I'd learned as a choreographer is to distinguish between what is complex and what is complicated. Complexity may have a lot going on but everything is interrelated. Complicatedness consists of disparate and conflicting parts."

Ada said, "Wow Dad, I didn't hear that last night while I was drooling and listening to your brain."

"What...?" Lucrezia said.

"Never mind," I said, frowning.

Lucrezia was still studying Ada, and I imagined her thoughts.

"Lucrezia, Let's go back to what you said our first evening together. You wanted to co-produce and co-direct a production with me for Spoleto, Yes?" (I could see Ada smirking out of the corner of my eye.)

"Yes."

"And you wanted to have, in that production, Ada, Blain, Mojobe, the Waldeebe, Sister Agnes, Father Joseph, and Vladimir (so you could torture him I presume)."

Lucrezia laughed at my mention of Vladimir, and I saw it as a good sign.

"Yes."

"Then listen to my idea."

I went through everything I'd told Ada about how we could pull this off, using Mojobe to lure the Waldeebe and Blain, etc. Lucrezia listened carefully and I could tell by her expression that she saw promise in what I was saying.

"I agree with all you've said but here's the complication. This man who has such power over Khalid wants Ada and Blain," she said.

"Why? Why does he want them?"

"Because he has carnal tastes to make the Marquis de Sade look like Mother Teresa. And he already has Blain."

"But does he have Blain in his custody?"

"No, she's being held separately by the Waldeebe."

"And they with her."

"Yes?" Lucrezia said.

"Look Lucrezia, let me simplify the situation. There are the good guys, us, and there are the bad guys, them. The bad guys have their sex nut and his obsession is fueling their side. But we have our own sex nut (two in fact) and with primal tastes, their bad guy could never imagine. The Waldeebe want their Mojobe back more than they want their next breath of air. And if they believe that they can trade Blain for Mojobe they are not letting anyone near Blain. Africans know the art of trade. All we have to do is convince them that Blain is their ticket to Mojobe."

Lucrezia walked to the window to survey her Rome and to consider what I'd said. After a few minutes, she turned. At that moment the sun broke through the clouds and streaks of light like stage spots struck her. Her curls were illuminated and her features clearly delineated in all their refinement, and the white silk pant-suit she was wearing seemed lit from within, as though she was an apparition. I was struck again at what a work of art she was. She walked toward me as she spoke.

"I believe you're right and I agree with your plan, and you know the reason is that I wish to make a great work of theater art with you."

When she was standing in front of me she lifted her arms and said, "Now up."

I reached down and lifted her, and monkey style, she wrapped her legs around me, reached up with her small hands behind my neck.."

At this, we heard the terrible crash of a Chinese vase on the marble floor that seconds before was on a table next to Ada, who stood in a sea of shards glaring at Lucrezia.

Lucrezia remained wrapped around me and turned to look at Ada. Then she slid down my body and walked to stand in front of Ada who was still angry but also uneasy with what she'd done. Lucrezia moved her arms out from her body and commanded, "Up!"

Ada glanced at me, then lifted Lucrezia. When Lucrezia was at eye level with Ada she leaned back. "I also want to make great theater art with you Ada, you're a remarkable dancer and a remarkable girl." She moved her mouth close to the corner of Ada's mouth and with her small tongue pushed out a little pool of saliva, which ran down Ada's chin. Then she slid slowly down, helping herself to a braille survey of Ada's body on the way.

Ada was obviously harboring conflicting impulses because she remained immobile, still with Lucrezia's drool on her chin. Finally, she wiped off her chin with the back of her hand, and said softly, "Sorry about the vase."

Lucrezia smiled, "Not to worry. It was a fake. You can't believe how many times people are provoked into breaking something of mine. I buy those vases six at a time." She sat in one of her little velvet chairs, crossed her legs, looked at us for a moment, then said, "So, our next move will be to bring Mojobe to Rome, yes?"

In the taxi on our way back to the hotel, Ada said, "You can't believe the effect it had on me when Lucrezia did that."

"Did what?"

"Climbed up me, stuck her wet tongue right next to my mouth, drooled on me, and then slid down me feeling my body like a blind man."

"Well, that's Lucrezia's style, her strategy is to catch people off guard, to surprise them, disorient them."

"Yeah, but to have the effect it had!..."

"Which was...?"

"It started when she stuck her tongue against the corner of my mouth, it was weird, like a kiss that missed the target, and then continued right down my body as she slid down. Do you think she knew what she was doing?"

"I don't think Lucrezia leaves much to chance."

"But why would she do that?"

"You could ask her, but make sure you want to hear the answer first."

"But what would be an answer I didn't want to hear?"

"That she's in love with you. That she wants to have you as her sex toy. That she wants to trade you to some decadent associate of Khalid."

Ada stared out the taxi window for the rest of the way, speculating probably on the mysteries of the body.

Going up in the elevator, Ada asked, "Do you think we can trust Lucrezia?"

"I would answer your question this way: Once we know exactly what Lucrezia wants for herself, we can trust her to act accordingly. Until then, I'd say, no."

"Do you like her, Dad?"

"I'm not sure. Do you?"

"I have a lot of different feelings that don't add up. I admire her. I'm scared of her. She's beautiful. She's mean. She's ambitious. She's fascinating to be with because she's so unpredictable. She makes me jealous."

"Jealous of what?"

"Jealous of how she might connect to you and you to her."

"Connect?"

"Yeah connect, you know like a man and a woman."

"You mean like a man and a midget."

"Don't tell me you're not attracted to her, that she's not beautiful."

"You mean beautiful like this?" I squatted down and did an exaggerated imitation of Lucrezia doing her wiggly monkey climb up. She screamed in hysterical laughter as the elevator door opened to a stern triad: a nun, a priest, a mother superior, all giving us an Inquisition stare that only fueled more hysterics from Ada.

When we were in our room Ada, still laughing, said, "Now it's my turn to do the Lucrezia imitation, and we'll see who does it best."

She squatted down, held her arms out, and commanded, "UP!"

I pulled her up and she climbed onto me with her arms and legs wrapped around me wiggling and climbing and giggling. As she began a tight descent she abruptly emitted a low intense "Ohhhh." Then she sat immobile on the floor catching her breath.

"Was that the difference one birthday makes?" I said softly.

Two hours later, there was a knock on our door. Ada looked through the peephole and whispered, "It's Rasputin and Aimee!"

I opened the door to Aimee, wearing a short white summer dress. From the edges of many parts of her dress, there was Rasputin's drawing skills in the form of green foliage creeping out. It was as though Rasputin had brought us a small garden wrapped in a dress. He had made some effort to meet the style standards of Rome but of course, fell far short. Nevertheless he looked more presentable than usual, in tan linen pants and a light blue silk shirt. But as usual, his long straggly hair, shaggy teeth, and curved yellow fingernails were still there. I had the feeling that he'd felt pressure to dress up for someone, certainly none of us. He motioned with his head for Aimee to come in first and I wondered if these two talked at all any more.

I played it straight. "Hello you two, sit down, what are you doing in Rome?"

When Aimee sat back in a chair her dress hiked up to reveal flora of all colors, growing progressively denser as it climbed up her thighs, like a garden leading to the forbidden fruit. Rasputin sat opposite Aimee looking at her legs as he spoke.

"I'd been invited to Rome to present my work (He nods toward Aimee) to a very important collector of... let's say, living art."

Ada and I exchanged glances.

"And how did you come across this collector?"

When Rasputin answered, "Through Khalid", Ada and I both knew who he was talking about.

"So, were you successful? Did he want your work?"

"Yes, my work and also the work of those two savages from Africa."

Aimee winces at Rasputin's words, and he responded with, "They *are* savages." and after a moment added, "Savages with impressive primitive skills, especially in the field of deep cuts resulting in beautiful hard raised scars, which combined with my color and imagery would be breathtaking." He pants briefly as though affected by his own words.

"So have you received a specific commission from the collector?" Still playing it straight I asked.

"Yes, he wanted to begin with fresh untouched subjects, to be embellished, totally embellished, as he participated as director. He wished for both tattoo and deep cuts, so it would be a collaboration between me and the savages. And that's why I'm here." He turned to Ada. "He also wanted you and your sister as our subjects, and he was offering an extraordinary amount of money."

"Yeah? Like how much are we worth?" Ada laughed.

Rasputin revealed a crooked stained incisor as he said, "He's serious. Three hundred grand for you, three for Blain, three for me, and a thousand for the savages."

Ada looked at me with raised eyebrows, turned to Rasputin, grinned, and said, "Gee, Rasputin, thanks for the offer to be immortalized but I don't think so."

Rasputin glowered at her.

To divert things I looked at Aimee and said, "What do you think?"

"I wouldn't be participating, I'm here just to show Rasputin's work, and this man was very impressed. He offered to buy me as I am."

"Buy you?"

"Yes, not to own, but just have in his collection to show occasionally to his friends."

Rasputin was still staring at Ada. He said, "Don't treat this as a joke. The collector wants this. The savages want this, a thousand dollars is an unimaginable amount of money to them and they are determined to have it and they already have Blain."

"You've talked to the Waldeebe?"

"Yes, it's all settled."

"We'll think it over. Give me a number where I can reach you," I said.

Rasputin, attempting to look like he was in control, said, "We'll reach you."

When Rasputin and Aimee had left, Ada asked, "Aside from this being too weird, do you think Rasputin was telling the truth?"

"Rasputin was bluffing. The Waldeebe haven't agreed to anything. He hasn't even talked to them. He said they were dazzled by a thousand dollars, but we know the Waldeebe are wealthy tribal royalty, so a thousand dollars would mean nothing to them. Besides, their interest is in trading Blain for Mojobe, not carving designs into people. Although I do believe the "Collector" wants to do this. It's consistent with all we know about him. And I would add that even though our Rasputin is a nut, he is dangerous because he's obsessed. It all goes back to my basic belief that anyone interesting has a screw loose, and given the personalities of our theater company, we've got enough loose screws to open a hardware store."

"Hey Dad, that was funny. Do you have a loose screw?"

"More than one."

"How come I haven't seen any?"

"Because your own loose screws have distorted your perception."

"Is that anything to say to your daughter?"

"Sure, because loose screws in an artist are a virtue. If all your screws were in-tact, you'd be back in Portland in high school, worrying about boyfriends and toenail polish."

Lucrezia had dispatched her brothers to the airport to meet Mojobe, because Lucrezia and Ada and I were under constant surveillance by the collector's people, and we didn't want him to know Mojobe was in Rome. She arrived under cover of darkness at the rear service entrance of Lucrezia's building. Mojobe was more startling in her beauty than ever. She was at first profusely apologetic to Lucrezia for abandoning her theater group when she first arrived from Africa. "Not to worry my dear, we are once again about to embark on an important stage adventure, with our artist friends here." Lucrezia gestured toward Ada and me. Mojobe seemed puzzled by Lucrezia's comment but didn't say anything.

Lucrezia's brothers were not what I expected, which were hard-eyed petty thugs. They were as stylish as Lucrezia, slim and handsome. But tall, like normal people. They were clearly packing heat as we say in American movies, but it seemed perfectly appropriate, as though since the whole world was not as refined as they, some protection was after all necessary. Brother One was immediately drawn to Ada, while Brother Two had it seemed already decided that Mojobe was just the woman to bring home to cause apoplexy in his mother. Ada was pleased by the attention of Brother One, and her cheeks were flushed pink. Now what?, is all I could think to think. When he offered Ada a cigarette, I immediately said, "She's only fif... sixteen." He shrugged genially.

We all had wine and cheese and bread and I found I liked these brothers. They were educated and had broad cultural interests but had decided to remain con-nected to the criminal activities that had been a tradition in their family. I specu-lated on whether they were selling heroin or just active in the business of "protec-tion." The one reassuring factor was that it was comforting to have these two on our side when it came to dealing with the Collector. My other thought was whether there would be some art to come out of all this.

When the brothers had left, we went over our plan with Mojobe, who had declined to go to bed until she heard the whole story. She seemed resigned to everything, and was looking forward to seeing the Waldeebe again.

"You have no idea what men they are," she said quietly with feeling.

Actually, I was beginning to have a very clear idea of what men they are, but I didn't say anything.

Ada had sleepily tucked her head against my neck as we all talked.

Mojobe smiled and in a slightly puzzled tone said, "You two seem quite close."

Ada said sleepily, taking my hand, "Yeah, he's my dad.", which only increased Mojobe's puzzlement. In her tribe, boys and girls pair up at adolescence or even before, so Mojobe was I'm sure imagining only one thing.

Back in our room, Ada said dreamily from beside me in bed, "What if I fall in love with him?"

"Who?"

"Lucrezia's beautiful brother."

"That's none of my business, I don't care."

"Oh yes, you do."

I remained silent and several minutes went by.

"Yes, you do."

More silence

"You do."

As Ada and I sat in the sunny parlor eating eggs and delicate pastries and sipping cappuccino, it seemed too idyllic, too much the proverbial paradise and the proverbial viper must be about to strike, and he did. There was a strange scratching sound at the door. Ada looked through the peephole and turned to me to do her Rasputin imitation.

When I opened the door, Rasputin smiled and I realized two things at once. I'd never seen him smile before, and his teeth were even worse than I imagined.

"What's with the scratching Rasputin? Don't you knock anymore?"

"The collector said to me 'Why don't you just scratch on the door when you come here, we'll always know who it is." and then everyone in the room laughed. I think they like me."

"Maybe they were ridiculing you, Rasputin."

A dark look came over his face.

"Why would they do that?"

"Jesus, Rasputin, look at those fingernails, you look like Howard Hughes with jaundice."

Ada laughed so hard she got the hiccups.

Rasputin glowered at her.

"Where's Aimee?" I asked.

He hesitated, then said, "She's with him."

"With whom?"

"The collector. He wanted to show my work to some acquaintances."

A trace of hope slipped into my mind.

"Your work? They just want to have her naked so they can gawk at her, staring at her private parts that she never lets you look at."

My words had just the effect I'd hoped.

Rasputin stared out the window and said, "You're right." He was visibly shaken.

As the Arabs say, 'The enemy of my enemy is my friend.' At least Rasputin was with us now, not plotting some stupid ploy like he was. And he might even be a useful double agent in all this if we could teach him a little subtlety.

I go further. "Let's be honest with each other Rasputin, you never did talk to the Waldeebe about some deal did you?"

"No."

"But the collector really does want to get his hands on Ada, right?"

"Yeah."

"And now all you want is to get your Aimee back, right?"

He nodded.

"We'll get her back, Rasputin. But for the time being, just lay low, OK?"

I realized I was sounding more and more like I was in some noire detective story.

Rasputin nodded and left.

I sat back in the chair, worn out by everything, all I wanted was to be back in Portland, working with our dancers and performers.

Ada said quietly, "Dad?"

"Yes."

"I have a date."

"A what?"

"I have a date to spend the afternoon with Luciano."

"Who the hell is Luciano?"

"Lucrezia's brother."

I stared at Ada in disbelief. We were both silent. Then I said, "Well, OK, I'm sure you'll be safe. He'll just blow anyone's brains out who comes near you."

Ada didn't know whether to laugh, and in fact, looked pretty guilty.

An hour later Luciano showed up, dressed casually but right out of Italian Vogue. Ada looked as stylish as he and they looked like a photo of the celebrity couple of the season as they headed out.

"What is happening to my life?" I said this to the remains of our luxurious breakfast.

The phone rang. It was Lucrezia. "The Waldeebe are here."

"Great", I said, but I don't know why.

Lucrezia went on, "But Blain is not with them."

"Can we switch to a different movie?", I said.

"What?"

"Never mind, I'll be right over."

When Maria let me in, I was met with the sound of rhythmically stomping feet, jingling ankle bracelets, and high- and low-pitched piercing songs. The three fiancées were in a state of supreme ecstasy. They continued to move against and away from each other and were totally unaware of my presence.

I talked to Lucrezia off to the side. "Where's Blain?"

"Some people in the middle have her, it's very complicated."

"I'd say."

"Where's Ada?" Lucrezia asked.

"With your brother."

"Ah yes, he's obsessed I'm afraid."

"What do you mean obsessed? He only met her last night."

"He told me he's convinced Ada's the woman he's destined to have for his wife."

"His wife? For Christ's sake Lucrezia, Ada is sixteen years old."

"Yes, but things happen early in Sicily where we grew up."

"What is this?, African natives and Sicilian mobsters all start sex at twelve years of age?"

Lucrezia was dangerously angry and I was half expecting a hairpin in the neck.

"Sorry Lucrezia, my nerves are frayed today."

"That's because you're in love with..."

"With...?" But I didn't finish because Lucrezia held out her arms and said softly, "Up, please." When I lifted her, she wrapped her legs around me and put her small perfect lips briefly on mine. When she descended it was like a firefighter in an emergency sliding down a pole.

She walked away saying, "Enough of that, yes? We need to make a plan to retrieve Blain."

My thought was that the only consistency with Lucrezia is that she's consistently an enigma.

Lucrezia's strategy on the matter of the Collector and Blain had taken on a new Sicilian dimension.

"I think he has to be eliminated," she said.

"Eliminated?"

"Killed."

"Why? How?"

"Why? Because he's not going to give up his obsession with Blain (or Ada too for that matter). He'll persist until he has them. I've never known him to not get what he wants. And, how will we do it? He'll have to be led into a trap, using the twins as bait and an intermediary whom he doesn't suspect. And it needs to be done soon, before he takes the initiative."

"Lucrezia, I won't be part of a scheme to murder someone, regardless of how evil he is. I'm a theater director not a director of assassinations."

"Well, Mr. Noble Theater Director, do you want to lose your drooly little girl? Do you want her drooling all over the collector because he orders her to? Do you want him drooling all over her because she's at his mercy?"

"OK, OK, OK, I get the picture! But he doesn't have Ada."

"No, but for all practical purposes he has Blain, and once he actually has his hands on Blain do you think Ada will walk away from her sister?"

"But why not just rescue Blain, from whoever has her now?"

"It's not that easily done. I'm still not sure what they want out of all this."

"Then why not just kill them?"

Lucrezia let loose her mirthful laughter, and said, "The man of fleeting principles."

I had to laugh, and I said, "It's because you have too strong an effect on me."

"You mean like this?" Lucrezia came over to the couch I'm sitting on and did a sit-down version of the clinging monkey.

We were interrupted by one more crashing Chinese vase and Ada stared at us speechless. Luciano was at her side bemused by the scene before him. He said, "Ah little sister, a new romance in life?" Ada turned on him, growling, "You fucking jerk." Luciano, in involuntary response to an insult from anyone, put his hand inside his jacket on the pistol side. Ada, her face red with rage said, "Now what, you going to shoot me?" She eyed an ancient Greek vase on a mantle, and walked toward it with her hand out. There was the unmistakable click of a pistol cocked and with it pointed at Ada with both hands, Luciano said, "That one's not fake."

Ada stopped dead in her tracks and said, "All we need now is Marlon Brando with his mouth full of cotton balls mumbling about family loyalty. Can we go home now Dad?"

All the way back in the taxi, Ada cried inconsolably, alternating between, "He said I had to marry him," and, "I'm only sixteen," and "I can't believe it, you and that midget monster"

As I opened the door to our room, the phone was ringing. I was Lucrezia. She apologized for her brother's actions. "He wouldn't have actually shot her you know, or if he had it would only be in an arm or leg. That vase is ancient and priceless."

When I said, "Arm or leg?" Lucrezia laughed and said, "Just kidding." She went on to say, "However, Luciano is probably out now as our man to do what we discussed needed to be done. He was pretty insulted by Ada."

"Machismo stuff, huh?"

"I'm afraid so."

Then she added, "By the way, as Narrator, aren't you going to let me know where our story is going? I'm curious to know."

"Our story?"

"Yours and mine."

I could see Ada staring at me.

"Not now, Lucrezia."

"I know, just teasing because I know she's listening."

When I hung up Ada said, "What did the midget monster want?"

"That's contradictory Ada, she can't be a midget *and* a monster, monster means big."

"Don't try and distract me, she's after you and she's a midget monster piece of shit."

"She was just teasing."

"She's a teasy twat."

"Ada dear, I have no interest in her, and besides, nothing would change the fact that you're my daughter."

"Well, she'd never be my mother."

"Isn't that a wild leap forward?"

"I don't know, you're the Narrator, you tell me what's going to happen. I'm not going to be sixteen for the rest of my life you know, and you and I are going to be together for the rest of your life, you know. Don't you plan ahead? There is a plot here, yes?"

At the last word, Ada got down on her knees and started moving around in circles, doing an imitation of Lucrezia's gestures as she walks.

I laugh.

"Or maybe we should have a conference, yes?"

In a running leap, her arms and legs were around me, Lucrezia style, and she started sobbing hysterically and slid down my body to the floor. I sat next to her and took her in my arms until she stopped crying. After a few minutes, she said quietly, "That was all an act, you know. It was my audition for when you're casting for a serious drama. OK, Dad? Did I pass?"

"You definitely passed."

She said, "I'm just overly sensitive. It's because I think I'm pregnant, Dad."

True alarm fills me.

"Who...?"

"Someone in our company, Dad, it happened before we left Portland."

"WHO?"

"I'm too embarrassed to tell, but here's a clue:"

Ada was up on her feet loping fast around the room, arms down, Rasputin-style, her hair pulled down wildly, an incisor poking out the corner of her mouth, her fingers curled in a ball as she leaped on and off furniture smiling mirthfully.

I laughed in huge relief.

Winded, Ada came over to kneel in front of me on the floor, and said, "Any questions, sir?"

"Yes, who's the Narrator, me or you?"

"Now, you're getting the point."

Ada lay down on the floor with her head in my lap and said, "OK if I take a little nap, Dad, this has been a tough day?"

She was asleep almost immediately. I studied her face. Her cheeks were flushed from exertion, childlike. Who is she? She's my daughter and she's not my daughter, nor could she ever be. She's my lover and she's not my lover, nor could she ever be. She has extraordinary skills and spirit as a dancer, perhaps a great dancer. She has a history I know virtually nothing of. Is there a God of Profound Enigmas who has delivered her into my care and into my life?

My thoughts were interrupted by scratching on the door. Ada opened her eyes and said, raising her lip over a tooth, "It's the father of my child, and I cannot face him." She walked to the bedroom and closed the door.

I opened the door to find Rasputin, and he was not alone. Aimee was beside him and behind them was an elderly man, in his early sixties I'd say, and well dressed, expensively dressed. He had thinning gray hair and a carefully trimmed mustache and beard. He looked to Rasputin for an introduction, but Rasputin is immobilized in figuring out what to say.

Finally, Rasputin says, nodding toward the visitor, "This is the Collector" and looking at me he says, "This is the Narrator."

The visitor was amused and said, "It seems we both have our aliases." He held out his hand and said, "I'm honored to meet you, I've heard a lot about you."

I took his hand and said, "Likewise."

Then an additional visitor came in from the hallway. He was one of the most menacing people I'd ever seen. He was not tall but he was wide and hard and his shaved head had little beads of perspiration as though it was a great effort to keep from just breaking everything in sight.

"Ah, this is Anton, my driver," the collector said,

"Is your car parked in the hallway?" I asked.

The collector laughed, "I've heard you're witty."

As Anton closed the door, the Collector said, "I have a simple request, I'd like to see Ada, have a look at her."

"She's not here."

"I know she's here. You were followed."

"She's sleeping, she's exhausted."

The collector looked at the bedroom and nodded toward Anton and the closed door.

Anton started toward the door and when I stepped forward, he took a pistol from his belt and aimed it at my head. I stopped. He pushed open the door to the dark room and stepped in.

There was a sickening sound that could only be compared to a watermelon dropped from a second floor, followed by a lot of weight hitting the floor. Ada emerged from the doorway holding in both hands a heavy-cut crystal pitcher streaked with blood.

"Jesus Ada," I said.

"Well, he didn't exactly knock, Dad."

"I'm not worried about him, sweetheart."

I put my arm around her and turned to Rasputin, who was, I was pleased to see, standing against the door to keep the Collector from leaving. I called the front desk.

Soon, the hotel security arrived and a doctor came in looking for a patient. We all nodded toward the bedroom. He emerged in one minute, and said, "*Morto.*"

"Dad, what does *morto* mean?"

"It means dead."

"You mean I didn't just knock him unconscious? I killed him"

"Yes, I'm afraid so."

Ada sat on the floor in shock. She was dry-eyed but stunned.

After some half-hour of dramatic discussion in Italian by the ever-increasing number of hotel officials, the police arrive in the form of two uniformed officers and the same inspector who responded to the bullet through the window. He looked at me, then went into the bedroom and returned to look at me again.

"More professional jealousy?," he asked.

Before I could answer, the Collector said to the detective, "I would like to leave. I had nothing to do with this murder, and I can be reached any time if you have any questions.." He handed the inspector a business card. The inspector took the card and said, "No, you may not leave."

The collector walked to the other side of the room to use his cell phone while the inspector turned back to me to ask his questions.

"I want to know exactly what has taken place here since your visitors arrived. We've already taken down names and contact information. We'll start with this, "Who hit this man on the head with the pitcher?"

"I did," Ada said softly from where she was still sitting on the floor.

The detective was skeptical. "This man was hit with the force of a strong grown man."

Ada spoke with more assertion. "I was standing on a chair and I used both hands. He was coming uninvited into my bedroom to abduct me so that this man

(Ada nodded toward the Collector) could use me as he pleased, and have me tattooed by this man (Ada nods toward Rasputin) and have my skin carved into designs by two African natives. And he had a gun in his hand."

The inspector turned to his police officers who had just come back out from the bedroom and said, "Gun?" They both shook their heads.

"He pointed the pistol at my head when I tried to stop him from going into the bedroom," I said, I got up to go check for myself but was stopped by the officers. I turned to Rasputin and Aimee who were sitting on the couch and asked, "Did that man have a pistol?" They both nodded.

"Who else was here before we arrived?" The inspector asked.

"About a dozen hotel officials in suits, and hotel security, all going in and out of the bedroom as they wished."

"You know the deceased?" The inspector turned to the Collector,

"Yes, he's my driver."

"Did he have a gun in his hand?"

"I didn't see a gun."

"What were you two doing here?"

"We were here for a visit."

"Did you invite him?" The inspector turned to me.

"Definitely not."

The inspector's cell phone rang. He listened, frowning slightly, then said, "Yes sir."

He turned to the Collector, stared at him for a moment and said, "You're free to leave."

Everyone else in the room was appalled, including the two uniformed officers.

As the Collector went out the door, I said to the inspector, "Connections at the top, I guess."

He looked frustrated, but ignored me.

After thorough statements were taken from everyone, the inspector turned to go, saying, "For the time being, I'm considering this an act of self-defense, but don't any of you leave Rome."

The body was removed and the hotel transferred us to yet another room, even more luxurious than the last, seemingly in an effort to help erase from our happy thoughts of the Excelsior any memory of a smashed cranium.

Once in our new room, Ada in a somber mood said, "I can't believe I took somebody's life."

"He would have taken yours. And the collector would have taken even more."

"I know. I was listening to everything before he came in. Who do you think took the gun, Dad? I saw it. I know he had it."

"I think one of the hotel executives. The Collector seems to be owed a lot of favors by a lot of people, including the inspector's boss."

"Yeah, that was really creepy and the inspector didn't like it at all when he had to let him go."

"I know. I think he's the only person we can trust. He seems honest."

"But what now Dad? Aren't we back where we started?"

"We've got to get Blain and get out of Italy fast. I have a plan."

"You're brilliant. Tell me the plan."

"After I've thought about it more. Now it's time to get some sleep."

In the morning I was awakened by the inspector on the phone. "Your guest last night, whom I was instructed to release, disappeared between the hotel and his destination. Eyewitnesses claim to have seen him intercepted by three tall Africans in native dress. Are you familiar with such people?"

"I've seen Africans in native dress in Rome, yes."

"I'm not talking generic. Do you know who these three Africans are?"

"How could I know? I wasn't there."

"Listen carefully. I'm one of the few people in this whole scenario who you can trust. I could help you a lot. I could hurt you a lot. My question again is, do you know who these Africans might be?"

"Yes."

"I'll be there in an hour."

When the inspector arrived, Ada and I were seated at our round table covered with one more spectacular breakfast spread. I asked him if he'd like coffee and he agreed. Ada got up to wash her cup for him and when he thanked her she smiled and said, "You're welcome. We think you're one of the few good guys, maybe the only one." He laughed.

After a few cursory questions about who Ada and I are to each other (I tell him the truth, and it seems to him a gesture of trust for me to answer his questions so frankly.)

"We have some overlapping interests," he said.

"Such as?"

"First, if anything I say here is quoted later on, I'll deny it and you'll have no 'good guy' to rely on, and in fact, you'll have a very 'bad guy' to deal with. Yes?"

"Agreed," I said and Ada nodded smiling.

"I know that this Collector wants your 'daughter.'" He smiled. "I know that he may have in his custody your other 'daughter.'" Smiled again. "You want to leave Rome with both your twin daughters."

"Yes."

He continued, "I want this Collector incarcerated, because his whims about your daughters are the least of his perversities and illegal trespasses. But he's well protected and has ties to many people of power, who would come down with him."

"May I ask you a question?" I asked.

"Go ahead."

"Are you really so altruistic a law enforcer, or will you benefit in other ways if the Collector is brought in? I ask this within the context of our already agreed upon confidentiality."

"The answer is both. I am an honest inspector. But I'm also an ambitious inspector. If I bring the Collector down, and along with him the power players mentioned, there will be no limit to my future in law enforcement in Rome. It is of course risky, and I could be gunned down in the process, but I like a challenge."

"And we could also be 'gunned down' as collaborators of yours."

"True. But you could be gunned down at any moment as it is."

"Now", he asked, "Who are these Africans and what do they want with the Collector?"

I hesitated for a moment, deciding how best to explain their relationship to each other, to me, and to the Collector. I decided the truth was probably the path of least resistance.

"There are three Africans. The woman is engaged to the two men, who are cousins. She is a member of our theater group. The cousins want to join our group so they can be with her. They are all three very gifted singers and dancers. Their interest in the Collector comes from wanting to retrieve Blain, Ada's sister, from the Collector or his people, wherever she is. Achieving that is a condition of their being allowed to come back to the U.S. with us. The cousins are warriors of extraordinary cunning, strength, and courage. They would have dispatched that thug driver of the Collector in a second like a soggy cannoli."

"The cousins are...?" The inspector stops, wisely deciding not to pursue the curious triad of the tribal liaison. He's too white, too Italian, too Catholic.

"OK," he said, "but who put them up to this, and where do you think they've taken the Collector?"

"The mighty midget put them up to it," Ada said with vehemence.

The inspector looked at her and said, "Sounds like an American comic book character."

"Italian comic book character, except she's not funny. She's trying to seduce my Father." Ada hesitated a moment and added, "She's a runt." She put out her hand at waist height.

"What's her name?" The inspector asked.

"Lucrezia."

"Ah, yes. I know of her. Impresario, yes?"

"That's her."

"And where do you think they're keeping the Collector?"

"Her criminal greasy wop brothers have him, I'm sure," Ada said.

The inspector's expression darkened.

Ada, embarrassed, said, "I'm sorry, please insult me and we'll be even. Call me 'Typical American Adolescent."

"Typical greasy American adolescent."

Ada laughed and said, "You're fantastic, we're going to be perfect crime-busting partners."

An expression came over the inspector's face that is very familiar to me. It could be translated as something like, "How did I suddenly get so under the influence of a sixteen-year-old?" I could imagine him adding, "Thank God, I'm not the 'father.'"

After some silence, Ada said, "How about this deal? You get us Blain and we'll get you the collector? We'll also get you evidence he kidnapped her, for his, you know, dirty sex stuff." After a moment she added, "I hope he hasn't done any of that to her already, she doesn't deal with that very well."

The inspector said, "What do you mean?"

"Never mind."

The inspector asked, "What makes you think it'll be so easy to extract your sister from the Collector's people?"

Ada brightened. "You know, the old swat team thing, a big bunch of cars, a big bunch of guys in black, with helmets, bulletproof vests, assault weapons, and all that, at four in the morning."

The inspector doesn't say anything but I imagine him thinking, 'not such a bad idea.' We are all silent and the detective was about to leave when we heard scratching at the door. He looked at me with a 'now what?' expression. Ada giggled and walking with her stomach pushed out in front of her, said, "It's the father of my child", and went toward the door. The inspector looked at me and I just shook my head, as in, 'Don't ask.'

Rasputin came in with Aimee trailing behind. When he saw the inspector he said, "It's good you're here. I have some important evidence." He opened a manila envelope of close-up photos of nudes with their legs spread. There were no faces shown. There were females and males all with their genitals pierced in some way with various hardware. Rasputin said, "I stole these from the Collector when I was there. Aimee will testify that this was done to her, without her consent, and that the Collector himself did it."

The inspector believed that the photos, plus Aimee's testimony, would be of extreme importance.

Rasputin added, "The Waldeebe have also witnessed some extreme things."

"The Waldeebe...?" The detective said.

"The African cousins," I said.

He nodded, lifting his eyebrows.

We made a plan to meet at Lucrezia's later in the afternoon. The inspector, Rasputin, and Aimee left. When I talked to Lucrezia on the phone she said she'd have Mojobe and the cousins there.

"I can't go over there and be around that midget. I'll get too angry." Ada said.

"You can't stay here by yourself. It's not safe."

"Oh yeah? So tell me Daddy how you would feel if I was abducted by that sex creep Collector or one of his sex creep friends?"

"I'd feel as though, to the extent you were violated, I too was violated."

"Just because those people are interested in my genitals?"

"Not just because, but yes."

"But you have no interest in my genitals."

"That doesn't mean someone else is allowed to."

"So then, you don't have interest in my genitals."

"I didn't say that, you did."

There is silence as I wait for more interrogation. But it doesn't come. Ada falls asleep.

When Ada and I arrived at Lucrezia's, everyone was there, all standing around the living room: Mojobe, The Waldeebe, Rasputin, Aimee, the Inspector. Only Lucrezia was sitting, and she was holding a cigar, which was a sure sign that she was about to launch into a proposed deal, and she did.

She delivered the first of several smoke rings and stated, "Everything is in place. We all have our various chattel and when the trades take place, we will all have what we want: The collector will be traded for Blain, and the inspector, here, will see to it that the Collector does not again have the opportunity to subject children to his jaded whims. Blain will be back with her twin. The Waldeebe will have their Mojobe, Rasputin will have his Aimee. And I'll have my theater company to return to America and produce our magnum opus for Spoleto, yes? This latter condition I expect you to fulfill on your word of honor with these people as witnesses." She looked at me as she spoke.

"You have my word, Lucrezia," I responded.

"How do I know you have the Collector?" The inspector asked.

Lucrezia nodded to the Waldeebe who left the room, and returned, each with one end of a pole on his shoulder and tied to the middle of the pole was indeed the Collector, with his hands and feet tied like a gazelle being brought home for dinner. There was a red cloth stuffed into his mouth, and his eyes were wide with terror.

We were all stunned.

Ada was the next to speak and she said to Lucrezia, "How do I know you have access to Blain, and that's she's OK?"

"I was with Blain privately last night for some time and she's fine." Lucrezia smiled.

Ada was troubled but said nothing.

I said, "Well we seem to have our deal in place. Does everyone agree to it?"

There were nods all around.

The Inspector said to Lucrezia, "Then you know where Blain is being held. Have you arranged with her captors to make the trade?"

"Yes, the trade is to take place here in my apartment."

"This is all well and good, but here's my condition for participating:" Ada said, "That Blain is safely traded and in our hands before any action is taken by your swat team." She looked at the Inspector...

"You're not in a position to declare 'conditions'," Lucrezia said coldly.

"Ada's condition is the condition of me and everyone in the company," I said. I looked around and everyone nodded.

"Thanks, Dad," Ada said.

"Lucrezia, you set up the timing and inform me of every detail immediately." The inspector said. "In the, meantime I will have your building clandestinely protected. What kind of timing do you have in mind?"

"The sooner the better. I'll make the call right now." She went into an adjoining room. While we waited we all notice that the Collector, who is suspended between two chairs, had wet his pants and the Waldeebe steadfastly ignored him.

Lucrezia returned. "It's on for tomorrow night, that is, 4:00 in the morning."

The Inspector nodded and left to arrange the necessary police scenario.

Everyone was milling around uneasily. Ada said softly, "Can we go, Dad?"

In the taxi Ada said, "Dad, we've been in Rome all this time and we haven't done any sightseeing. There's something I want to see."

"What's that?"

"It's a sculpture in a church. I saw it when I was about nine and it was very important to us, Blain and me."

"You didn't tell me you'd been in Rome before."

"I haven't told you a lot of things Dad."

"Who were you with?"

"That's the creepy part. It was one of those times in my life I try not to think about too much. I'll tell you about it when we see the sculpture."

"Where is the sculpture? Do you remember anything about it?"

"I just remember that it was huge and white marble with sculpted gold rays of sun pouring down. It was a woman with robes on being stuck with a spear by an angel. She was pretty emotional about the whole thing. I don't remember the name of it or where it was, but I know it's very famous."

"Ah, I know what it is. It's called the Ecstasy of St. Teresa," I said.

"That's right Dad, I remember now. I remember the word 'ecstasy.'"

When we got to the hotel I asked the concierge where the sculpture was. He responded immediately, giving me the name and location of the church.

When Ada and I got out of the taxi at the church of St. Maria Della Vittoria, a mass had just ended. We waited until the last parishioners had left and then entered the small church. The light was low but it was easy to find Bernini's sculpture. The chapel is in the left transept, and light floods down from above on the two marble figures. St. Teresa is in voluminous robes and hood, and has her head tilted back with her mouth open as though emitting a moan of ecstasy (as per the title of the sculpture). A smiling angel is lifting her robe to expose (to himself) her bare midriff which seems to be the target of his spear.

There were two elderly women in black kneeling at the main altar off to our right, murmuring prayers. Ada glanced at them and stepped close to me to whisper. "When Blain and I first saw this sculpture we were nine and it was during the period when we had been experiencing the sexuality of our bodies for the first time. That was after one of the adults caring for us had been touching us slyly in a way that excited us. We returned to the church a few days later and brought with us a 'spear' that Blain had made. It was a straight stick of wood with a rounded end, short enough so Blain could conceal it under her clothes. When we were alone we did our imitation of the sculpture. It was just like a spear sticking into me. I cried out in pain. We had come here with a young priest who was a kind of temporary guardian for us. He'd overheard us and rushed us out of the church and didn't ask for any explanation about what we were doing. I think he knew and couldn't handle it. Also, he was often leering at us with what we thought were his own dark fantasies. Don't you think the Church is steeped in sex, Dad?

Afterwards I told Blain that the pain was part of the pleasure I felt and I couldn't understand how such pain could be so pleasurable. It was very mysterious. Every time later when we saw this sculpture we both became very serious because it seemed to be us. It was a time when a lot of change was going on in our lives."

There were postcards of the sculpture and a booklet in several languages about St. Teresa and Bernini. We bought several things and left. In the taxi, Ada read the booklet to me. There was a quote from St. Teresa herself:

Beside me on the left appeared an angel in bodily form...He was short and very beautiful and his face was aflame. In his hands I saw a great golden spear. This he plunged into me several times so that it penetrated my entrails. When he pulled it out I felt that he took them with it, and left me utterly confused by the great love of God. The pain was so severe that it made me utter several moans. The sweetness caused by the intense pain is so severe that one cannot possibly wish it to cease. This is not a physical but a spiritual pain, though the body has some share in it, even a considerable share.

After thinking for a moment, Ada said, "That's exactly how I felt with Blain."

"You know what I want to do Dad? I want to choreograph a dance piece for Blain and me once we get back to Portland, on the theme of the ecstasy of St. Teresa for us to perform at Spoleto. What do you think?"

"I think it's a brilliant idea, sweetheart."

"Really? and you'll let me do it myself?"

"Yes, but I'll be available to consult with if you wish."

"Of course, I'll consult with you, Daddy love."

Back at the hotel, Ada spent the day exploring movements for her St. Teresa dance piece. As I watched her go from one tentative gesture to another, each more sophisticated, I realized again how much natural sense of performance she had and how great her potential was. Her power of concentration was amazing, even including soft conversations with herself as if she was the only person in the room. She went back and forth between her role and Blain's, registering intense emotion in each part. Late in the day, she asked to show me some movements. Her choreography was raw but charged with originality and I could visualize the finished piece, especially since I already knew the content.

"What do you think, Dad?"

"I think it's original and engaging."

Ada laughed happily, "And I think you're original and engaging. Do you think we should get engaged since we're both so engaging?"

"We are engaged, in each other's art."

"And each other's souls, don't you think Dad?"

"Yes"

"So if our souls are engaged, someday they'll be married, right?"

"Possibly."

"And our bodies too."

"That's another matter."

"I can never trick you."

"Not verbally."

"Then can I trick you with my art?"

"Possibly, I don't know yet."

Ada smiled.

The much-anticipated prisoner exchange of Blain for the Collector turned out to be not very reciprocal. In spite of the presence of police in large numbers and the supposed evil of the captors of Blain, the exchange was made with only one mishap, albeit an unfortunate one for the Collector. As the trade of Collector for Blain was taking place on the balcony of Lucrezia's apartment, as soon as the Waldeebe cousin in front had a strong grip on the wrist of Blain, he pulled her aside and released his grip on the pole from which the Collector was suspended, thus creating a fire pole at a ninety-degree angle down which the Collector shot like a highly motivated firefighter. The Waldeebe managed to emit a very unconvincing "OOPS" before we all heard the unequivocal thud of the now lifeless body on the concrete below.

The heavy police presence was now apparent to the Collector's thugs and they could only look down in horror at the demise of their ex-source of considerable monetary reward. The detective was furious, having lost the prize on which his future success was to be based. When he confronted the Waldeebe, the latter said lamely, "I was soooo nervous I lost my grip."

The police were relieved to be rid of us all but had promised protection until we were all on a plane the next day. I splurged with the rest of Khalid's money to have the concierge buy up the necessary tickets on several flights the next day to take us all home...Ada, Blain, Mojobe, the Waldeebe, Rasputin, Aimee, and me. Lucrezia said she'd join us within days, and added, looking at me, "I expect you to keep your word on our arrangement."

I assured her I would, and I was surprised to realize that I was looking forward to working with her because she was the perfect wild card element to keep our production on edge and create a tension that would feed all the players, especially Ada, resulting in a production with an element of menace right below the surface. Why did I want an element of menace? It just seemed right for the history of all of us together.

When the inspector released everyone, Ada and Blain and I returned to the hotel, exhausted. We'd all been up more than 24 hours. In the taxi, I was sitting with Ada on my right and Blain on my left, an arrangement Blain seemed to prefer as we were getting into the taxi.

"Are you OK? Do you need anything? Need to see anyone? A doctor?" I asked Blain.

"Why a doctor?" Blain said.

"My question is, were you harmed in any way?"

"You're not *my* father, you know."

"I don't claim to be."

"Sorry, thanks for asking, I'm OK."

After some silence, Blain, in a softer more conciliatory tone asked, "So have you two done any sightseeing in Rome?"

I waited for Ada to tell about our visit to see St. Teresa, and when she answered, "Nothing special," I offered, "Well the Ecstasy of St. Teresa was pretty interesting."

"Ecstasy of St. Teresa? What's that?" Blain said.

Ada remained silent looking out the window, and I was thinking maybe I'd made a blunder, maybe the experience they had in the church at age nine was too personal for Blain to think about, let alone talk about. So I said, "It's a famous sculpture by Bernini in a church here in the city."

"Oh," Blain said.

When we got up to our room, Blain did a circular tour looking out the windows and seemed relieved to have her freedom back. She said, "As tired as I am, I'm even more hungry, I bet they have good breakfasts here, can we have some?"

I called room service.

Blain and Ada decided on showers before eating and headed for different bathrooms. There was an unmistakable tension in the air, whose nature I was too tired to try and understand.

When the same elderly waiter rolled in our breakfast, he seemed discreetly disappointed that I'm the only one in sight. However (and I hoped his heart could take it) he was soon confronted with two of the ones he'd been anticipating. They were both flush-faced pink from hot water and not totally tucked into their thick white terry robes, displaying bits of bare limb here and there as they took over the setting out of the food. He was assaulted by four hands tucking flowers from the vase into as many of his button holes as the twins could find. I gave him an even bigger tip than usual and he left our penthouse heaven for the work-a-day world of Rome, beaming and calling out "Grazie!, Grazie!, Grazie!" The twins tore into the food with total abandon and seemed years younger than their sixteen. When everything was consumed, they sat immobile with half-closed eyes. The plan was to sleep till late afternoon. Our flight was early the next morning. I left it to them to decide on sleeping arrangements. There were two bedrooms and two beds in each. I headed for the shower.

When I came out of the shower, I looked into the room Ada and I had been sharing and it was empty. The door to the other room was closed. I was relieved. Ada had decided to keep our former sleeping arrangement a secret. And now with Blain part of our lives and hopefully part of our theater company, maybe my life was going to return to its pre-Rome equilibrium. I closed the door and immediately plunged into the sleep of one who had not only been sleepless for too long but who'd been faced with the kind of threatening circumstances that totally drained one's reserves.

"Since you're Ada's father, does that make me your daughter?" It's the first thing Blain said when I waken to find her sitting at the foot of my bed watching me.

"It's too early in the morning for conversation."

"It's 4:30 in the afternoon."

"Then it's too late. Now, if you'll please allow me to get out of bed and put a robe on..."

"Anyway, we're starved, Dad."

Blain was looking at me with her eyebrows raised and her lower lip between her teeth. "I just wanted to hear what it sounded like."

"Yeah? So how did it sound?" I said this with helpless resignation.

"It sounded cool; I've never had a father before."

"You have a biological father."

"Yeah, but who knows who he is?"

I can only think, why am I bombarded with *deja vu* before I'm even out of bed?

Blain went over to a chair and picked up my robe to hand to me. She held it out and said, "I'll avert my eyes, Dad."

With my robe on, I stood facing Blain. I took both her hands. "Answer this question for me, have you really never seen the sculpture of St. Teresa?"

"Oh, I've seen it."

"With Ada, when you were nine?"

"Yes."

"Why did you tell me yesterday that you knew nothing about it?"

"Because I hardly knew you yesterday and it's too personal to talk about."

We were both silent and I decided not to ask anything more. But Blain said, "And besides, she probably told it to you all backwards, with the roles reversed. She does that."

My role as Narrator urged me not to ask more.

Blain leaned against me. "OK, Dad?"

I put my arms around her in once again what I assumed was a fatherly way, but what was I supposed to use as a criterion? She put her arms around me in what I'm imagining she assumed was a daughterly way, and wondered what she was supposed to use as a criterion. Being a person whose primary weakness of the senses is olfactory, and to which I have little resistance, I inhaled deeply and was flooded with Ada-like and non-Ada-like scents that caused me acute lightheadedness.

I said, "I think I need some food too."

After a long classic multi-course Italian dinner, we walked back to the hotel, attracting considerable attention on the way. Ada and Blain had dressed for an evening out in light summer dresses that clung and didn't cling to their young lanky bodies. I was in the middle as we walked down via Veneto, with a matching redhead holding each hand in a studied daughterly way, one with shorter hair, both flushed with the possibilities of life. When we passed our police protection near the hotel, the Inspector was checking on them. He looked at us and nodded once, slowly.

"What do you think, Dad?"

Ada had led me into the bedroom where the two king-sized beds had been pushed together making a sleeping arena the size of a soccer field.

"It's as big as a soccer field," I said.

"More than enough room for our little family, yes?"

"Actually, I was thinking of sleeping..." I nodded toward the other room.

"No, we have to return to Portland as a family and this is our last night in Rome."

Ada said this with firm resolve and Blain stepped forward as though to bar me from leaving. I elected the path of least resistance.

"OK, OK, OK"

"One OK for each of us, huh Dad?"

I had been delegated to occupy the center of the bed, which meant I had to make a series of diplomatic moves during the night, to keep both political factions content, because the neutral territory, the crack where the two mattresses met would not be comfortable. My modest stab at optimism before I drifted off, was "There's got to be some brilliant art to come out of all this." Another thought I had for the millionth time was that it must be very gratifying to have the capacity to clearly define everything in life and choose accordingly, a capacity that seemed more fugitive than ever. In the sleep of night, I could only tell whose territory I was in by smell. At least I was getting familiar with my family.

In the morning, there was a pile-up of bodies like a three-car collision. The covers were twisted in and around limbs. It had been a restless dream laden Rome to Portland night for all of us. I was also aware there were two droolers in the family, not one, and I left the bed midst of an argument about who drooled on whom, aware of an ample puddle in the concavity of my own clavicle. Shouted at me as I left was, "You drool too!"

"When in Rome..." was all I could come up with.

Standing in the shower and striving to wake up for the fifteen-hour flight back home, the thought that came to my mind was that Ada and Blain together were pure animalism. And what do you get when you combine that with the Ecstasy of St. Teresa of Avila? A unique multidimensional pas de deux. I was inspired. I wrapped a towel around myself and walked into the bedroom and abruptly pulled the covers off the bed, to prompt squealing and to reveal red hair, red hair, red hair, red hair, and a mélange of smooth sixteen-year-old angles and curves.

"Up my children, we're going home to make art."

Part Three

"Minuscule Mussolini is not here to torment me?"

Vladimir was smiling as he watched us all straggle into the brewery with our luggage and our jet lag. He was flat on his back on a kind of hospital gurney, and seemed to have added great girth while we'd been in Rome. In fact, every detail of his body seemed to have expanded. He watched me and said, "Yes, I know, I've advanced in quantity of flesh as well as quality of soul."

'Unfortunately, Vladimir, Lucrezia will be here in three days."

"Oh. I'll have to leave."

"Again, unfortunately, you'll have to stay. That was a condition of Lucrezia's agreement in doing her part to arrange the release of Blain."

"How dreadful."

I asked "Vladimir, are you ill?"

"Oh, this you mean?" He patted his great protruding middle. "A tiresome business, I'll give you a full report in due time."

"Is it OK if I stay here now?" Ada asked.

"It's all right if you ask your family," I said.

"Excuse me", she said, "What do you think I'm doing?"

"Oh, yeah", I said, returning from my thoughts of choreography. "Sure, pick any unoccupied room."

"And me?" Blain asked with an open amused face.

"Are you going to be one of our company? Under my direction?"

"Do you want me?"

"Definitely, but we have to spend time together so you can show me the results of all that dance training you've mentioned."

"Am I St. Teresa or the Angel?"

"That remains to be seen, doesn't it?"

Blain smiled.

Everyone settled in and began working on their own individual performance pieces. I was leaving it to each group or pair to do the groundwork for their own performance and I was coordinating them into a whole. The theme was emerging from the nature of the pieces themselves. It explored the relationship between human animalism and human spirituality. Spirituality not as religion, but as transcendent art.

Father Joseph and Sister Agnes were continuing their flights of fantasy and I was encouraging them to think in terms of elevated spirits not just elevated bodies and they were very responsive to my idea. Their crashing orgasms however seemed to be an inevitable part of their performance and since it's animalism on the cusp of absurdity, I loved it.

The nature of Mojobe and the Waldeebe's performance is so out of the tradition of western dance and music that I'd decided to leave them alone at this point and weave it into our overall performance later, making as small adjustments as possible to make it work. I don't want to lose any of its exotic uniqueness.

Rasputin and Aimee had been keeping to themselves. Aimee was working on a life-size ceramic self-portrait sculpture which was supposedly going to be integrated into their performance. I'd had some glimpses of it and it was intriguing. Rasputin was obsessed with it and had developed a dark attitude about having access to the sculpture with or without Aimee.

Ada had asked me to work daily with her and Blain. She'd overcome her original proprietary attitude and admitted that she needed help. Blain was cool. She was bemused by Ada's intensity but worked hard at what she'd been asked to do. She didn't have Ada's wealth of movement virtuosity but had a quiet, assumed grace that was beautiful and a perfect complement to Ada.

Vladimir was anxiety personified. He dreaded the appearance of Lucrezia and felt trapped, which of course he was. I was filled with curiosity about what Lucrezia had in mind for him as one aspect of her contribution to our company.

There was the feeling on the part of everyone that our progress was suspended until Lucrezia arrived from Rome because the agreement we made obligates us to her. The suspense ended on the fourth day after our return, when Lucrezia walked into the brewery followed by a taxi driver making the first of three trips in with her luggage. She was stunning in a black silk pants suit, tailored to perfectly present her perfect proportions.

"I'm in black to anticipate the bleak dark weather of this part of the world." She said smiling.

Her smile disappeared when she saw Vladimir. "Hello, Vladimir."

Vladimir could manage only a subdued, "Hello Lucrezia." He looked like he believed his days were numbered, and maybe they were.

"But enough of that, we're here to make joyous art together, yes?" Lucrezia said brightly.

We ordered out for Thai dinner from a local restaurant and ate at a long table made of saw horses, old doors, and odd fabrics from around the world. Sister Agnes went out for flowers and the table was festive and filled with excellent food and wine. Everything was so congenial and the air so filled with enthusiastic talk of art and theater that we seemed like a company working together happily for years, rather than what we were: a disparate group of highly gifted neurotic performers just beginning to accommodate each other, all of us apprehensive about working with our temperamental midget from Rome.

Lucrezia was staying at a small nearby hotel, and after dinner asked that I accompany her there. She was tired but wanted to talk briefly about our plan for the Spoleto piece.

"Not to worry, I'm exhausted. We won't be up late," she said.

"*We* won't be up late? *Who* won't be up late?" Ada immediately said.

"Ah, the *daughter*, will you be insecure here without your daddy?" Lucrezia answered.

"A. I'm never insecure and, B. I'm not going to *be* without my *daddy*, he lives here."

Lucrezia smiled, seeming pleased to have stirred up a little trouble so quickly. I picked up one of her bags to walk with her the three blocks to the hotel. Ada came up close to me to whisper in my ear, "You better not stay there with her tonight."

"Don't worry, I'll be back to tuck in my little girl," I said, with a straight face. Her expression said, you better not be mocking me, and you better be back here, or there'll be hell to pay. But she only said, "Thanks, Dad."

At the hotel, Lucrezia said, "I want to change, I've been traveling for fifteen hours. Help yourself to the bar."

Lucrezia ran a shower and I opened a beer. There was a new mood between Lucrezia and me. The threats of Rome were behind us and Blain was with us, and there seemed to be a neutral sense of artistic pursuit now that the Italian comic book characters were out of our lives. The whole context of our being together seemed different.

"I'm sorry to have picked on Ada, but the temptation was too great. She seemed to have a serious, what do you say, crushed schoolgirl obsession with you." Lucrezia was walking out of the bathroom in a cream silk robe and was drying her wild black curls.

"A schoolgirl crush, it's called," I said.

"Ah, yes." She laughed. "Well, I won't keep you long. I just wanted to talk a little in advance about how we'll proceed with the Spoleto piece, so we're not arguing in front of the company."

"How would you like to proceed, Lucrezia?"

"I would like pure collaboration, as though you and I are one person."

"But we're not one person."

"I think as we proceed, you'll find we're more one person than you would have imagined."

"How so?"

"We each have a theatrical dark side, that places us closer to each other than to any of the others."

I considered Lucrezia's words for a minute and I knew she was right. We looked into each other's eyes for a moment. She was all seriousness, but not in the threatening or hostile way she constantly was in Rome. She seemed to be opening herself up to me by setting aside her former imperial self. She said, "Let's connect through that darkness, search it out in each other, and we'll produce a beautiful, strong, performance piece."

"OK."

When I left the hotel, I saw Ada and Blain across the street. They smiled as I approached. They come up close. "You smell like a French brothel," Ada said. "Italian brothel," Blain said. "I know what happened, UP!" Ada said.

She was squatting down to Lucrezia's height and had her arms out.

"You're right and you look just like her."

"What an insult!" She punched me in the arm, a little too hard for kidding around.

Lucrezia was right about my dark side, and I was thinking, what I really needed to do was combine these two with Lucrezia in one dance piece. As we walked back to the brewery I thought how close my dark side is to my light (Illuminated) side, and that there couldn't be one without the other. I took turns giving Ada and Blain piggyback rides on the way, because they insisted on it.

"You have to decide if you're kids or adults, I can't do this and marry you too," I said.

"Why not, you'd be the first to say there are no rules to art," Ada said.

"This is art? Marriage is art?"

"Don't you always say that unexpected combinations make for interesting experiences?" Blain said.

"Do I?"

"Who do you think we are, your biographers?" Ada said.

"Well, you did seem to be spying on me."

"You mean because of tonight?" Blain said.

"Yes."

"The only reason we were spying on you and the midget was to make sure she doesn't become our mother, in which case we'd have to kill you both," Ada said cheerfully.

In the morning after Lucrezia arrived, we had what can only be described as our version of the mosh pit. It's something we do periodically anyway to keep us from becoming too intellectual about dance, but this morning it's also to introduce Lucrezia to the range of talent in our group. The idea was to pile (sometimes literally) one act upon another. Ada and Blain had volunteered to start it off with their embryonic version of St. Teresa and the Angel. Ada slid in on the floor as St. Teresa on her knees, her head thrown back, awaiting Blain in the form of Angel. Blain strode up purposefully with arms raised and the imagined spear raised over her head to thrust into Ada again and again as Ada opened her mouth in a moan of ecstasy. The Waldeebe moved into the arena from one side and Mojobe from the other, stomping their feet and bending and raising their bodies and arms to mimic the Angel. Mojobe began a blood-curdling African howl of pleasure/pain. From above Sister Agnes sailed down on her trapeze with Father Joseph running under her as she approached the cluster of players. They slid into the Waldeebe with just enough force to tip them over like giant black redwoods. It was totally improvised but already there was a natural anticipation among the company of the moves of each other. Everyone was required to participate and Lucrezia had looped a length of rope onto Vladimir's rolling bed to pull him in like a soft round Goliath, captive of a minute David in drag. That left only Rasputin and Aimee. He began a rolling harp partita improvised to relate to Aimee who had assumed the form of something like a drifting ball of tumbleweed approaching the players. As she got nearer she lifted herself partly out of her clothes to reveal Rasputin's flora tattoos in all their glory. It was quite extraordinary in that it looked more like flora imitating a person than the reverse. I too had to participate and I loped toward the players with increasing speed and leaped up with total faith I'd be caught creatively and securely and I was, by everyone it seemed. Our moshing today served the purpose it always has. There was nothing like physical contact to break down barriers. This was the high point of our players' purely cooperative attitudes toward each other. From here on it's moving toward dark individual depths as personalities emerge to declare their creative selves.

In the evening, Ada, Blain, and I accompanied Lucrezia to her hotel, carrying all her baggage between us. There was an edge to the twins' mood toward Lucrezia, who finally said, "Look, there's no competition between the three of us you know."

Ada said, "Not anymore. Blain and I tied for first place last night."

Lucrezia asked, "First place?"

On the way back, Ada said, "We've decided to narrow down the possibilities, Dad. Tonight you have to decide which of us sleeps in your bed. The bed's too small for three people and you have to pick one of us,"

"Or?"

"Or we go on a rehearsal strike tomorrow."

I looked at Blain who shrugged, as in, don't look at me, it wasn't my idea. I knew it was a power play on Ada's part, and too much power in her hands would be counterproductive, so I said, "OK, I'll take Blain."

Ada was not surprised. She knew I wouldn't be manipulated. But I think it had more to do with Lucrezia than Blain. There was something burning inside Ada that she hadn't figured out yet.

In bed, Blain was the opposite of Ada. She lay still and with space between us, and spoke softly only after a long silence. I realized that most of her extroverted playfulness was borrowed from Ada and she needed Ada by her side to keep it up.

"You know Ada and I are sixteen, but we could be a hundred given what we've experienced so far from life. I don't know what the core of me is or even if I *have* a core. Unlike Ada, who is really defined by her dance talent, genius maybe. Do you think she has genius in her?"

"Keep it between us, but yes I do think she has genius in her, at least potential genius. She's probably the most natural dancer at her age I've ever encountered. I already depend on her to set a criterion for quality in the company. By that, I mean a potential for a level of art. She inspires others because her gifts are so fresh, even as others know her talent is still raw and undeveloped, and none of them have what she has. We have a rich mix of talent and together we'll produce a brilliant piece for Spoleto, but Ada's something else entirely."

"You know, I went to live in Switzerland, to go to school there again, because I wanted to get away from Ada, to try and find what kind of 'fire' I might have in myself to make my life worth living. But I found no fire (Switzerland's too cold) and I just ended up missing Ada which made me feel insecure and incomplete, and that made me want to stay away from her even more."

"And how do you feel now that you're here?"

"You mean in bed with you?"

"No, no, I mean here in this city with everyone around you."

"Oh, I'm happier than I've ever been before in my life. But I feel like it will just disappear in a second. I think I'll always feel like a fugitive, like an outlaw."

"Why an outlaw?"

"Because I am an outlaw."

"No, not just a rebellious sixteen-year-old, I mean an outlaw in the sense that you've done something egregious and you know that if it was known, you'd be considered outside of the law, a criminal."

"You sound like you know something about me that I didn't know you knew."

"Like what?"

Blain was silent for a few minutes and I was beginning to think she'd fallen asleep, but then she said "I want to ask you something."

"OK."

"When Ada hit the Collector's driver on the head and killed him?"

"Yes?"

"Did you wonder how a fifteen-year-old girl could have done that, so decisively, so efficiently?"

"Yes, as a matter of fact, I did and so did the Inspector."

"And did you wonder how she could have gotten over it so quickly?"

"Yes." I was beginning to feel uneasy.

"Ada hasn't told you anything about this?"

"About what?"

"About the Boa Constrictors?"

'What are the Boa Constrictors?"

"Our code name."

"Code name, for what?"

"For what we did. In the Middle East. For Khalid."

"Such as?"

"Such as carrying out paid assassinations."

"Assassinations of whom? By whom?"

"People who Khalid was paid to eliminate."

"And what did you have to do with it?"

"We did it."

"Did what?"

"Killed people, hit 'em over the head."

I lay still and silent, determined not to say another word.

"You don't believe me?"

"Of course I don't believe you, and it's not the kind of fantasy I would expect of you. Ada may be in one of her noire moods, but not you."

"Suit yourself."

I said nothing more and eventually, I fell asleep.

Several hours later, Blain wakened me.

"Dad?"

"Yes."

"It's true."

"What's true?"

"The assassination thing."

"OK, tell me."

"But don't interrupt me?"

"OK."

"Khalid and the Collector worked together. I didn't know that then but have found out since. The Collector moved in a circle of hugely wealthy Arab perverts, some of whom barely knew each other or didn't know each other at all, but what they had in common was that they were competing for large amounts of illicit oil money going through government and private hands. What else they had in common was obsessive interest in young Caucasian girls, by that I mean the bodies of young Caucasian girls, which was the Collectors specialty as you know. It started when Ada and I were eleven and we had just come into the guardianship of Khalid, which is a long story I'll tell you another time. Khalid asked that we accompany a man he knew, and whom we'd seen before, to some kind of Arab social event. We were totally new to Khalid's house and life and were trying to find some security so we tried to do what he wanted. At this event, Ada and I were taken to a room where some Sheik was waiting. He must have been very rich and influential because everyone seemed scared of him. He ordered everyone out of the room except Ada and me. He told a bodyguard to wait outside the door. He spoke stiff but clear English. He told us to take off our clothes. We both said no. Like a bad Hollywood movie, he pulled out of his robe a curved sharp knife and said he could cut us up any way he wanted and nobody would ever know about it. He said we'd just disappear. So we took off our clothes, except our white socks, which he insisted we keep on. He told Ada to get down on her hands and knees and stick her "bootooks" up in the air. Afterwards it was the only thing Ada and I could laugh at "bootooks." Ada did what he told her to. He stared at her bottom like he was in a trance. Then he spit on his index finger looking at her asshole. He never got it there because in the meantime I was aiming a stone statuette at his head I held in both my hands and bringing it down with strength I never knew I had. He went over with a crash and a crater in his head that held the statuette. The door burst open and in rushed the bodyguard who stared at us and pulled the statue out of its resting place inside the Sheiks cranium, as though that might save the Sheik's life. In another second, others ran into the room and stood shocked at the carnage and child nudity. Ada, in the great dramatic performance of her life, pointed at the body guard and started screaming, "He killed the Sheik. He tried to stick his thing in us but the Sheik wouldn't let him!" That was it. The body guard was hanged two days later, and no other version of the event was ever considered. We were turned over to the man who brought us and he took us home to Khalid. We told Khalid what had happened. It was the start of our hatred of him. A few days later, Khalid received a package containing an enormous amount of cash and a note, which read, "My sincerest gratitude. I thought you were just joking." He later explained to us that at a gathering of powerful oil people a man of great wealth who was an enemy of the Sheik had told Khalid that he wished the Sheik dead. Khalid, in what he thought was a humorously exaggerated manner said, "Consider it done." That was the beginning of our life as hit girls and it lasted three years off and on. I know what your first question is going to be so I'll answer it before you ask. You want to know why we agreed to do what we did. When Khalid told us after the first time that he was setting up another social event, we said we'd refuse to kill anyone else and he couldn't do anything about it. He said, 'Fine, if you don't mind the consequences then don't defend yourselves, just do what these people tell you to do.' So we felt we had no choice, and in addition, we were given a large amount of money each time that was deposited into a Swiss bank account in our names. You see the amount of money being paid Khalid was huge, hundreds of thousands each time. He had found a perfect niche for his particular kind of entrepreneurship, involving two powerful forces, Arab oil magnates' bottomless greed for money and Arab magnates bottomless lust for the bottoms of pale young girls. There is a primitive image of the eye of God in a triangle that symbolizes the center of the universe. Khalid said, replace that eye with the pink anus of a twelve-year-old girl and you have the true center of the Arab universe."

Blain was silent as I began to process everything she'd said. I was still thinking of what to say when she asked, "Do you think I'm evil?"

"I think Khalid is evil, and worse. I think you are amazing to have come through all this, and be as together as you are, as stable."

"What about all those dead people?"

"Khalid killed them, you didn't. Anyway, judging from how you've described their priorities in life, the world's better off without them."

"What about the so-called sanctity of life?"

"The only sanctity of life I'm concerned about in this story is yours. It was a question of them or you, and I can't imagine what my life would be like now if you two weren't in it, in the center of it."

"Yeah but you're really talking about Ada, and her dancing, I'm just a hanger on."

"I don't lump you together with Ada. In the beginning, I did because I knew nothing about you. But now you have as strong a presence as Ada."

"But I don't dance with her talent and inspiration."

"You dance with a classic beautiful grace, and you are what you are."

"But what is that?"

"We don't know yet, do we?"

"Hmm, well, I am your daughter, anyway, right?"

"Yes."

"Can I make an honest confession, Dad?"

"Go ahead."

"I'd rather be your lover than your daughter."

"Now I can lump you together with Ada."

"No, there's a big difference. Ada wants to marry you. I want to be your lover."

"And what's the difference?"

"Toward the end of our time as killer girls, because we were getting despondent, Khalid arranged for us to see a Jungian analyst, a man so mixed up in illicit transfers of money that he could be trusted not to report Khalid for what he was doing. Setting aside his lack of morals and ethics, he was known as a brilliant analyst. He saw my response to what we'd experienced as totally different from Ada's. Ada had built a defense against what was happening by separating her mind from her body. I, on the other hand, was being 'eroticized' (that was the term he used) by these constant threats of being violated sexually. But he said that I would probably never be able to act them out because I'd never be able to trust a man enough to give myself over to him."

"And I'm the man you could trust?"

"Yes, but not just trust in the usual sense. I mean trust you to *understand* why I want *you* to be the one who actually did what we protected ourselves against by being killers. I'm talking about having *you* put whatever part of yourself you'd like in me." Blain was looking at me with an open childlike expression that she might have worn when she asked for something exorbitant for Christmas. She added, "Please don't just reject what I'm saying automatically. Don't say no. In fact don't say anything yet, Okay?"

"Okay."

"After a moment I said, "Why 'Boa Constrictors'? Why was that your code name?"

"Well, Boa stood for Blunt Object Assassinations."

"Ah yes, and 'Constrictors?'"

"Well, Dad, think about the anatomical center of all this, and what it does to express itself... I mean..."

"That's OK, I get the picture."

Blain said sleepily, "Now I'm really exhausted." She rolled over to put her face against my neck, an arm over my chest and a leg over mine. She was asleep almost immediately.

To relate the thoughts that passed through my mind as I waited for my own sleep would test my veracity as narrator. I like to think of myself as a civilized person and I also like to think of myself as an honest person, so I'll let the reader speculate.

The next day I said to Ada, "Boa Constrictors?"

She looked at me blankly. "What about Boa Constrictors?"

"Blain told me everything."

"Everything about what?"

"Your life as assassins."

"What do you mean, assassins?"

"Since I'm your father and since you want to marry me, shouldn't I know about an important part of your history?"

"Does that mean if I tell you my secret history, then you'll marry me?"

"No."

"Then forget it."

"But it does mean that if you don't tell me, I can't even consider the possibility of marrying you."

"Meaning, if I don't tell you, it's no, and if I do tell you, it's maybe?"

"Something like that."

"I'll think about it."

Until I can hear Ada's point of view I can't imagine her being part of the story as Blain told it. The other question is, what about Khalid? The man should be in prison.

I was beginning to form a larger picture of our efforts to form a whole performance for Spoleto. Lucrezia and I have talked and she asked about Rasputin and Aimee. We both wondered what they were up to, so I asked Aimee if we could look at her sculptural self-portrait. She was surprisingly agreeable to the idea.

"It's almost ready to fire," Aimee said this as she pulled a damp cloth off the ceramic sculpture. The life-size figure was standing and in a posture that would be natural also if it was lying down. She said, "I haven't decided yet whether I should be standing or prone." For her to refer to the sculpture as "I" was appropriate because it was a dead ringer for her. I'd never seen her totally nude but I felt like I was now. All of Rasputin's tattooed flora was exquisitely reproduced with incised marks, some of which had color added.

Rasputin was standing off to the side seemingly entranced by the display of his tattoo work and the figure itself.

In her forthright manner, Aimee explained the function of the sculpture in their performance. "In real life as in our act, he (she nods toward Rasputin) is not permitted to touch me other than with his needles. His obsession is to put his mouth on my body, which will never happen except in his fantasies, because he repulses me. In our act he manages to put his mouth on my thigh, that is *this* thigh." She points to the leg of the sculpture. "And because the flowers have just been painted with a glaze that is toxic until fired he almost dies of poisoning. Later in the performance he does it again, this time ingesting the most toxic of all glazes, and dies a grueling death onstage. Hopefully, at Spoleto, I can arrange the real thing."

Lucrezia and I left Aimee's studio with her still staring at her sculpture and Rasputin staring at Aimee, unfazed by what she'd just said.

"You know her better than I do, did she mean what she said?" Lucrezia asked.

"I think that's an unknown and I don't think even she knows. Everyone in this company has their dangerous obsessions, but she's the most enigmatic by far."

Lucrezia shrugged as though Aimee was no different than people she'd been around her whole life in the theater. "Speaking of obsessions, I love being picked up by you. You have no idea how dreary it can be to always be looking up at people. Just pick me up like a sack of flour and throw me over your shoulder and give me a ride to your room so I can take a nap. I'm exhausted and I don't want to go all the way back to the hotel."

I did as she asked, being none to gentle which thrilled her and she unleashed her high pealing laugh to fill the brewery. I had hold of her legs and her head was swaying behind my back. Across the brewery floor, Ada and Blain were working on St. Teresa and both stopped to stare. In my room and by the bed, I said, "Do you want a gentle landing or shall I drop you like a bomb?"

"Like a bomb!"

She bounced twice. "I love being your little kid."

"Excuse me, there are only two kids in this family and we are they."

I turned to see Ada in the doorway and Blain behind her.

"Ah, the jealous siblings!" Lucrezia said, pleased.

"We're no siblings of yours," Ada says.

I could see a storm brewing so I said, "Lucrezia's taking a nap, so let's leave her in peace." I eased Ada and Blain out and after closing the door, said, "I need a little siesta myself, whose room do I get?"

"Mine." "Mine."

We ended up in Blain's room. And until I fell asleep, I heard many competing versions of "I love being your little kid!" in absurdly high voices. During my nap, I had a dream about Lucrezia who was squirming around in my arms like some other form of life than human, like a seal. I realized upon waking that her minute size did not keep me from being attracted to her smooth perfect proportions, and in fact was a contributing factor. I also realized that I'd been having these thoughts for some time but not acknowledging them. As though reading my mind, Ada suddenly sat on top of me and pinned my arms down.

She said, "Marry me," but was immediately dislodged forcefully and replaced by Blain who also pinned down my arms. She pressed into me and leaned down hissing softly, "But with me, there are no obligations."

I pushed Blain off. "What do I have, a family of sex maniacs?"

Ada was delighted, "Sex Maniacs! Sex Maniacs! SM, SM, S and M, Sado-masochistic Sex Maniacs." She started out the door like the head of a conga line singing and dancing and Blain joined in from behind holding onto Ada's hips, both kicking out a foot at key sounds like 'Sado,' 'Maso,' 'Chiastic,' 'Sex,' laughing hysterically. Soon everyone who had been working out on the floor, joined the line, hands on each other's hips, kicking out a foot at key lyrics and calling them out with total abandon.

As I stood watching, I was suddenly struck by the power these twins had over all of us. This group of adults would have followed Ada right out the door and down the street. It's the kind of power a Japanese horror film demon might have, defying logic but still believable because it's happening before one's eyes. Even more alarming was the rapidly increasing effect they were having on me, without my having stopped to register each increment of increase. The constant aura of cheeky, erotic, intensity surrounding them now seemed, and only partly because of their age, threatening, and dangerous. The playfulness was becoming something else. I needed to put something, or someone, between them and me.

As though on cue, Lucrezia walked over beside me. I was still filled with my dream of her. I leaned down and picked her up and on impulse, kissed her on the mouth. She wrapped around me like the half monkey she is, wiggled like the seal of my dream, and slipped her tongue into my mouth.

"So? I'm on the other side of your defenses now, yes?"

"It seems that way."

She placed her face against my neck and seemed to melt into softness. I had a hard time remembering the menacing, cigar-smoking Sicilian impresario.

"Are we going to be lovers?" she whispers.

"Possibly."

"Promise me one thing, Narrator"

"Yes?"

"That in your narration about us, you do not use the word 'love,' because one should do not say."

Within days, we did in fact 'do.' We spent the night passionately entwined, and I dreamed of seals in warm ocean waters.

I had shimmed in between the twins and me, a wall of protection, because I knew they would not abide what I had done and would cease their assaults on me. Assaults I knew I would at some point be unable to resist, just as those in the Japanese film cannot resist the demons imbued with their peculiar powers.

Ada and Blain did indeed step back from me, but not without a scene of near hysterics that ultimately ended with Ada announcing, "You have no idea how much you want us." As proof of what she'd said, I almost said, 'I do know how much I want you' but the Gods of Self-Protection intervened to save me by insisting, 'Don't say a word' and I didn't.

The weeks sped by, and our individual performance pieces coalesced into an impressive whole, interlacing personal exposure with artistic dimension smoothly, all evolving from a surprisingly easy collaboration between Lucrezia and me. We were ready for Spoleto.

Part Four

"An Enormous Success by a Diminutive Artist."

Lucrezia was reading from a Roman newspaper.

"Any other time I'd be put off by any reference to my size, but this review is so positive and well written, I have to forgive. But aren't you offended, Narrator? To have your name hardly mentioned?"

"No Lucrezia, this was your success in finally being seen at the cutting edge of Italian theater, where you should be. And except for the unfortunate role that Rasputin played in the end, and Aimee's narrow escape from the law, it was a very transcendent piece of theater."

It's been three weeks since the end of the Spoleto Festival, and we were all now beginning to disperse to whatever came next in our lives. Ada and Blain left the day after the performance, still speaking to me only when necessary. My Lucrezia liaison saved me (at least that was my sanguine and naive assessment at the time). Their last words were threats ranging from terrible retribution to declarations that I would one day be married to one of them and the other would be my mistress after all. As a further provocation, they left with Waldeebe II, who had been turned away by Mojobe because she felt now, living in the west she wanted to have only one husband. Waldeebe II was understandably upset, and when he left with the twins, he said, "Oh yes? Well, that won't keep me from having two wives."

I know I had been derelict in my role as Narrator and have a lot of catching up to do, but all in due time, yes? as my diminutive partner in passion would say (passion, because as you'll remember, 'love' is forbidden).

Preceding our performance at the Festival we were the guests of an old friend of Lucrezia's, Signore Ponzza, a financier and lover of theater (and I suspected a possible past lover of Lucrezia as well) who owned a large villa at the edge of

Spoleto. He also, I believe, was influential in having Lucrezia's performance chosen by the festival.

It was in Signore Ponzza's villa that some last-minute changes were made to our planned performance. One of them involved Vladimir. His steady increase in size baffled the doctors, but they agreed on one thing. His condition was increasingly a threat to his heart and in fact, one doctor believed he had already crossed a line of no return. This was the prognosis Vladimir chose to believe.

"If it's my heart that's going to take me out," He said, "I want to go out as a participant, not as a victim. I want it to be part of the performance. After all, we decided to make as great a mark as possible at this festival. Here's my plan: If I know anything, I know my heart and I know my own little perverse fetishes, and the best example of the latter is *The Perfect Adolescent Thigh*. My cardiologist believes that sexual stimulation would be the 'kiss of death', his exact words, amazingly. So in my performance, I want a bare thigh descending from above as I lie on my gurney reciting my lines which I have yet to write, but will be appropriate I assure you. Of course, this thigh belongs to a live girl and that can only be Ada. No other thigh will do. I've had my glimpses and full exposure will be as the doctor says, my undoing. And I would add, It will be a great gift to me from all of you if you'll agree to this because I am at present suffering greatly and don't wish to go on."

Vladimir had made his statement to the whole company and Ada happened to be standing next to me.

"What do you think, Ada?" I said quietly.

"It's too bad the sight of my bare thigh didn't give you a heart attack Mr. Narrator, you deserved it. But my answer to Vladimir is, sure, I've killed enough men who didn't want to die, why not kill the one who does?"

"Ada has agreed, if everyone else is willing to go for it."

There was no dissent and I thought, what a wonderfully unsentimental company we have. Ada and I agreed that Sister Agnes should be the choreographer for

Ada's death descent. We talked about Ada's costume with Vladimir. He immediately responded, "School girl uniform! There must be total taboo!"

That night in bed, Lucrezia and I were lying quietly against each other. As often happened, she'd then bring up a serious subject, and it was always hard for me to concentrate. She justified it by saying, "This is when we're most one person, so there's minimal dissent. So now we have two promises of death in our performance, one from Aimee, one from Vladimir. Aimee is determined to poison Rasputin, and Vladimir is determined to kill himself by flying thigh. Exciting, yes?"

A woman had been hired by Signore Ponzza as nurse to care for Vladimir, of whom he had become very fond. She was a qualified nurse, but she was also a member of an obscure pagan cult of healing that Signore Ponzza had taken an interest in. We'd not seen much of Vladimir since we all arrived here a week ago because we'd been rehearsing every day at a theater space in town.

One evening after rehearsal, we all went out on a side terrace of the villa to greet Vladimir, who was waiting on his gurney, with his nurse at his side. He gestured toward the nurse who was not wearing a white nurse uniform, but a peculiar blousy costume of black pantaloons, green and purple horizontally striped shirt, and a pointed silver hat with several blue stars of various sizes.

"This is Marconia, who usually wears the reassuring white uniform of the registered nurse she is, but today she is attired for the ritual we're about to participate in." Vladimir said, "We're just waiting for our transportation."

Marconia nodded to us without a smile. She was dark and thin and had the stance of a circus acrobat. Her face was plain except for a mole above her lip, from which sprouted a cluster of fine black curly hairs like a miniature head of Medusa.

We all turned at the sound of a vehicle that pulled up the driveway alongside the terrace. We looked over the marble balustrade to see an antique hearse, painted silver. Two women, stouter than Marconia and costumed the same came up the three steps of the terrace and without a word and with Marconia's help, bumped

Vladimir's gurney down the steps to the rear of the hearse where he and his mattress were shoved inside with some grunting, the door was closed and the hearse pulled away. We looked at each other with expressions ranging from mild bemusement to seriously raised eyebrows. In the end, we all agreed that it was Vladimir's call on how he chose to spend his final days.

A week later the Festival was in full swing. On the night of our performance, after the hugely successful acts by Sister Agnes and Father Joseph, and the three Waldeebe, Vladimir was pulled across the stage by Marconia and six of her cult all costumed in their pointy hats and pantaloons, adding an element of unintended farce not lost upon the audience. The stage was dark and the only sound was the voice of Mojobe singing with simple clarity a Nigerian lament of loss. Vladimir was on his back covered by black fabric and wore his own pointed silver hat. He was reciting in Russian the poem he had written to describe the perfect thigh that was about to take his life and why it must be so. He had abandoned the idea of providing the audience with a translation and had decided instead to have a series of English words, large, projected onto a hanging white fabric floating against the back wall of the stage. The pagans pulled Vladimir in a slow circle and when they stopped, a single spotlight high above revealed Ada suspended by a cable. She was dressed as a pure school girl in a white blouse, plaid skirt, and gray knee-length socks. Mojobe sang, Vladimir recited, and Ada was very slowly lowered. As she approached Vladimir she had begun to slowly lift her skirt demurely. She moved closer to Vladimir and her skirt was above one hip. Mojobe's lament grew louder and the projected words appeared seemingly suspended in the air, one after the other, Vestal... White... Chaste... Savor... Life...

Ada's thigh was shown like smooth white marble in the spotlight, a work of art in motion. Vladimir was looking up.

Odalisque... Exposed... Lush... Piquant...

The pagans were all in a circle around Vladimir, following his eyes. Ada's thigh now wiggled overhead like a pale worm dangling over a nest of hatchlings, their pointed beaks in the air. The lights were dimming and Ada's legs were in a slow swinging motion just above Vladimir's eyes.

Sully... Taboo... Dew... Dark... Die...

Marconia had quickly leaned her face over Vladimir's and he felt her Medusa mustache crawling across his cheek toward his ear, like a tarantula bringing the final word of death. But instead, he heard...

"Vladimir, don't go, I love you, I will heal you."

But Ada's thigh was just a wish away, in all its terrible curvy glory. Vladimir's eyes were wide, his forehead glistened with perspiration, he was gasping for breath loudly enough to compete with Mojobe, and he unleashed a loud "Arrggg!" His body was trembling, convulsing, and then was abruptly stone still after a last eerie wheeze of breath.

The lights went out and fat candles were lit by the pagans at the four corners of Vladimir's gurney before it was drawn slowly toward the wings as a Russian requiem poured out over the theater. The audience was silent and troubled. They could hear sobbing backstage. Just before the candlelit body of Vladimir reached the wings, the body sat abruptly upright and shouted, "Stop!" A spotlight came on, moving quickly across the stage in search of Vladimir who was in the process of sliding off his bed to stand, his black robe only partially covering his pale corpulence. Marconia was at his side holding him steadily by one arm, the other pagans clustered nearby to catch him if he toppled.

Vladimir's pointed silver hat had been knocked askew and as he carefully straightened it he said, "I'm sorry, I'm so sorry, I've let you all down." He hesitated a moment and then went on, "So there we were, in the world of art, and now back in the world of life, while I should be in the world of death."

The audience was perplexed, and had begun to look at each other and question whether this was life, or just one more unexpected turn in this original piece of theater. They were waiting for a clue from Vladimir.

He continued, "Yes, from art to life that should have been death. My great countryman, Fyodor Dostoyevsky, whom I might add, ha!, was referred to by that other Vladimir Nabokov in a letter to his friend Edmund Wilson, as 'a third-rate writer' ...where was I, oh yes, in Dostoyevsky's novel, *The Idiot*, there was an event that gave me some solace. One of his characters, Ippolit, had decided to take his own life in the presence of his acquaintances. His pistol misfired, well, actually he forgot to put in a firing pin...”

Vladimir hesitated for a moment, organizing his words to continue his story. From above, where Ada was slowly turning, suspended, came her clear voice, “Look Vladimir, I’m sorry my thigh’s not enticing enough to trigger your coveted coronary, but this is getting boring.”

At that, the balance was tipped for the audience and there was loud and appreciative laughter. Vladimir was taken aback by the laughter but continued on, “Ippolit had said, ‘I shall die gazing straight into the source of power and life.” The audience was still laughing and Lucrezia in a moment of theater savvy, ordered that the curtain be brought down and the lights diminished to darkness as though this were the planned climax of the act. The last words heard from Vladimir were, “And Ippolit, in his embarrassment apologized for still being alive, as it seems I am...”

More and louder laughter. In the darkness, Vladimir crawled back onto his bed and said to Marconia, “How humiliating, get me out of here.”

While Vladimir’s failed death performance had its element of levity, Rasputin’s performance did not. The act which was brief but intense consisted of the three players, Aimee, the surrogate Aimee in the form of her sculpture, and Rasputin on the stage in a series of puppet-like attempts at contact and rejection between Rasputin and the two Aimees. At the climax, Rasputin having been rejected by the live Aimee took solace in the form of a passionate embrace of surrogate Aimee. In the act of kissing the sculpture high on the inside of the thigh, he was seized by gagging and convulsions and thrashed in a circle on the floor, which the audience took for part of the planned drama. Again, Lucrezia, who was ready for anything brought down the curtain as the closure of the act, and the audience was moved and applauded enthusiastically.

On the other side of the curtain, Rasputin was still on the floor, now in a fetal position, gasping and gasping for breath. A doctor was called. "It looks like he's been poisoned," He said.

In the meantime, the audience was applauding fervently and our performance came to a close, with the cast, sans Rasputin, out on the stage bowing. I urged Lucrezia to join them. I stayed in the wings.

The Spoleto police were called in and they, in turn, called for the Inspector from Rome to investigate, because Rasputin was on the edge of death.

"He was poisoned by chrome oxide. This is a pigment you used on your sculpture?"

This was the Inspector, now investigating a possible impending homicide. When he arrived at the villa and saw me and the other players from Rome, he shook his head incredulously. He was seated now across from Aimee in the library of Signore Ponzza. Lucrezia and I were sitting on either side of Aimee on the couch.

"Yes, I use chrome oxide."

"But you always fire it to make it permanent, correct?"

"Yes."

"And unfired chrome oxide is extremely toxic."

"Yes."

"But the chrome oxide that may be killing this man, Rasputin, it was not fired."

"No."

"Why not?"

Aimee hesitated, then said, "I added it the night before the performance and there was no time to fire it."

"Then why did you add it?" The Inspector was soft-spoken but was looking hard at Aimee.

"Because I wanted the green on the vines to be brighter."

"But the only area where the chrome oxide was added is high up on the inside of the thigh of the sculpture where it would not have been seen by the audience."

"But I would see it."

The inspector was silent for a few moments looking out the window. Then he asked in a neutral tone, "The exact events of your act, they were carefully planned beforehand, and carried out as planned? I mean precisely where Rasputin was to put his mouth on..."

"Me."

"You?"

"Yes."

"You mean the sculptural replica of you."

'It's not a replica, she has her own existence, life, persona."

"And you feel responsible for her?"

"I am responsible for her existence, yes, I created her."

"No, I mean do you feel a responsibility to take care of her, look after her?"

Aimee shrugged her shoulder slightly.

The inspector continued, "Getting back to the performance, you knew Rasputin would have his mouth on...her, you?"

"Yes, it was carefully worked out."

"Then why did you add the chrome oxide, a deadly toxin when not fired, to the sculpture the night before the performance?"

"Because I wanted the green to be brighter."

"But if you knew Rasputin's mouth was going to be..."

"It wasn't supposed to be there! So close to..."

"To what?"

"My private place." Aimee's cheeks were flushed and she was staring angrily at the inspector.

The inspector had his eyebrows raised as he said, "Do you mean that according to the choreography, Rasputin's mouth wasn't supposed to be that high on 'her' leg, and therefore you thought it was safe to put the chrome oxide there? or do you mean it was morally wrong for Rasputin to put his mouth there, and therefore he got what he deserved?"

Aimee was silent and staring at the floor while Lucrezia and I waited for her to provide the answer that would declare her innocence.

But Aimee said softly, "Both." Then she looked up at the inspector and said defiantly, "Both!"

The inspector studied Aimee's face. Even he, after decades of investigating the crimes of high passion of his compatriots, seemed surprised.

Aimee was charged with attempted murder and led from the library, past the other players on the terrace to the police car waiting in the driveway.

Vladimir had been steadily losing weight and gaining strength and moving about like his old self, at least the self we discovered on our butterfly outing when he first appeared in our lives. One evening after he'd recovered enough to walk on his own, he and I strolled through the villa gardens.

"Vladimir, I have to ask, what does Marconia's treatment consist of, that it's so successful?"

"Ah, I'm sworn to secrecy on that subject, at least medically. But this much I can say. I'm driven in our wonderfully decorated vintage hearse (surely a sign of defiance of death), to a structure in a remote hilltop location and I'm marinated shall we say in a cistern of natural substance inhabited by crawly things that I can feel around me. It's all-natural, and it smells dreadful. Afterwards I'm rinsed in clear water and then left out in the sun to dry. In terms of the biochemical inter-actions between myself and all that, I can tell you nothing, although I do know a fair amount, thanks to Marconia who it seems is turning out to also be..., well, more about that another time."

"Is it fair to use the word romance, here, Vladimir?"

"If you insist."

"I thought so. You seem to be more at peace with the world than any time since we've met."

"That's partly due to you."

"How so?"

"Well, Lucrezia seems to be so totally enamored of you that she's found it difficult to keep active hate for me alive, so I feel safe from threat for the first time since our marriage ended so many years ago. You know, her brothers and all. And, Lucrezia and Khalid have a long history together, about which I don't know much. I've wanted to caution you about these things for some time, because you've, well, you've saved me."

"Saved you? How?"

"You've saved me from émigré purgatory. I'd been floating in between my two countries and my two selves and frankly, in and out of sanity. By adopting me into your theater world, you've given me a context for my life for the first time, perhaps ever. So, ha!, don't kick me out."

"Well, Vladimir, I can't adopt you."

"Why not? You've adopted two daughters who are not your daughters, why not a father who's not your father?"

"I'm only the Narrator, Vladimir. I don't write plots. I report plots. And even there, I've been lax lately."

"Fine, Narrator, but we're all together for the time being, aren't we?"

Vladimir's eyes were glistening with emotion. I've always disliked being responsible for the well-being of others.

"Yes, Vladimir, for the time being, everyone's together who wants to be."

"Ah, thank you. And on that subject, don't you miss Ada and Blain?"

Only after being asked that question do I allow myself to feel my true yearning for the twins, particularly Ada.

"Yes, I miss them."

Unexpected visitors arrived at the villa. The Nelsons are Aimee's parents. They had been on their first guided tour of Europe, where they saw their daughter's photo in the paper in connection with the Spoleto Festival and the mishap with Rasputin. After meeting Lucrezia, as co-director of the company, and finding it too awkward to carry on a conversation with a 'freak' (the word actually slipped out), they have asked to talk to me.

"Hello, I'm Bob Nelson and this is my wife Joan. We expected to find Jane here and now we've been told she's in Rome, in the custody of the police. Is that correct?"

My reply to these people to whom I had taken an instant dislike was, "Who's Jane?"

"Our daughter, Jane. I don't know where she picked up this Aimee business." Mrs. Nelson said impatiently.

"I see. Yes, your daughter is in Rome."

"And what has she been charged with?"

"I'm not the magistrate."

The ever-gracious Signore Ponzza intervenes. "It's all a bit complicated. We'll put you in touch with an Inspector in Rome and he can give you the most accurate and current information. What you've probably read in the paper is all we know here, and that is that there was an accident and a misunderstanding about some poisonous pigments ingested off of one of your daughter's sculptures."

"Sculpture? What kind of sculpture?"

"How long has it been since you last saw your daughter?" I asked.

"It's been a while now." Mrs. Nelson says.

"How long a while?"

"Eight years. What business is it of yours?" Mr. Nelson asked.

"I just wondered how close a family you are."

"Very close."

Signore Ponzza invited the Nelsons to spend the night and leave for Rome in the morning. "Since you're unfamiliar with your daughter's sculpture, we can show you a piece that's in a room upstairs." I accompany him and the Nelsons up to a room where Aimee's sculpture from the performance had been laid out on top of the bed for safe keeping. The Nelsons were shocked by the nudity and the simulated tattoos and especially by the similarity to Aimee.

"It could actually be her", Mr. Nelson said, in an incredulous whisper. He was mesmerized, and reluctant to leave the room.

Part Five

Six months had passed since we all left Spoleto. Rasputin had recovered from his brush with death, and Aimee had been cleared of all charges. We were in the center of the Brewery, witnessing the marriage of Aimee and Rasputin. Father Joseph was officiating after agreeing not to mention God. Aimee had chosen to wear a pale yellow, very sheer translucent, short, sleeveless dress which provided the perfect arena for Rasputin's baroque multi-color flora which covered her body. Her tattoos now seemed as full of life as they seemed full of death in Spoleto. Art is always a matter of context.

Everyone had returned except Vladimir, who would not leave Marconia, who would not leave Italy for the US. "Too barbaric", she said. Lucrezia too chose to stay in Rome, where her success at Spoleto had brought her the artistic attention she coveted her whole life. She had said to me in true Lucrezia tradition, "Well, I seem to have gotten from you all I can get in this lifetime. Maybe in another life, we'll stay together, yes?"

At the same time that I felt the terrible blow of rejection from someone for whom I'd come to have feelings of love (although of course I never told her that), a part of me I held in reserve was quick to acknowledge that Lucrezia, like some dark fairy tale princess, would in the end, kill me if she could, emotionally if not mortally. And while she didn't kill me emotionally, she severely wounded me, and reminded me that my only safe place in this story is as Narrator.

Ada and Blain had returned for the wedding. Waldeebe II had gone back to Africa. With eleven stitches in his head.

"He said we were his property, that his cousin had given us to him in exchange for Mojobe." Ada explained. "We pointed out that his cousin didn't own us to give away. He said that all women were owned by some man. We probably could have worked it out with him, he was really very sweet, not to mention very sexy, not to mention he had the biggest..." Ada and Blain become hysterical with laughter. Blain continued the story, "The main problem was that he had some pretty strange ideas about what to do with it..." Then more soberly she went on, "First he asked nicely for what he wanted, which appalled both of us. Then he said it was his right. Then he became forceful, and wham!, he got it on the head with a flower pot. We both said after, that if one of us had been alone with him, we'd have been split in two."

I couldn't help but wonder as I listened to them, if they would always associate sex (or, almost sex) with smashed male crania. In any event, their attitude toward me was back to its former familial self. When they heard about Lucrezia, they performed a little circle dance around me accompanied by a chorus of, "Dumped by the midget, dumped by the midget, dumped by the midget..."

Even I had to laugh.

That night, Ada and Blain stood in the doorway of my room reading out a list, alternating from one to the other: "France, 15, Guyana, 13, Italy, 14, Montenegro, 14, Korea, 13, Chile, 12."

"Age of consent, Dad." Ada said, adding, "And in case you've lost count, we're seventeen now."

I was close to incredulous. Were they really two years older than when we met? As I stared at them carefully, it was uncanny and frightening. They were young women and even worse they were like works of art.

After too long a silence, I laughed and said, "Speaking of age of consent, and more to the point, age of non-consent, tomorrow we're going to pay a visit to Khalid."

Khalid was pacing the floor in his office tower.

"So the score is even all around. Lucrezia had her moment of glory in Spoleto, sponsored by me. You had a lessor moment of glory in Spoleto sponsored by me. Lucrezia has dumped you, romantically, and has forgiven me for dumping her, financially. You have funding to keep your dance company going. Ada and Blain have been adopted by you, relieving me of a responsibility I never much cared for. Anything I've left out?"

Ada and Blain were watching me to see how I'd respond to Khalid's self-assured incantation.

"Yes, you've left out the killings that Ada and Blain were coerced into, as a result of which you became a wealthy man."

Khalid was surprised by my bluntness, but not unnerved.

"Yes, there were some unfortunate incidents in which my young and fragile daughters defended themselves against some barbaric Middle Eastern characters. Incidents that were consistently judged as acts of self-defense. And I would add, incidents in which generous compensation was provided by the parties involved."

"Compensation to you."

"And to them." Khalid nodded toward the twins.

"They've seen none of that 'generous compensation.'"

"Oh, this is about money?"

"It's about manipulating children into acts of murder, for your financial gain."

"Listen, my friend, all of this took place in another country and years ago. If this business were to be reopened, these two girls would be far more vulnerable criminally than I, and I have numerous witnesses to prove the veracity of that statement."

I knew that what Khalid said was true. I was quiet for a moment, thinking.

"Dad, find out where our mother is," Ada said.

I was relieved to have something to say. "Where, is the twins' mother?"

"I'm under no obligation to give anyone any information. You've come in here accusing me of egregious acts and now you want me to give you information?"

"Look Khalid, forget our past as Murder, Inc. and just tell us how to contact our mother," Blain said.

Khalid looked at the three of us. "Is this an agreement then that we forget the past and I graciously provide your mother's contact information?"

I looked at Ada, then Blain, and they both nodded.

"Yes, that's our agreement," I responded.

We were given an address in Zurich and we left. In the elevator, Ada said, "Dad, promise me we never have to see that man again."

'I promise."

The twins accosted me with fervent borderline affection, to the consternation of a young business type sharing our elevator who'd been ogling them since we got on. I thought of all the possibilities he could imagine of how and why the twins and I were together, and knew how far he'd be from the truth. I also considered that when this story is done, I too will know the outcome of all this. When the twins are adults, which is no longer in the far distant future, will I marry one and be lovers with the other as they have insisted? Will we at some inevitable point part ways and be but memories to each other? And what about the myriad of possibilities in between? I wished I knew but we all had to wait to find out, yes? Speaking of memories, will I ever be able to find the right resting place in my archives for Lucrezia? Would you really like to know how I could have allowed myself to become so vulnerable to her as to result in what she did to me in the end? I'll tell you. Imagine this: a perfect small-scale model of a perfect human being, a model made of real human parts. A minuscule work of art professing such adoration for me and my creativity that I couldn't help but believe her. A writhing, smooth, maquette of an adult with the whole history of Italy seemingly inside of her, whose tininess engulfed me desperately in a frenzied mix of pleasure and pain. A mind and imagination so relentlessly provocative that my own was constantly nurtured and never relaxed. That was Lucrezia, whose smallness seemed to make her gifts seem larger than ever. In a sense, you could say Lucrezia was constant illusion, which in the end is the essence of art anyway, yes?

The letter I sent to the twins' mother in Zurich was answered promptly, and was very businesslike. So much so that I was hesitant to show it to them. One more example of clinical disinterest on the part of an adult who should have felt something for them. No wonder they stick to me like Velcro. In the letter, there was the acknowledgment of facts and not much more. "Yes it is true I am the biological mother to them. Yes, it is true there is a bank account here of considerable size in their names of which they take possession at the age of eighteen. No, It is not a good time for them to come here, but it is necessary for me to be in your country (New York City) in one week, we could meet then. And finally, no, there will be no information forthcoming as to the identity of the biological father."

After Ada read the letter, she said, "Just what I've always dreamed of, a warm, loving mother. Jesus, *the* biological father? She couldn't even say, *their* biological father."

"The hell with her," Blain said, "How much money do you think we have there, Dad?"

"I don't know, but if you were getting anywhere near your fair share of Khalid's entrepreneurship in Arab eliminations, you should be a couple of rich babes."

They both broke into peals of laughter and encircled me chanting, "Arab eliminations, Arab eliminations, Arab eliminations..."

"That's really funny, sounds like a fairy tale where a giant ogre eats Arabs and poops them out!" Ada said.

As I watched and listened to Ada and Blain, I realized their resiliency came from their capacity (need, probably) to turn every bad bit of news into cause for vaudevillian antics. If they ever lost that they'd be in for a big crash because their archives were filled with the malice of the dregs of humanity.

We had arranged to meet the twins' mother, Leanda, in New York, at the Metropolitan Museum. It was to be a brief and one-time meeting to receive documents, and she said, some advice. She had chosen a specific painting she asked us to stand in front of. It was a fifteenth-century Flemish Virgin and Child by Memling that I'm quite familiar with. After a night flight (because it's all we could get on short notice) we were fairly fatigued when we made it to the Metropolitan. We walked slowly up the grand staircase to the second-floor Renaissance galleries. Slowly because, we were tired and slowly because none of us was very keen on the idea of one more bizarre chapter in the life of the twins (and me as *Dad*). As though reading my mind Ada said, "Maybe she'll turn out to be just a regular person, a sort of grouchy regular person."

There was no one standing by the painting, and no one else in the room who could possibly be Leanda. Ada and Blain were absorbed by the painting and what I told them about it, including a story that had recently emerged about a second, similar Memling Virgin and Child, in the national museum in Zurich, which had just been declared a forgery, a very accomplished forgery. While we were admiring the painting as best as our jet-lagged eyes could, a figure quietly appeared by our side. We turned to look, and saw a woman whose face was strikingly similar to the painted Virgin, except for... Well, I'll have to get to that in a moment because she was speaking to us. It was not often that I saw the twins struck dumb, that is speechless, but they were, as they looked at and listened to their mother.

"Hello, I'm Leanda."

She was staring at Ada and Blain who could only stare back.

"I haven't seen you two for over fourteen years."

Still no sound from the twins.

Leanda looked at me, with slightly raised eyebrows.

"Hello, I'm, well, the Narrator."

To her credit, she saw nothing peculiar or flippant in my statement.

"Hello," she said and held out her hand.

Because I'd been staring at the Virgin's hand just before she walked up, I could not help but now stare at her own perfect replica.

"I've been watching you three since you arrived. It was my intention to simply give you the documents I have for you and leave. But seeing the intense exchange you've had over the painting, my selfishness took over. That is, I thought, I like the look of these three people together, totally separate from any blood relation, and perhaps I'd like to know them."

At this Ada opened her mouth, I'm sure with the intention of delivering a searing diatribe against Leanda on the theme of who do you think you are that you think you get to decide whether or not we are to be privileged to make your acquaintance. But at the last moment, she closed her mouth and remained silent. This both surprised me and relieved me. I couldn't let this person just disappear without knowing what happened to her.

We were scheduled to fly back to our respective cities tomorrow.

"I know of an excellent restaurant nearby," Leanda said.

I was relieved by her words.

Over dinner, Leanda went over the paperwork she'd brought.

"Here's the number and password for your bank account. I didn't keep track of the balance. Given that there were large deposits made by Khalid repeatedly and given the accumulated interest, the balance, which I had my lawyer check before I left Switzerland three days ago was larger than I expected: About three and a half million dollars."

At this Ada and Blain stared at Leanda and then at each other and then at me.

Raised eyebrows was all they could come up with.

I was pleased to see that the money didn't seriously faze them.

Leanda went on, "Here are the birth certificates. Here is a signed form that Khalid no longer has legal guardianship over the twins. And here is a signed form that I make no claim to custody of the twins."

Again, Ada opened her mouth to let loose some ripe opinion, but thought better of it and remained silent.

A silence fell over the table. We were all pretty tired, had eaten well, and shared excellent wine. After a moment of looking at Leanda, Blain spoke.

"What happened to your face?"

Now that the primary question on the mind of all three of us since we first caught sight of Leanda had been asked, I felt free to look unblinkingly at her. She had a classically refined northern European face with delicate features, intense dark eyes, and the high round forehead of the Flemish women who appeared in paintings. In fact, there was a startling resemblance to the Memling Madonna. However, and there's no other way to put it, all this had been X'd out, Literally. There was a perfectly symmetrical scar remaining from what had to have been a carefully incised X across her face, executed by the steady hand of an artist. The center of the X was on her left cheek, well to the side of her nose and well below her eye. No reckless slash this. The scar extended into the hairline at the top and across the sides of her face on the bottom. The right edge of her upper lip was clipped as was the top of her left ear. The careful incision that left this scar was made by a master draftsman.

Leanda looked at Blain without judgment "To answer that question, we must all either stay here in New York for longer or go back to Portland together."

That night as I lay in bed with Ada on one side and Blain on the other, each resting slightly over me as though they'd been washed up by the tide, I said to the darkness, "You know of all the scenarios I could have imagined in meeting Leanda, this could not have been one of them."

"You're right, Dad," Ada said sleepily

"You're always right, Dad," Blain said.

"Will you marry me, Dad?" Ada said.

"Can I be your mistress, Dad?" Blain said.

We all sigh at the familiar mantra.

"You know, her scar has X'd out all the animosity I felt toward her," Ada said.

I felt Blain nodding in agreement, her head on my shoulder.

In the morning, Leanda seemed to know that the twins had forgiven her for her abandonment even though no words were exchanged on the subject. Over breakfast, she decided that she would come to Portland with us. She had completed her business in New York, about which no information was offered, and she wanted to see the brewery and the dance company that was so important to

Ada and Blain and she wanted to see Ada dance. I'd explained to her that Ada was on her way to possible world-class status, lacking only some more formal training.

"I was determined to go back to Zurich right away but as I said there's something about how the three of you are together that I wanted to know more about. Also, I have decided that I have some business to take care of with Khalid."

I realized from being with Leanda in public that she had no self-consciousness at all about her scar. It was true that the scar was a refined line almost in the category of exotic body piercing, but nonetheless it was a scar, and clearly wasn't created with her consent. Part of the startling effect she has is that beneath the scar there is such refined and intelligent beauty that the scar seemed almost as though it could just be lifted off like a veil. If she were not such a beautiful woman, she would be considered grotesque by most people, possibly myself included. There's something about the violence of the cut combined with the poetry of her face, that's so compelling.

Leanda was unable to get a seat on our flight and we arranged to meet when she arrived the next day at the brewery. On our flight, I was flanked by Ada and Blain and the subject of conversation was of course Leanda.

"All my life I'd had blank feelings about her because I couldn't even remember what she looked like," Ada said. "When we got the letter from her I hated her because she sounded so cold. When I first saw her in the museum I pitied her, and was repulsed by her. Now, I'm intrigued by her and for some reason feel as though I owe her something rather than the other way around. Why do you suppose that is, Dad?"

"I feel the same way. Why?" Blain said.

I think I understood. Because Leanda had made no apology for abandoning them, I sensed she had made serious sacrifices for them, somehow related to her scar. Like a survivor from some private hell, she felt she owed no apologies to anyone. After I'd attempted to explain all this to the twins, they reflected on it for a moment and Ada said, "You're a smart guy, Dad."

"You're a really smart guy, Dad," Blain said.

"Will you marry me, Dad?" Ada said.

"Can I be your..." Blain said.

She didn't finish because the flight attendant was leaning over us with lunch, and with the quizzical expression, people wore when observing the three of us together, especially if they'd overheard bits of conversation.

When Leanda arrived at the brewery, we all saw her from a distance, as we were rehearsing on the far side of the room. She was wearing a soft linen dress and heels and strode across the floor as rhythmically and gracefully as a lanky model. We'd said nothing to anyone about her scar, because she'd have known if we had and we wanted her to think it was a non-issue to us. She was an impressive and beautiful image. Everyone welcomed her warmly, as the twins' mother and also as people who admired style.

Ada and Blain surprised Leanda by immediately embracing her and she blushed slightly. She was clearly pleased by their gesture. I had the feeling there was not much of that in her life.

I noticed no change in expression as people registered her scar. The members of our theater company have seen everything.

"My bags are just inside the door, would you get them for me?" She said to the twins,

There was a race between them to get to the bags first, at which everyone laughed, relieved at the acceptance of Leanda by the twins.

After greeting everyone individually, Leanda asked that we continue our rehearsal so she could see us working. She said that meeting new people exhausted her and she'd like to not have to talk for a while. I sat silently with her on a bench as everyone went back to work on a new dance piece we'd just begun to explore, in which people were improvising moves. When Ada began to move in her own choreographed piece, I could sense Leanda watching carefully. Ada's steps involved a range of movements from writhing curlicues of motion on the floor to her signature fleet-footed leaps and turns. She had been doing this impressively earlier today but now, because of Leanda I was sure, she was outdoing herself to the appreciation and applause of everyone not least of whom was Leanda.

"I see what you meant," Leanda said to me with quiet awe.

After an hour of work, the company broke for a rest. Ada came over to sit by Leanda. Her face was flushed from exertion and she was radiant with enthusiasm about her piece. She knew how good it was. She knew how good she was.

Leanda put her hand over Ada's. "You were wonderful."

Ada burst into tears (the only time I'd ever seen her really cry). "Really?"

Leanda put her arms around Ada, and had tears in her eyes.

I looked across the room to where Blain was sitting on the floor among the others, watching Leanda and Ada with an expression I'd never seen before, a maturity that had only appeared before in brief fleeting glimpses. I caught her eye and motioned for her to come over, which she did. She sat on the other side of me and looked across at Leanda and Ada and held onto me with the most intensity I'd ever felt from her. I was filled with sympathy for her but there was nothing I could say.

Leanda turned to her and said, "You were wonderful too."

"Thank you", Blain said with her quiet new resolve.

Leanda was staying at the small boutique hotel three blocks away, where Lucrezia stayed. Ada, Blain, and I had dinner with her and walked her back to the hotel. There was none of the childish competition that went on with Lucrezia. The twins both knew that when Leanda told her story, it would be to me alone so that she wouldn't have to censor it for two seventeen-year-olds. And since they were anxious to know that story, there was no resistance to my going up with Leanda alone to her room.

We sipped brandy and she talked about her response to the brewery experience and she told me a little about what she did in Zurich and New York and other cities around the world.

"I'm trained as a lawyer and as a mathematician. International law. Financial investment math. I put together deals for hard-headed and hard-hearted moguls from one country to another. I speak four languages. My scar has served as a kind of abstract credential. Much as a saber scar served its purpose in the past between Prussian military men. No one had ever asked its origin. What they imagine is, I'm sure, far more impressive from their point of view than its actual provenance. No one, before Blain, had ever actually asked me what happened. Speaking of Blain, she suffers doesn't she, beside Ada's brilliance as a dancer?"

"Actually, today was the first time I saw it to that extent."

"Hmm, I suppose it had to do with me."

"I think so."

We were both silent for a minute. Then Leanda started the story of her scar with a resigned tone.

"What happened to me was a long and complicated story. No one but I knew the full story, but a number of people knew parts. It's so long I may have to tell it to you over a period of time."

"But in the end, I too will know the whole story?"

"That remains to be seen. It depends on my level of trust in you as I proceed. You see, the justification for my telling you is that you are father to Ada and Blain, father in a way that I'd never seen before, even between a man and his actual children. And I believe it's because you're not their actual father and therefore you don't see them as chattel, something that even the most dedicated of fathers have a hard time avoiding. It's built into our culture."

After a re-pouring of brandy and a bathroom break for both of us, Leanda began her story.

"Let me start by asking if you knew of the painting at the museum in Zurich recently declared a forgery?"

"Yes, actually I was telling the twins about it when you walked up in New York. A Memling Virgin and Child. In fact, very similar to the one we were standing in front of at the Metropolitan."

"That's right. You see the painting had just been declared a forgery but had been under suspicion for many years. The forger, a brilliant virtuoso, had used me as a model for the Virgin. He's a man whose greatest gift is his greatest enemy and whose greatest enemy is his greatest gift."

"Sorry?"

"It's not a riddle. Let me explain. This is a painter who was born five hundred years too late. All his sensibilities are focused on fifteenth-century Flemish painting. His capacity to paint as a Flemish master was his great gift, but was his great enemy because it had no place in the twentieth century. It was also his great enemy because it was all he could think about. So he settled into making forgeries and knew so much about the history of the period, he invented very convincing 'histories' for the previously unknown masterpieces he made. He's a brilliant man all around."

"You knew him well?"

"Oh yes. And like most obsessive, gifted artists, he had a few screws loose. I'm sure in your work, you're familiar with that."

"On a daily basis."

She laughed.

"And the Zurich Memling was not his first use of me as a model in a forgery. You see he believed that because the primary figure in the painting was painted from a live contemporary woman, it gave the painting legitimacy as a work of art in our present-day culture, and therefore legitimized his place on earth as an artist of the twentieth century. But his frustration was that he couldn't tell anyone that the Virgin was a modern woman, and in fact couldn't even paint me as a contemporary woman because I was in this context, a fifteenth-century woman."

Leanda sipped her brandy and went on.

"And to further complicate things, he fell in love with me, and I with him."

"That seems fairly counterproductive, given his criminal activities." I couldn't help but say.

"Oh indeed, but who has ever been able to assess love in terms of what is productive?"

"I know, but you seem like a pretty rational person, and it sounds like you had a pretty good idea that this man would be trouble down the line."

"Yes, but this was sixteen years ago, and he was a gorgeous brilliant gifted man."

"I have to ask how old you are. You're very worldly and very young at the same time."

"I'm thirty-eight. And you?"

"I'm forty-seven."

We poured more brandy and she continued her story.

"It's a good thing I'm getting a little drunk because this all gets harder to talk about as I go on. So we went on together, he making his forgeries and making a small fortune off of them, and I finishing up graduate school. We knew some other artists and there was one who was almost as gifted as my forger, but painted in a contemporary style, but too was a naturalistic figurative painter. He was obsessed with painting me nude and I discussed it with the forger. "Sure, go ahead", he said in his cavalier bohemian manner. So I did. The paintings were very successful and the painter had a show which caused a stir. He became a celebrity and the work was reviewed all over and reproduced all over. A lot of it had to do with how I looked in the paintings. I wore an expression of "So?", and my nudity in the paintings was really more a nakedness, which people saw as extremely provocative. At about the same time, one of the forger's earlier paintings was labeled a fake and he became a fugitive. And as he hid because his paintings of me were contraband, the other painter thrived on my appearance in his paintings."

Leanda had become agitated as she talked and I asked if she'd like to stop and continue another time. She shook her head. She sipped her brandy, looking out the window at Portland's night lights. Then she continued.

"So the forger snapped. It's the only way to put it."

I waited for her to continue.

"The next night, he seemed calmer. We had dinner and wine as usual, and when I began to feel extremely dizzy and then barely conscious, the last thing I remembered him saying was, "I'm crossing you out as model for anyone else.""

"He had drugged me, and then he did what you see."

"That's my story. As much as you'll hear tonight. The rest, the worst part really, I'll tell you another time."

She was silent for a long time. Finally, she said quietly, "I'm so tired."

"Shall I help you to bed?"

"Yes, please."

Holding onto her I led her to the closest bed and turned back the covers. She got in and said, "Will you stay here, on the other bed? At least for a while?"

"Of course."

When I finally fell asleep, I slept till morning as did Leanda. I showered and dressed while she continued to sleep. When she had showered and dressed we went out for breakfast. Her attitude toward me and life, in general, was as it was before she told her story. She was cheery and responsive. It was as though the subject of her story last night had never come up, and I realized her resilience is similar to the twins' and as strong. On the way to the brewery, I asked how much I should tell the twins.

"As much as you want, you know them better than I."

But after a moment, she said, "On second thought, tell them nothing until I've told you the whole story, then we'll decide how much they should know."

When we arrived at the brewery, Ada immediately came to me when Leanda went over to talk to others.

"Did she tell you how she got her scar?"

"Yes, it was from a bizarre encounter with a man from her youth. She doesn't wish to discuss the details right now. We'll know more soon."

"Oh, Okay."

Blain had stayed off to the side and I was beginning to worry about her, that is, worry about the effect on her of Leanda's appearance in our lives.

I found her in her room. "Not rehearsing today?"

"No, I want some time to myself."

"Would you like to talk?"

"No, I'm okay."

When I turned to leave she said, "Dad, you won't abandon me will you?"

"Abandon you in what way?"

"I mean will I always be part of your life?"

"Unless you abandon me."

She smiled in a shy way and said, "Thanks."

I was worried about her.

I spent some time working with Father Joseph and Sister Agnes. They were exploring new directions. There was no trapeze, but instead, a kind of rolling colliding series of encounters. They were pushing their interest in the interaction between erotics and physical violence. They were in a perpetual state of charged arousal combined with a new, feigned (I hoped) hostility toward each other. It was pretty crazy. In fact, everyone now seemed to be releasing remembered energies from Spoleto. Things that couldn't be assimilated while we were still there. All somehow violence-related. I think it stemmed from Vladimir's and Rasputin's near deaths on stage. And also the actual death of Aimee's father in Spoleto. What happened in Signore Ponzza's villa was this: In the morning after the Nelsons slept there and Mr. Nelson saw Aimee's sculpture lying on the bed, the body of Mr. Nelson was found, in his pajamas, in a contorted fetal posture on the floor of the upstairs hallway. There was a smear of green across his mouth. A more eloquent narrator might have said, "The green key to the mystery of everything Aimee." But I'll just quote my daughters, "Seemed obvious to us."

"You said you were withholding the worst part of your story of the forger. I don't know what could be worse than what you'd told me."

Leanda and I were walking along the river. After my question to her, and during her long hesitation in answering me, I looked up and down the river at the many bridges, each of a very different design and I thought of all the different ways the players in my narration attempt to connect to each other.

Leanda broke the silence.

"The worst part is that the forger is the twins' father."

"Jesus!"

"Yes, a few weeks before his cutting of me, we slept together many nights in a row. He was very insistent and passionate. I realized after that he had planned to impregnate me and did not use protection even though he said he did. When I found out I was pregnant, my parents urged me to get an abortion because I was mentally falling apart. I refused, and when the twins were born, they managed to legally remove them from me. My father is a judge and my family has huge wealth and influence in Switzerland. I was so traumatized and unstable. I just let things go. After much psychiatric treatment, I ceased to even believe I was a mother. Much later I was made aware that my children were brought up somewhere by some distant relatives of my family, and at some point, there was a complicated interconnection between my family and Khalid and a man called the Collector. I was warned not to interfere. I didn't see the twins again until we met at the Metropolitan Museum."

After a silence while I tried to deal with this news, I asked, "Who else knows about this?

"No one knows, only me. And now you."

Again some silence. Then I said, "I don't think Ada and Blain need this information, at least not at this point."

"I agree. But there is another complication."

"Yes?"

"The forger is at large. He disappeared years ago because he was a fugitive, wanted by Interpol for the forgeries. The last I heard from him was that he would have his revenge on me."

"Have his revenge on *you*? Wasn't dis..." I caught myself before saying 'disfiguring you' and said instead, "'cutting you,' enough?"

She went on, "And he added that he'd 'have his daughters.' What he meant by that I don't know, and it was so long ago I'd really ceased to think about it. He could even be dead for all I know. It's been fifteen years. But now I am worried about something. I'm wondering if Khalid is potentially a link between the forger, the twins, and me. The forger was involved with Khalid in one of his forgeries that was sold to a rich Arab known to Khalid."

I was suddenly struck by the realization that Leanda knew nothing about the nature of Khalid's connection to Ada and Blain and the killings.

"What do you know about what went on in the lives of the twins under Khalid's tutelage, and where all that money came from that was deposited for them?"

"I know nothing about it. I'd essentially abandoned the twins, and because of my mental state at the time, I chose to know nothing."

"Would you like to know now?"

"Yes, what information do you have?"

"I'm going to let Ada and Blain tell you. I think they need to. And I think you need to know."

"All right, I trust your judgment. Is it bad?"

"As bad as the forger."

That evening, when Leanda emerged from Ada's room where the twins had told her their story of Khalid and the killings, she was ashen. Ada and Blain too were upset, having gone over their history one more time. We all went back to Leanda's hotel room after dinner together. Ada and Blain were each lying on a bed. Leanda and I were sitting in chairs. After a settling-in silence, Ada said to Leanda, "We want to talk about our father."

I could sense Leanda's panic, but she showed nothing as she answered, "Yes? What about him?"

Blain took over. She looked at me and said, "If you're our father..." then looked at Leanda and said, "And you're our mother..."

Ada took over, "Then what's the connection between the two of you?"

Leanda smiled in great relief. "Well, I haven't thought about that."

Ada continued, "There's something you should know. This man, my father the narrator, he and I are going to be married."

"And I'm going to be his mistress," Blain said.

Leanda was a little baffled but was taking it lightly.

"I see, and have you slept together?"

"Many times." Both twins simultaneously.

Leanda looked at me, smiling, "Is this true?"

"Yes, literally, but not figuratively."

Because the twins seemed serious, Leanda's expression changed.

"OK, so is there a conflict here?"

"Only if you're planning on Dad marrying you."

Because Ada's tone was challenging, Leanda became slightly impatient and said, "No man is marrying me."

"Why not?"

Leanda drew an X in the air.

The twins looked stricken. They'd gone too far.

Ada and Blain wanted to go back to the brewery and wanted me to go with them.

I said I'll be along soon and they left after giving Leanda conciliatory hugs. Leanda said, "Today when they told me their horror story of life with Khalid, as they got more into their story, they seemed transformed. A hardness gradually appeared as they talked. It didn't surprise me to see it. I have the same thing in me. Their story worried me though, and I don't think we're through yet with Khalid. Does he know I'm here?"

"I don't know. He always seemed to know more about what was going on than I would have expected, and certainly, more than I would have liked."

Leanda nodded. "Enough of Khalid. I'm curious about Ada's fantasy of marrying you and Blain's of being your mistress. Where does that come from? And what's this business of you sleeping together?"

"Well, it's all connected. It started in Rome with Ada. There was so much stress there in dealing with Lucrezia, and the Collector, in rescuing Blain. She originally asked to sleep in my bed for security. But you know they're both tough girls, assertive, and obviously sexually precocious. Then Blain, in competition with Ada got into the act. But in spite of what they were implying, there's been no sex."

"That's reassuring to hear. Things are complicated enough on their own."

"Complicated in what way?"

"My life before your letter and before I came to New York was much more in my control. In my work, I could be as tough as I wished, and in fact, the tougher I was the more successful I was. And there were never any feelings to deal with. No vulnerability."

"And now you are vulnerable to the fact that you have two daughters."

"Yes, but what's interesting is that there's no sentimentality involved. I think I'm too hardened to have family feelings. I feel like I'm relating to them as you do, not because they're blood relatives but because they're fascinating and endearing. I even suspect that if they didn't fascinate me I wouldn't have much feeling for them at all."

"You are a tough babe."

"And you are a detached narrator, Stephen." I was surprised at her using my name.

"Are they the same thing?"

"Pretty close I think. Close because neither of us will initiate anything with others, but instead allow life to happen to us, or not, as we chose."

"I initiate some things with my dancers. I'm involved there."

"That's your work."

"And you initiate a lot in your work I would assume."

"True, but you believe in your work, and I don't believe in mine."

"So we're not the same."

"I think we're the same, just not in how we're each living our lives in the present."

"Would you like to believe in your work, Leanda?"

"Yes."

"Maybe you should join our theater company."

"With this...?" She drew her X in the air. It was not a self-pitying gesture. It was a gesture of fact.

"You should spend some time with Aimee and Mojobe."

Leanda had seen Mojobe's scars and Aimee's tattoos. She thought for a moment.

"Maybe I will."

I heard three different versions of the show and tell meeting between Leanda, Mojobe, and Aimee. I think it was because I'm the narrator and the event was too important and interesting to go unrecorded. One by one they came to me.

Mojobe: "You know, for a mark done out of retribution, it was very carefully executed. Not that it didn't cause pain, but aesthetically it is elegant. More sweeping, spontaneous, and emotional than my carefully executed system of geometric scars. It would not be appropriate for me and my culture, but for her and her circumstances, that's a whole different matter. I thought she should come to respect them. They are her mark of distinction, her story. They are not going to go away. She must have power over them and use them, or they will have power over her, and use her. They have presence and persona. They will not be ignored."

Aimee: "When Rasputin began tattooing me, it was out of confusion and self-loathing that I went along with it. It meant different things at different times. His obsession with it fascinated me even though I was repulsed by him. He really is a greaser you know, even though he is now my husband. The whole process took over my life and I thought it was going to be a fast spiral down for me. I wouldn't have minded dying along the way. Then it occurred to me that it was Rasputin who should die, and I did my best along those lines in Spoleto. And voila! The right death did occur, but never would have without my tattoos. In the end, it's our scars that tell our history."

Leanda: "As the three of us stood in a circle, naked, observing each other it was a moment of epiphanies for me. I looked at Mojobe and her deep black skin and high raised scars like a geometric army marching across her abdomen and I thought three things: It is beautiful. It surely hurt more than mine. And I'm thankful it's not on me. Then I looked at Aimee. A person hidden in a jungle really. And when she told the story of Rasputin and her during this whole process and the constantly changing emotions involved, I thought what a long litany of contradictions. Then I turned to the full-length mirror in Aimee's room and looked at myself as I had looked at them. I was seeing a simple truth, so simple as to be almost abstract and impossible to verbalize. That truth is in me and I can't explain it."

"No need to explain anything to me."

"I know that and I appreciate that. I can say anything to you and I don't feel judged."

"Narrators don't judge, they just narrate."

"You are more than a narrator, my friend."

"Not to me."

"You are to me."

"I've not initiated anything with you."

"Yes, you have."

Leanda took my hand and holding out my index finger slowly traced the scar over her face.

"No one has ever touched my scar before."

"I didn't touch them, you did, using my finger."

"And you felt nothing?"

"I felt a lot, but I didn't initiate it."

"What did you feel?"

"Your history."

Leanda smiled the smile of the accomplished lawyer in a courtroom after she had conveyed a very complex important point.

The eighteenth birthday of the twins came and went without much fanfare. There were jokes about their new status as millionaires, but to them, it was only numbers on paper. We had a party at the brewery and it was a festive event. Everyone loved Ada and Blain. At the party, Ada announced that she'd been accepted as an advanced student at the most respected modern dance company in San Francisco, and that she'd be going back and forth between here and there. Everyone looked to Blain to see how this affected her plans, but she gave no clues. They looked at me and I felt my face was ashen. But we all thought that this next chapter in Ada's dance career would be the one that would propel her into stardom.

One morning a disquieting event emerged from the news. There was a small item in the paper about a man who appeared at an important art dealer's in New York with a small, incomplete study for a well-known Flemish painting, purportedly by the fifteenth-century painter. It was so convincing and beautiful a work that the dealer made an offer to purchase it. In the course of further research on the part of the dealer, he was apparently alerted to a series of these attempted sales of similarly stunning pieces in the European market. Because they were only studies, their provenance was impossible to trace. And because they were only small studies and the price was moderate, the temptation to purchase was strong. The dealer, in describing his encounter said, "He was so erudite and charming, I was convinced it was the real thing." Then he added, laughing, "So art dealers of the world, watch out for a very intelligent purveyor of small beautiful studies of Flemish Masters, a man with an intense attitude to match his intense red hair."

We were all convinced of the identity of this purveyor of forgeries, but the odds of his happening on the twins and Leanda seemed remote. Still, the knowledge that he was alive and out there was disquieting.

Leanda had returned to Zurich on urgent business, and took Blain with her. Blain was becoming progressively more detached from everyone. However, after three weeks Leanda wrote to say that Blain had left to go visit friends from her school years there and she hadn't heard from her since. Mojobe and Waldeebe One had returned to Africa for family and tribal matters. They said they'll be back. Father Joseph and Sister Agnes were in Nepal on a spiritual quest. Aimee and Rasputin had gone to visit his family about whom I'd heard nothing before. Ada had spent progressively more time in San Francisco where she was the principal dancer in a production in rehearsal. Her rapid rise there surprised none of us. She had been written about a number of times. The nest was empty. Or I should say, the brewery was empty. Nothing was brewing here. And just as well. I was burnt out. With everyone gone, there was nothing to respond to, and since I don't initiate, I'd reached a plateau. It was time for one of my periodic aimless odysseys. Aimless because the only decision I made (initiated) was where to go, and even that must have some reason for being before I started. The rule after that was that I only go where I'm led, for whatever reason. I had been reading the real Nabokov's memoir, Speak Memory, and I found myself thinking of our ersatz Nabokov in Italy and I decided that thinking about someone was a legitimate reason for starting my journey and Spoleto should be my first destination. I called Signore Ponzza and asked if I might visit. He was delighted, and I was off.

I had been at Signore Ponzza's villa for a week and had no luck in tracking down Vladimir and Marconia and the cult. Signore Ponzza was not surprised. "You didn't really expect them to be in the phone book now did you?"

On my eighth day, as I was coming out of the Duomo after looking at the great Fra Filippo Lippi fresco on the subject of the life of the Virgin, I caught just a glimpse of the silver hearse rounding a corner of the square. I ran, waving my arms for some distance before someone looked in the rear-view mirror and saw me. The silver vehicle coasted to a halt and waited. It was filled to capacity with pointy hatted pagans. Marconia was in the front seat and remembering me greeted me with an odd smile. She said, nodding to the rear, "Vladimir has had a relapse." I looked back to see Vladimir on his back and he raised his hand weakly in greeting. I said, "Hello Vladimir, how are you?"

"Oh, I've been better."

I looked over the other passengers inside and was stunned to see Blain, her red hair protruding out from under her silver hat, calmly observing me with a bemused smile. Then I noticed an odd aura of celebration in the hearse with pagans looking at each other. Marconia said, "I'm glad you could make it. Now we must go. We have an urgent ceremony."

I said to Blain, "I'm at the Ponzza villa."

"I'll come there."

And they were off. And I was baffled. What did Marconia mean, "I'm glad you could make it?"

Two days passed before Blain appeared. It was just after dawn and she was standing in the garden outside my tall bedroom window, rapping lightly on the glass. From the bed, she seemed a strange apparition, with the rising sun reflecting off her silver pointed hat. I opened the window and she stepped in, fully costumed in her blousy black pantaloons, bright striped shirt, and gold slippers. She was exhausted, and said, "Trick or treat." It was at that moment I realized how much I'd missed her, and what strong feelings I had for her.

She walked up to lean against me, her pointed hat falling to the floor.

"I'm exhausted, Dad, I haven't slept in two days. I haven't washed in two days. Vladimir might be dying. Take off my clothes and bathe me and put me to bed. Please, Dad."

I led her leaning body to the bathroom, turned on the tub water, and began to peel off her clothes. When I pulled off her shirt I got the first whiff of her unbathed self, and when I pulled down her pantaloons it was in full glory.

She said sleepily, "Pretty stinky huh, we even ran out of toilet paper up there. I think the cheeks of my bottom are stuck together."

In the tub, as I washed her, she said, "We can't be apart."

I continued washing her. I said, "I think you're right."

"That we can't be apart?"

"That you're stuck together.

"I love you, Daddy." She laughed softly.

Blain slept for eighteen hours. When she woke it was after midnight and an almost full moon was spilling its blue light over us. We were on our sides, facing each other.

"Can you feel the difference Dad?"

"Difference?"

"Can you feel that now we should be together?"

"Well, things do feel different."

"Does it surprise you?"

"Well, I don't know how it happened."

"Vladimir almost lost his life in the sacrifice. In fact, he may be dead."

"Vladimir? How? Why?"

"I'm too hungry to explain right now. Can we go to the kitchen and eat everything in Signore Ponzza's refrigerator?"

Watching Blain, in the light of the open refrigerator door, eating with the voracious efficiency of an eighteen-year-old, I asked myself, am I still only the narrator?

"We'll see."

Startled, I ask Blain, "See what?"

"Whether you're still only the narrator."

When we were back in bed, Blain said, "Now we'll see." She was on her back, arms and legs relaxed, lighted softly by the moon.

"See what?"

"Whether you only narrate, or whether you initiate."

I pushed into Blain midst much excited touching and soft sounds.

In the morning, she was gone. She had left behind her pointed silver hat on my writing table. Inside, tucked into a seam, was a reference to our conversation last night,

On the subject of feelings.

"Does it seem our feelings have evolved?"

"Maybe."

"Then maybe I'm right, and maybe our feelings have evolved into something new?"

"Yes."

"So now what?"

"Now, we see what else evolves."

"You see what else evolves, as narrator?"

"Yes."

"So, we're back where we started."

"No, my feelings seem real enough, but I need to know what Vladimir and Marconia had to do with all this."

"With my wanting us to be a couple?"

"No, with my wanting us to be a couple. When I understand that, then we'll see."

"You sound like you think a spell has been cast over you."

"Has one? Tell me the truth."

"Yes." Tears filled her eyes.

I noticed another note in another seam inside: "To whomever finds this hat, please return it to the following address (listed was a remote crossroads outside of Spoleto). A small heart was drawn.

I asked Signore Ponzza where the address was (he had to find out from his cook) and If I could borrow a car (he has a collection). He graciously agrees to my use of the car, but says, "My cook says to be careful up there."

I frown and raise my eyebrows as a question.

He says, "I don't know."

After an hour of asking for directions I finally found the crossroads written down by Blain. I was driving a very old but perfectly maintained silver Audi. I picked the car because the color, matched the pagans' hearse and I thought I might be viewed as less of an intruder as a result. Peculiar logic I know but I was uneasy about even being here. I was well up in the Umbrian hills and the road I had just turned off of was unpaved and uneven, but the road I turned onto was more like a goat path than a road. Even though I did see tire tracks, I didn't want to chance damaging Signore Ponzza's antique so I left it by the side of the road and continued on foot. The road formed a large spiral up so I was always on a curve and couldn't see much ahead of me. I was torn between calling out as I walked up so as not to startle them, and remaining silent so I could get a clearer picture of what went on up there without their knowing. The narrator won out for the sake of the best possible story to tell after. He was not disappointed.

There was a cluster of low twisted pine trees through which the road passed, concealing me as I first saw a thick and high stone wall with an arched entry opening sealed by an ornate iron gate, through which I saw the tops of silver pointed hats moving back and forth behind a second lower wall. The gate had a large very old key hole with a key in it about eight inches long. I decided to walk around the wall looking for a way to look over it. I found I was very excited about this voyeuristic outing. Ahead I saw a dead tree that looked like I could shimmy up it. I did so with some effort and could see over both walls to the pagans in a circle around Vladimir who was stark naked on his back in the sun apparently drying off after a dip in some liquid. His body was still glistening with moisture. Then all the pagans began taking off their clothes. At the instant when there was a circle surrounding Vladimir, of naked and quite hairy pagans of all shapes, there was also a blow of searing pain to my ankle that caused me to lose my grip and crash to the rocky ground. I looked up to see a muscular pagan about to deliver another blow with the same pole when I heard Blain's voice call out, "Stop, Fantula!"

Blain ran over to tell the pagan she knew me.

"Thank you, I think you saved your father's life," I say.

Blain looked totally perplexed. "What the hell were you doing up in that tree, Dad?"

"Well you know I did have a spell cast over me."

Supported by Blain and the pagan warrior guard (who offered no apology for her actions), I'm led, limping, into the pagan compound where I'm greeted with hostility all around. Vladimir is out cold, covered by a white sheet, so no help forthcoming there. Blain was embarrassed by my peeping tom activities, but does admit she gave me directions up here. I'm led into one of the low stone buildings (the place seems to have been a farm in the past), so I could get out of the sun. There was the sweet smell of old stone, old straw, and sheep manure. My ankle had swollen dramatically and my body had raw abrasions from scraping down the tree. Marconia was called in since she was the senior healer.

"Your ankle was sprained but you have no broken bones. Your cuts we will wash and dress. Why were you spying on us?"

By now there were many pagans surrounding me and Blain looked guilty and ashamed. I decided to play a long shot. I knew that these people and especially Marconia took great pride in their mystical powers.

"I'm very sorry for my intrusion, but it's not my fault." I see annoyance growing in the expressions around me. "You see, some kind of powerful spell had been cast over me and I'd become obsessed with Blain. My heart is filled with passionate love for her, well beyond my role as her father. I would follow her to the ends of the earth."

I hesitated, to see how well I was doing. Very well indeed.

Marconia said, "It's we who owe you an apology. Because Blain loves you and because Vladimir so admires you and feels so in your debt, we decided to bring you back to Italy. But I must admit I had no idea our powers had become so strong. I can see from your tree climbing how obsessed we've made you, and I also know how difficult it is to even find this place. I don't like good people living not according to their own free will, because of us. I will remove your spell."

"Can't you just lessen its strength? I love having power over my daddy. I want him as my lover." Blain says

In unison like a Greek chorus, the stunned pagans spoke, "She wants her daddy to be her lover!"

Before my laughter could escape, I disguised it as a sneeze.

"He's getting a chill from the dampness here, move him out into the sun." Marconia commands.

Outside, Vladimir had regained consciousness and was delighted to see me.

By God, it worked, but it almost killed me," he said.

"Almost killed you, how?"

"Dealing with that concentration of willpower drained my energies. Marconia said it was because I wasn't used to it, that I don't know how to regulate my willpower, using no more than necessary."

I was sitting next to him and he was leaning up on one elbow.

"But it worked, that's the important thing." He repeated.

"What worked?" I asked. I wanted to hear his explanation.

"Tell me, my friend, what were you reading when you decided to return to Italy?"

"Well, the last thing I read was Nabokov's Speak Memory."

Vladimir looked around smiling in triumph. The pagans nodded.

"That's what I suggested to you from the cauldron," he said.

"The cauldron?"

"Never mind about that right now. Don't you think it's phenomenal that you read Speak Memory when I suggested it to you from many thousands of miles away?"

"I often picked up that book."

"But did you always fly to Italy after you'd been reading it?" He smiled.

The pagans snickered knowingly. It was the first time I'd ever seen any of them smile. I also remembered that their spell was my defense against accusations of lurid spying on their naked ritual.

"You're right, Vladimir, with your spell you've all made me totally obsessed with Blain. She's all I can think of."

Blain was watching me quizzically, knowing that I was playing on their pride, but also hoping some of what I was saying was true. And alarmingly, it was. Looking at Blain in her silly pagan outfit, I was filled with adoration for her and I thought about my having bathed her. My theory that the pagans would be too embarrassed to stand around and stare at me, was true and they wandered off leaving me with Blain and Vladimir.

"Brilliant performance old boy," Vladimir said laughing.

"Was it a performance Dad?" Blain asked quietly

"No, I'm under everybody's spell it seems."

"Everybody's?"

"Yours, you are everything."

"I love you, Stephen."

Stunned, I stared at Blain. Vladimir was stunned. There was a moment of silence.

"I'm no longer Dad?"

"No."

I kissed Blain softly on the mouth.

"If this is still a spell, God help us all", Vladimir said with his eyes on the sky.

The pagans were gathered in a circle thirty feet away staring at us expressionless.

The next question is what to do about my ankle which now looks like I have a tennis ball stuffed into my sock.

We called Marconia over for a consultation.

"We could pull you down to Signore Ponzza's car in a cart and one of us could drive you back, but your ankle wouldn't return to normal for weeks. What's called for is treatment in the cauldron."

I was filled with alarm after having heard Vladimir's references to the cauldron. "I don't think so."

"It's not so bad my friend, I'm due for a treatment at dawn. We could do it together, couldn't we Marconia, dear?"

I was amazed to see Marconia stroke Vladimir's cheek tenderly and say, "Yes, if you'd like."

I had to ask, "Does everyone here dip in the cauldron?" I was thinking something remarkable must be affecting these people.

"Yes, regularly, it's the source of bodily healing, well-being, and spiritual power," Marconia said this with a tone of intimate confiding that made me wonder if I'd ever be allowed to leave this place, or even desire to.

In the largest of the ancient stone farm buildings, we had an evening meal. Small windows faced west and crimson rays of setting sun streamed in. Everyone was dressed in full costume, including me, I must confess, with my own pointed silver hat and a black robe that matched Vladimir's. We were seated at a thick old wood table big enough to accommodate a dozen people. We were all lined up on two long benches. Blain was seated opposite me and the sun was striking her hair beneath the edge of her hat so it seemed aflame, like a true sorceress, and I was wondering if that is in fact what she is, and has been from the moment I first saw her in Rome so many years ago. She was smiling at me with a serenity I'd never seen in her before, and I was momentarily unable to recall my life before this evening. The pagans were quiet. Other than Marconia none speak English and they said little to each other. After the meal, all of the cult except Marconia went off to a long low building where apparently they slept.

"Let's sleep outside tonight," Blain said. "We can bring a mattress up to the roof of the shed. It'll be a great star show."

Vladimir and Marconia were going off together to a remote small building.

"We'll be by for you at dawn to heal your ankle," Vladimir said.

"Dawn? How about something more civilized like mid-morning after coffee?"

"No, it's dawn for physical repairs and midnight for spiritual repairs."

"How about casting spells?"

"Ah, they can take twenty-four hours."

When we were alone on the roof of the shed I asked Blain, "Did the casting of my spell really take twenty-four hours?"

"And more. Vladimir and I were totally wiped out. That's how he got sick again, and my skin was like a prune after all that soaking."

"You and Vladimir were in the cauldron together?"

"No, we alternated. He did his casting and I did mine."

"And what does casting consist of?"

"Well, I can't speak for Vladimir. It sounded like his was more cerebral than mine."

"And yours?"

"I concentrated on making you uneasy, making you want to leave the brewery. And then after you were on your way I concentrated on making you feel you had to have physical contact with me, not sexual necessarily, but just having to hold onto me and smell me. I knew my pheromones would do you in. And they did, didn't they?"

"Yes, your pheromones are killers. But where did you learn about casting spells?"

"Marconia. She has amazing powers and for people she cares about she's willing to share them, teach them."

"And now you have those powers independent of Marconia?"

"I don't know. I have the feeling that these powers and their spells are fleeting. That they need to be fed to keep them going. I don't know what's left in the person experiencing the spell after it's run its course."

"So are you saying that after my spell is removed, your pheromones will no longer have an effect on me?"

"I don't know, this is all new to me."

"Hmm, and why did Vladimir want me back here?"

"He said you saved him. That if he hadn't run into you in the butterfly forest, he'd still be wandering around there. Also, he knows he's a bit of a nut, and he said you never judged him for it."

"We're all a bit of a nut, at least all of the people who interest me. I mean look at everybody in our company, look at Leanda. Speaking of Leanda, how was it being with her for a few weeks in Zurich?"

"She talked about you a lot. She said you were the only person to have talked to her in-depth about her scar, until she showed it to Mojobe and Aimee. She said you're the only one to have touched it. That made me very jealous. I asked if I could touch it (I thought it would erase any power she had over you from your touching them). She refused. That's when I left. Did you two make love? "

"No."

"How about her pheromones?"

"What about them?"

"Did they affect you?"

"No, they didn't seem to have."

"Good. One more question. In all the time you and Ada and I were hanging out and sharing beds in Rome and Portland, which of course was before the spell was cast on you, did my scent affect you?"

"I'd have to say yes."

"That's excellent news. It means that when the spell is gone, you'll still be drawn to my scent."

"Probably."

"One more question, did Ada's smell affect you?"

"Yes."

"Hmm, now I'm afraid to ask my next question, but I have to. Did the scent of one of us affect you more than the other?"

"Do you want the truth?"

"Of course."

"Yes, considerably more."

"Please Dad, tell me I'm the..."

"You sure you want the truth?"

"Yes!" Blain's face is serious.

"You're the stinker. You're the stinkiest stinker of my experience."

"You have a way with words."

We were silent for several minutes, each of us dazzled by the intensity of the stars out here where there's so little man-made light. Without our clothes, we felt like totally natural participants.

"You know Stephen, we could have been out here together at any time in history and this star performance would have been the same. And on the other hand, by the time I finish this sentence we've spent a moment of our history together never to be had again. Isn't it sad to be spending our time because eventually, we'll run out of it?"

"Well, I'll run out of time long before you do."

"That's too sad to even think about."

"Well unless I drown in the cauldron tomorrow I'll still be around for a while."

"I know, and the important thing is how we spend the time we have, don't you think."

"I agree."

"So on that subject, is it okay if I lie on top of you on my back? That way we can both still see the stars. Even though the air's still pretty warm on my skin, some exchange of body heat would be nice, don't you think? And I have to say, what a treat it would be for a girl to be on the roof of a centuries-old stone building in the hills of Umbria naked with her lover. Can I get on top?"

"Is this part of your spell?"

"I don't know."

"let's just lie against each other on our backs and watch the sky."

"Oh, okay, this is sweet."

"There, now you have to admit Dad, this feels pretty good right?"

"I can't quarrel with that."

"OK Dad, you win, I don't want to get into a long philosophical discussion about definitions of relationships, and right and wrong."

"That's good. And as for your use of words, I think one day you'll be a great narrator."

"Jesus, with all due respect, I can't imagine anything worse."

A thin slice of moon had risen in the eastern sky and it was like a light rendition of a finger curving lightly over skin.

"The one thing I didn't tell you, is that this spell cast over you is also a spell over me. I've never felt anything like this. Do you think this is a kind of love never experienced by anyone before? A love that has as its necessary ingredients, you, me, this sky, this shed roof, the fragrances of Umbria wafting over us and combining with our own, not to mention the spell and being surrounded by all these peculiar pagan women and dear Vladimir? If it can only exist under these circumstances then isn't its ending doubly sad? It makes me want to live on top of this roof forever."

After a short silence, Blain turned with her back to me. "Slip inside of me and hold me tightly."

I did and the only movement remaining happened inside.

Finally, we lay silently until sleep overtook us.

We woke to the racket of wooden wheels grinding over the rocky ground below.

"Time to rise old boy, your limousine is here to deliver you for your ankle repair."

I looked down from our shed penthouse to see Vladimir and Marconia and several pagans, fully costumed, standing around the cart that's to deliver me to the cauldron. There was only a streak of red in the sky to announce a new morning. With every ones' help, I descended the crude wood ladder to the ground without further damage to my ankle which this morning seemed bigger than ever.

"Don't let them take away the spell."

Blain was looking over the edge of the roof above. The first streaks of dawn light illuminated her hair.

I looked at Marconia and her expression was neutral.

Then with urgency in her voice, Blain said, "Wait, I'm coming too."

"No," Marconia said simply.

Sitting side by side in the bumping cart, Vladimir and I looked back at Blain standing on the roof and exquisite in the low sun. I wondered if all that happened last night was a dream.

"No, it wasn't a dream, if that's what you're thinking," Vladimir said, "Marconia cast the same spell on me in the beginning. It was necessary or I couldn't have believed she could save my life."

"And are you still under her spell?"

"No, we are totally together now." After a moment of thought though he said, "Well actually every once in a while, I suddenly ask myself, 'What am I doing here?' and then I have a suspicion that Marconia does a little bit of supplementary spell casting to keep me attached to her, but I have no way of knowing for sure."

"How does she remove a spell?"

"I've never known the answer to that question. She's a person with terrifying strength of will. She has a great deal of Gypsy blood in her, and I know very little about her history."

We arrived at yet another low ancient stone building with a door at an angle like a cellar door. We all had to stoop to get in the doorway and by candlelight, I saw a round room with a dirt floor and a round wood cover over the stone cauldron which was lifted by a rope pulley with much heavy breathing on the part of the pagans.

Marconia said to me, "Disrobe."

I did and I was handed a black cotton cape-like robe to cover myself. There was a quiet seriousness now to everything going on. I was told to sit at the edge of the cauldron, which was about eight feet in diameter, and lower my leg in the liquid. I expected a shock of cold but no, the water was quite warm. I sat very still with everyone watching me, and then I felt a light movement around the flesh of my foot and ankle, and lower leg. I grimaced and opened my mouth to comment but Marconia shook her head. "Do not speak," she said.

Once it was clear that I was going to be an obedient participant, their attention was turned to Vladimir who was being lowered into the liquid to be fully submerged except for his head. He was suspended there with cloth straps under his arms.

Marconia offered, in a milder tone, "This sharing of the cauldron will enrich the connection between you two, enrich your friendship." I couldn't help but wonder what she was really up to. I tried not to speculate about what was moving around on my flesh, and gave myself over to my treatment. After some time, I was told to remove my leg from the cauldron. My ankle was considerably smaller, almost normal size. I noticed some worm-like forms suspended from my skin. In disgust, I looked to Marconia, who said in a calm voice, "Leeches, totally harmless, do not panic." She sat down next to me and explained. "They are only attracted to damaged tissue and they extract blood coagulated that causes swelling. They inject natural morphine that eliminates any pain or discomfort. When they are sated, they will drop off and your ankle will be healed. It will take perhaps another hour. Please lie back and think only of healing."

"Marconia, does Vladimir have leaches all over himself in there?" I had to ask,

"No, they are selective in his case. I'm not sure why it's effective for him but it is. I think it has to do with blood circulation."

"And they go everywhere on his body?"

"Almost everywhere. We plug his anus and wrap his penis to protect his urethra. Leaches will happily escape into any orifice."

I lay back down on the ground to continue healing and I resolved to myself no matter how ill I may ever be, I'm not going to be submerged in that cauldron. Soon, Marconia told me that the leeches had dropped off and I should move out in the sun. I was amazed that I could walk with almost no discomfort. My ankle was almost its normal size, and I was very impressed with Marconia. She stayed with me outside for a minute, and told me to walk very little for the next few hours, and then I should be totally healed. When she stood to leave, I said, "I don't understand how that cauldron can be used to cast spells on people."

"Oh, it's a totally different cauldron we use for spells."

"Ah, I see, and where is that cauldron?"

"It has a secret location. Spells are serious. I don't want anyone by chance happening on it. It takes knowledge and experience to cast spells, and someone with just a small amount of knowledge could do serious harm there."

She looked at me pointedly as she said this. But it was not me she was thinking of, it was Blain I was sure. I wondered if I should talk to her about Blain and me. It would be good if I didn't feel she was an adversary. I decided I didn't know her well enough. But I did ask her one question.

"Are spells removed in the same cauldron where they are cast?"

"Oh no, they are removed by will, and sometimes from great distances away."

She was watching me carefully and it made me uneasy.

I decided to ask one more question. "Why would one remove a spell?"

"Oh, for any number of reasons. If the spell had been cast to punish someone, and the person no longer deserved punishment then the spell would be removed."

Against my better judgment, I ask my next question.

"And what if it was a love spell?"

Marconia surprised me by smiling. "Every love is different. Some loves cannot prevail even with a spell. Some loves created with a spell, will continue to exist after the spell is removed. Sometimes the spell is a source of information. Sometimes the spell is a source of deception."

"And how do you judge, Marconia?"

"I don't judge. I'm not God, Mr. Narrator, I'm just a manipulator."

"I'm surprised to hear you use that term about what you do."

"Oh, I'm not using the word in the derogatory sense. I manipulated your ankle to heal it."

"The leeches manipulated my ankle."

"I taught them everything they know."

She laughed. I laughed.

"Then you don't have any opinion on the nature of my relationship with Blain?" I said.

"That's right."

"And if she wanted to keep the spell over me, that would be OK with you?"

"Yes, she asked me for it and I gave it to her because I like her."

"And what if I wanted the spell removed because I didn't want her to have power over me, would you remove it?"

"If she were grossly misusing it I might. But usually, the casting of the spell is a matter between me and the person to whom I've given the power of the spell. I don't cast spells for just anyone. I would also add that in the case of love, if there's not something like love in each of the two people it doesn't work."

"Something like love?"

"Don't sound like such a purist, Mr. Narrator, we all know there are a million kinds of love, maybe as many different kinds of love as there are people on earth."

"So you're saying that it's up to Blain to give up the spell voluntarily."

"Yes."

"Does she know that?"

"No, I think it's good for people to feel their power over another person is tentative. Then they're more careful. And I would add, nothing is absolute, sometimes spells just dissipate on their own. Not enough juice to keep them going."

"Juice?"

Marconia laughed. "Sometimes literally."

I thanked Marconia for my ankle healing and asked if it was healed enough for me to walk slowly back down the hill to the shed.

"Yes, just rest a few times on the way."

I found myself staring at Marconia. Something was very different. Then I realized her tarantula mole above her lip was gone. I stared at where it was.

"I let the leeches eat it. They didn't care for the hair but they really loved the mole," she said.

Blain was on the roof of the shed watching the path down from the cauldron building. She was astounded to see me walking on my own when I came around the turn of the path. She called out, "I'd come to help you but obviously you don't need help, plus there's some spell keeping me here." She laughed happily.

I climbed the ladder easily and when I was at eye level Blain said, "Let's be like we were when all those people showed up so early this morning." She was unbuttoning my shirt as she spoke. We were soon entwined under the warm Umbrian sun and were slippery by the time we lay still again After our breathing calmed, Blain said, "I want to show you a secret very cool place."

A short path through cypress trees led us to a small very secluded pond. We slipped into the wonderfully cool water and floated with our fingers just touching. When we stepped out of the water, Blair said "Oh", and pointed toward the calf of my leg from which a leech was dangling. We laughed.

It was late afternoon when we woke from our last intermittent sleep. It was a voice from below that woke us. An unmistakable voice.

"So this is the center of familial love, yes?"

We looked over the edge of the roof to see Lucrezia. Lucrezia and, how to put it? An heir to be. She looked like a child who'd swallowed a watermelon.

She continued, "And speaking of familial, see what I've brought you!" She affectionately patted her protruding middle.

Blain and I looked at each other. "Let's pretend it's a mirage," She said.

But the mirage continued, "And who's the co-author? Too early to tell, yes? But you'll be the first to know."

The last time we were together was long ago. Knowing Lucrezia's fondness for impulsive sex, I felt pretty safe.

We watched her waddle off to a waiting car, where she had a brief conversation with Marconia, before getting in. Signore Ponzza was in the driver's seat. He waved lightly, shrugged sympathetically, and then they were gone.

"Yikes!" Blain said.

"I know, I thought we were through with her for life."

"I wonder what she had to say to Marconia."

"Let's go see."

"You mean, we have to leave our paradisiacal penthouse?"

"We'll be back."

Marconia lifted her eyes comically when I asked her what Lucrezia had to say.

"Well, she said she needed to decide with whom to "celebrate parenthood", or one could say, knowing her, whom to punish with parenthood. I have the impression there are more candidates than just you. I wouldn't worry too much."

"Why shouldn't I worry?

"It's complicated, but the short answer is that if she caused you trouble, she'd end up with a spell, and one not as benign as yours."

"And how about Signore Ponzza, why was he here?" I asked.

"She asked him to bring her here after he'd told her you were here. Also, he wanted to make sure you were okay, since you hadn't returned to the villa. He's a good person, one to be trusted and he likes you. Everyone seems to like you."

"That's because I try to only narrate, not participate. I'm neutral, I don't interfere in peoples' lives."

"Neutral?, I don't think so. You haven't interfered in my life, you've become my life." Blain said.

Marconia asked me, "How do you feel about your spell?"

"It's difficult to answer because I'm under the spell as I consider your question."

"Yes, that's true."

"How do you feel about the spell?" Marconia says to Blain.

"I love it."

Marconia continued, "Do you wonder if he loves you beyond the spell?"

"Of course."

"Would you like to know?"

Blain thinks for a few moments. "Yes, I would like to know, but I couldn't know unless the spell was removed, and then I might not like what I found out."

Marconia looked at me. "Would you like to know how it would feel now to not be under the spell?"

There was alarm in Blain's face.

"I'd have to say yes, because I was happy with Blain before the spell as well as during the spell, so I don't have anything to lose."

Tears were in Blain's eyes. "You don't have anything to lose? What about our passion?"

"Well, maybe the passion won't be lost, maybe the passion is no longer dependent on the spell. That's possible isn't it Marconia?"

"Yes."

"It is?" Blain seemed skeptical but hopeful.

"Yes, it is," Marconia said.

"If we found out that the passion existed without the spell, what next?" Blain said to me.

"We'd be where we are right now, except we'd know there was no artificial ingredient."

"But what would come next?" Blain persisted.

"I don't know what would come next just as I don't know what will come next, as things are now."

"And if we found that without the spell, the passion no longer existed, what would come next then?" Blain asked.

"I don't know, just as we didn't know what was going to come next before the spell was cast."

"I certainly have nothing to gain by having the spell removed, do I?" Blain said.

"You have a great deal to gain my dear, you'll know what his true feelings are," Marconia said.

"And what if his true feelings are that I'm just some eighteen-year-old, make-believe daughter!"

Marconia said patiently, "Now listen, let's assume the worst-case scenario. The spell is removed and the Narrator finds that he loves you as he did before the spell, which it seems to me was a fair amount, not to mention that he adopted you as his daughter. What might be missing is the present erotic feelings that he was unable to act on, but it seems to me from what I've heard and observed, there was no small amount of that before, Is that not so?" She looked at me.

"Well, I don't know how much erotic feeling there was before because I felt bound to contain it. But I have to admit there was a lot of something, which maybe I declined to put a name on. I mean who could help but be drawn to this exquisite creature?" I put my hand tenderly on Blain's cheek.

"Jesus, is that the spell talking or you?"

"That's what we don't know sweetheart. Probably both."

Marconia says, "Exactly, I can't create something out of nothing."

Blain was silent, staring off at the hills of Umbria. She turned to me with tears in her eyes. "OK, what do you want, spell off, or spell on?"

"Off."

"Shit."

She turned to Marconia, "OK, do it."

Marconia was silent, watching us both.

"Go on do it!" Blain said.

"I can't just do it like that, it's not a TV," Marconia said.

There was an odd moment, then we all burst out laughing.

Still smiling, Blain hugged Marconia and said to me, "Come on, let's get back to the penthouse during the break for commercials"

"Good idea."

"Let's bring some food, I want to stay a while."

Loaded up with cheese and bread and fruit and water and wine, we returned to our roof garden. Once we'd eaten, and were lying back watching the emerging stars, Blain said, "Do you feel any different? Do you think she's done anything yet?"

I responded by kissing her as neutrally as possible.

"Yum", she said, wrapping around me, "Marconia must be busy doing other stuff."

Part Six

"So, yet another daughter, yes?"

I was in Rome and Lucrezia was presenting to me a tiny dark beauty in her crib, staring out with all the appropriate puzzlement of anyone closely connected to Lucrezia. I had submitted to DNA testing and we were waiting for the results.

She went on, "You'll be happy to know that I have as little interest in being involved with you as you have with me. But, I wanted my daughter to have a connection to a father worthy of her and you are that. And to underline this conviction that we are not for each other it's important to know that she was conceived after we'd decided that you and I were not right for each other. It was the last time we made love."

"Correction, it was after you decided that we were not right for each other. I wanted you then Lucrezia."

"Ah yes, that happens to men. I guess I just have too much brilliance and too much beauty compressed in this small package to resist."

This self-assessment of Lucrezia's should have put me off, but I found myself as attracted to her as ever.

"However, my body has returned to normal, and there's no man in my life. Would you care to make love to the mother of your daughter?" Lucrezia said languidly.

She pulled off her light summer dress under which there was nothing but too much brilliance and too much beauty compressed in her small package. The only change was her swollen breasts.

We were interrupted by a phone call delivering the news that I was not in fact the father of this child.

Six hours later I was at the airport outside Rome for my flight to Zurich, where Leanda awaited me. She had called me in Umbria with disconcerting news. Ada, who was now a famous dancer in San Francisco, had gotten involved with an older man, whom Leanda thought might be the Forger.

What happened to my quiet life as director and choreographer in the brewery? What happened indeed? The twins that's what happened.

When I awoke on the roof of the shed in Umbria, Blain was watching me carefully. Nothing had changed. She was lovelier than ever and the low sun on her hair gave her a rosy halo like a Fra Angelico angel. That I felt a strong love for her was undeniable. A love I'd never felt before?

"It's not over is it? I feel the same with you, the same passion, it's inside me and it's alive," Blain said.

"Maybe Marconia just hasn't done anything yet," I said.

"Oh yeah, then we better not waste any time." She said, rolling over on top of me and squirming wildly.

When we parted, Blain went back to Leanda in Zurich. She said she wanted to know more about her mother. She is amazing, an eighteen-year-old with a world-liness twice her age.

I went to Rome, where I had business to attend to. But I've already reported on that, yes?

In Zurich, when I arrived at Leanda's apartment, I was met with more than I'd bargained for: In addition to Leanda and Blain, there was Ada and there was the Forger.

"Hello, I'm Romain," Said the Forger, and every previous image of the man I'd had disappeared. He held out his hand, and I took it. He was obviously the father of the twins, complete with luminous red hair and features as refined as his daughters.' He radiated sensitivity and intelligence... "And you are of course the Narrator, but you do have a name?...

"Yes, I'm Stephen."

Leanda, Ada, and Blain relaxed immediately.

Romain went on, "Why are you called the Narrator?

"I report on events such as this one."

He smiled, "Report? To whom?"

"To the readers."

"What readers?"

"The readers of this book."

"What book?"

"Our story, of all of us who are connected. Life is a story, is it not? You certainly have your story, right?"

"What do you mean I have my story?"

"Well, you have what happens in your life and you have why it happens, and you have what effect it has on those around you. If that's not a story, what is?"

"You really know nothing about my story."

"On the contrary, I may know more than you."

"Like what?"

At this point, Leanda and the twins were watching intensely. There was a sense of impending confrontation in the air.

"Like what?" He repeats, smiling pleasantly.

"Like what you did to Leanda." I drew an X in the air..

He was surprised, but said politely, "I believe what I did was for Leanda, not to Leanda. I added beauty to beauty."

Leanda actually blushed slightly.

"But I see that's a sensitive subject," He said, "Best postponed until we know each other better."

At that, he walked to the door and left.

All during our conversation, the twins seemed mesmerized by their father.

"For all your talk about being the passive observer, that seemed like pretty active participation to me," Leanda said.

"I agree," Ada said, "It's good it happened now, after I found out who he is, and not when I was about to get involved with him. I would have considered you a meddling father. I was thoroughly charmed by him, and he pursued me like a madman."

"Like a narcissistic madman, who saw himself in you," I said.

"I never thought of that. Do you think we look that much alike?" Ada said.

"No, he was flattering himself."

"Well, he was flattering me, I think he's beautiful."

I could only think what is going on here?

"What do you think?" I asked Blain.

She shrugged her shoulders, but seemed puzzled.

"Why did you bring up my scars before you even had a chance to talk to him?" Leanda said.

"He wasn't really interested in talking to me, and besides I hate him for what he did to you. He should be in prison for life."

"Do you care that much about what he did to me?" Leanda said.

"Of course I do."

"Because it so disfigured me for life?"

"You're not disfigured, you're exquisitely beautiful. No, I hate him for the suffering he caused you."

Leanda walked to me and embraced me and pushed her face into my neck, and kissed me there with increasing feeling. Over her shoulder, I saw Ada and Blain exchanging a look of 'What's this?' Blain especially was troubled.

"Well here we are, Mommy and Daddy and the two little girls," Ada said snidely

Leanda and I turned and opened our arms, and Ada and Blain, surprisingly, were quick to join the embrace. The only thing altering this configuration of a happy nuclear family was when Blain put her mouth on mine and kissed me leaving no doubt about what it meant. I could not alter it, not after all that happened on our roof garden in Umbria.

When Blain ended her kiss, she said, "I love you."

Ada watching carefully said, "I'm afraid to ask."

"I'm not, what's going on between you two?" Leanda asked.

"It's private. Marconia cast a love spell over us in Umbria. That's all I'll say," Blain said.

Leanda looked at me.

"I have nothing more to add," I said.

"Is the spell still working?" Ada asked.

"Partly."

"I would say, partly! I'm curious about the part that was there and isn't anymore. I think we should invite Marconia to Zurich and she can turn all these cold fish Swiss into passionate human beings," Ada said.

Leanda's apartment was huge and filled with elegant European antique furniture. There were a number of bedrooms, but Ada and Blain chose to share one. I was sure Ada wanted to interrogate Blain on the subject of love spells, and probably Blain, wanted to share her secrets with her sister.

When Leanda and I were alone, she asked what we should do about Romain.

"We could report him to Interpol. He is wanted for forgery after all."

"I'd thought of that, but I didn't want to do it if I was here alone. I think he's dangerous, because he thinks he has nothing to lose, that he's lost everything already."

Leanda and I talked for a while. She was telling me about various characters she's encountered in her work as an investment lawyer. The story always seemed the same: "The people most obsessed with money are the ones with the most screws loose. Unfortunately for them, the screws that are loose don't make them particularly interesting as happens with the artists that populate my world."

"Would you like to sleep with me? Not sexually, just for companionship." Leanda said.

"I would like that if it weren't for Ada and Blain being here. My relationship with them is so complicated and peculiar, I'm afraid they'd just make a big deal out of it."

"I understand. You're right."

After a moment, Leanda said, "May I ask what happened with you and Blain in Italy with that strange love spell? Sounds like a children's fairy tale."

"I know. It was like that, but it was more complicated than I would have liked. I would add that the spell was cast on me, not at my request. I literally woke up with it one day."

"What do you think about the woman who cast the spell?"

"She's brilliant and has extraordinary powers. She's also a person with strong integrity. She does these things only for people she admires, and only if some good can come from it. Although I did get the impression that she was also capable of casting a destructive spell, and maybe has now and then, if she believed it was called for. It's all pretty secretive."

"Is it a matter of either good spell or bad spell, or are there many kinds of spells with many kinds of effects?"

"I have the impression she could do anything she wanted."

"If I met her and she liked me, do you think she'd cast a spell for me if I convinced her some good could come from it?"

"Leanda, what in the world do you have in mind here? Or I should say, who do you have in mind?"

She was quiet for a moment and then said, "Romain."

I was stunned enough by her answer that I could do no more than just stare at her.

"Is this to help him or hurt him?" I said Finally.

"It's more complicated than that. I have to think about it more and I'm tired now. I'll tell you in the morning."

I was awakened in the morning by Leanda holding two notes. She handed me one.

"This is from Ada."

I read:

Good morning Mommy one and Daddy two. I've decided to go off on an adventure with Daddy one. Don't worry, he is my Daddy, so he'll do no harm, although I have to admit he can be scary, but that can be exciting too.
PS: Blain has come with us.

Leanda handed me the second note, "This is from Romain."

There was a fifteenth-century Renaissance painter named Fra Filippo Lippi. "Fra" because he was a priest as well as a remarkable painter. He was obsessed with a young nun in a nearby convent, whom he wanted to use as a model for the Virgin in an Annunciation fresco he was painting. So he absconded with the young nun, right out from under the nose of the Mother Superior. And for good measure, he took along her sister, whom he used as the Archangel Gabriel. In Vasari's 'Life of the Painters', we learn that the young nun soon after gave birth to Lippi's son, Filipino Lippi, who also became a great painter.

Yours, The Forger, formerly of Northern Renaissance paintings, currently of 'Southern' Renaissance paintings.

I lay in bed staring at Leanda. She was standing, wearing a silk dressing gown.

"I would remind you of this." She said, pointing to the X on her face, shocking at any time but doubly so in their significance this morning.

"He wouldn't dare," I said.

"Do you think that before he did what he did to me I would have thought he would dare?"

We discussed whether to report him to an array of possible law enforcement agencies, from Interpol to the Swiss police to the Italian police. The latter because I sensed that's where he'd be headed with the twins, because Switzerland was too small and because he wanted to be in Italy to paint his ersatz Italian Renaissance magnum opus. Ultimately we decided against any of it. Since the twins went with him willingly we couldn't report a kidnapping. And to report him to Interpol would only antagonize him, and anyway, the issue at hand was getting the twins back not making him pay for his forgeries. I believed his plan was to immerse himself in the persona of Filippo Lippi, so he could be convinced he was painting as Lippi did. And that meant researching Lippi's life and finding out where he did his work and especially finding out where he did his absconding from the Sisters in order to paint his Annunciation, early in his life and career. I considered momentarily the Duomo at Spoleto, but that fresco was his last.

Leanda had a good idea. She believed Romain also wanted access to the twin's Swiss bank account because as a perpetual fugitive he was probably running low on the proceeds from his forgeries of years ago. She had a client who was an executive at the bank in question, whom she said, "Owed me one...a big one." She'd ask him for any recent records of money wired from that account. If we could establish where the money had been sent, we'd know where they were or at least the route of their travels. The only thing we could do in the meantime was wait. After discussing all the worst possible things we could imagine that could happen, we took a fatalistic stance. One fact that helped was that in the past when the twins were threatened with harm, they disposed of their threateners with an efficiently executed cranium smashing, and the forger knew nothing about that. As the saying goes, he wouldn't have known what hit him. However, it's taken years for the twins to get over all that carnage and another killing at this point would do them no good at all.

We researched Filippo Lippi and found that his painting activities and his mischief took place in a number of areas of Tuscany and Umbria. We decided to give the banker some time before we set out. We were rewarded for our patience when three days later we received word of a money transfer to a bank in Perugia. I realized immediately that Spoleto is right down the train line from Perugia. Then I remembered the Annunciation in one side panel of the Duomo where the model for the young Virgin was known to be the nun he ran off with, in spite of the fact that the Duomo fresco was the last of his life. I couldn't believe it, Spoleto, the site of the festival and our performance, complete with two near deaths. I was right in the first place.

"This is remarkable, Marconia and her pagan followers live outside of Spoleto up in the hills," I said to Leanda.

"Marconia?"

"The woman who casts the spells."

"This is amazing," she said.

"I know, and I was just there less than a week ago."

Leanda and I were in her bed where I had been sleeping the past three nights, 'for comfort' as she characterized it. The only intimacy we had allowed ourselves was a morning ritual where I systematically kissed her scar to 'exorcise' it. And while we had ruled out sex because of the complexity of our connection to Blain and Ada, the ritual drove Leanda crazy, and it had become a source of humor between us, a levity appreciated in the tense present circumstances.

"The Alps are like life," Leanda said as we looked out the window of our compartment at dramatic snow-covered peaks. "The train moves through them so swiftly that suddenly one is in Italy, mild, full of the warmth of life. In an hour we'll be in Milan." Leanda kissed me richly and I her. The X kissing routine got

slightly out of hand this morning, slightly more expansive and we ended up referring to it as Xs without borders. It seemed important to keep humor an active
ingredient in what was happening between us, as though it would keep things from
getting too serious and complicated. A naive notion really. The excitement of new
love often releases the most outrageous humor, or maybe it's just my own self-
defense ploy.

Our plan was to go first to Signore Ponzza's villa. I had called him and as always
he made me feel like I'm the one person in the world he'd be most happy to hear
from. Then we'd drive up to see Marconia. Her wisdom and her uncanny powers
seemed like they would be very helpful in our present quest. In fact, she might
even know something. I had a sense that Blain would try to contact her, maybe
even had. Blain had mixed feelings about Marconia. Because of the spell, she loved
her, but because of the spell's tentative nature, she resented her. In any event, felt
tied to her in complex ways.

After warm greetings all around with Signore Ponzza and his fleeting troubled
response to seeing Leanda's face for the first time, we drove up to the compound.
When Leanda saw one of the cults in full costume inside she burst into laughter.
"I thought you were kidding me about how these people dressed. My God, this is
a riot."

"Spend your humor now, they won't take kindly to being seen as a joke."

"I'm sorry, I just hope I can take them seriously."

"Oh, you will, believe me, once you've met Marconia."

When Marconia came out to greet us, after warmly embracing me, and I her,
she turned to Leanda. Unlike any other person I'd ever seen meeting Leanda for
the first time, Marconia doesn't avert her gaze from the scar. On the contrary, she
immediately reached up and carefully ran a finger over every inch of her scar, feeling the surface and even gently pinching the skin together to get a sense of the
thickness. Marconia had so much innate authority in her presence Leanda submitted to this careful examination seemingly without resentment.

"I can remove this," Marconia said this evenly while looking into Leanda's eyes.

Leanda was very moved, and confused, and said with a shrug of acquiescence, "But how?"

Marconia turned to one side and lifted her stripped shirt, ignoring the fact that her breast was bared, and pointed to a very faint long line over her ribs that was just slightly pinker than her skin, and was in fact almost imperceptible. She said, "If we weren't in bright sun, you wouldn't be able to see this at all."

"But what is it?" Leanda said.

"It is where a very deep scar, deeper than yours, used to be. A scar resulting from a knife wound, but I won't go into that story, except to say that my wound was delivered with malice, as I'm certain yours was. Is that not so?"

"Yes, that's true," Leanda said.

"That's good."

"Good? Why good?"

"Because that fact makes your scar more eligible for treatment."

Leanda was confused and troubled. She turned to me looking for reassurance that she was not being made the brunt of some horrible joke. She had tears in her eyes and I'd never seen that in her before. She raised her eyebrows instead of verbalizing a question.

"You can believe Marconia," I said.

It was the only thing I could say, even though I didn't have the faintest idea what Marconia was up to.

"But how is it done?" Leanda says to Marconia.

"Ask him." Marconia turned her head toward me.

I knew then that Marconia was talking about the leeches but it was too soon to say that word to Leanda.

"I'll tell you after we get settled a little, OK?" I say to Leanda, as I stroke her face with affection.

"OK," she said.

There was silence and Leanda looked to me to break it.

"Have you seen anything of Blàin, or Ada?" I ask Marconia.

"No. Should I? Had they come to see me?"

"I'm not sure." I then proceeded to tell her all that had transpired with Romain. Leanda gave some information too, I think in order to have some regular conversation with Marconia, to reassure herself. When Leanda mentioned Romain, Marconia says, "Does he have red hair?"

"Yes."

"He's in Spoleto, I know the sextant at the church, and he mentioned someone making drawings in the apse of the church, where the frescoes are. He attracted the attention of the sextant because of his intensity, and his ability to draw."

"He didn't mention the twins?"

"No."

"Could we get someone to follow him when he leaves the church, like maybe a kid so as not to attract attention, to find out where he's staying?"

"I can arrange that. I know a boy who will stay in the area of the church and the next time this man comes, follow him home."

"Perfect."

Marconia had been watching Leanda carefully while we'd been talking.

"This is the man who cut you isn't it?" She said.

Leanda was stunned. "Yes."

"When you talked of this man your scars got redder," Marconia said.

We returned to the villa for the night. We were both tired from traveling. Signore Ponzza joined us for a late supper, served by his very old and faithful personal housekeeper. Whenever this housekeeper heard Marconia's name she raised her eyebrows and crossed herself. I asked him about this when we were alone.

"I believe the word in English is xenophobia. This Marconia has a reputation for strange powers and she's such a pagan, a bad combination among these simple people."

Signore Ponzza was clearly upset about Leanda's scars. When he talked to her or listened to her his eyes moved around so deliberately trying to avoid looking at the scars, he seemed to be watching a fly buzzing around her face. In sympathy, Leanda brought up the subject. A sweet thing that I'd never seen her do before.

"Speaking of Marconia's powers," She said, "She believes she can heal my scar so it doesn't show. A miracle certainly to be appreciated, I've had it for almost twenty years. A man who lost his senses did it."

Signore Ponzza graciously made all the appropriate observations and thanked her for bringing it up. Everyone was more comfortable. Later he said to me alone, "I've seen plenty of scars and disfigurement in life, but with Leanda it's so upsetting because she's so extraordinarily sensitive and beautiful."

In bed, Leanda says, "OK, let's have it."

"Marconia?"

"What else?"

With Leanda, if she asked a question, you come right to the point, or receive a barrage of verbal abuse. Too many years of dealing with evasive people of power.

"Do you know what leeches are?"

"Oh God, when I was little we vacationed on a lake where inevitably you got a leech stuck to your skin sucking away, *blood-sucking* away! I'd always scream, 'Get it off of me or cut off my foot!' It became a family joke. So what about leeches?"

Not a propitious start thought the narrator.

"Well, Marconia in all her powers of spells, curses, and healing uses many different approaches, and the medical use of leeches is one of them. I'm not sure exactly what she has in mind for you, so it's best to let her explain it."

"You knew it involved leeches or you wouldn't have brought it up."

"I'm assuming it does, because she did say ask me about the healing process. When I was here before, I fell and seriously injured my ankle. She totally healed it with leeches on it for a couple of hours. It was miraculous."

"Leeches on your ankle, Oh my God!"

"Here's another example even more impressive. Marconia used to have a mole above her upper lip that was really grotesque. It was large, black, and had stiff hairs growing out of it. It looked like a scorpion. She totally eliminated it with leeches, there's not even any scar."

"She put leeches on her lip?"

"Yes."

"Forget it, I'll keep my scars. Anyway, I don't believe she could succeed in doing it and I'm not going to be her Guinea Pig. Every plastic surgeon I've talked to has said the scars cannot be totally removed

"That's fine. No one's going to try and coerce you."

"I'm not going to do it."

"Fine."

"I'm definitely not going to do it."

"I know."

"Do you think she could do it?"

"I'd put it this way, I believe there's a possibility she could do it."

"Would you do it if you were me?"

"I don't know. If I'd accepted the scars the way you have, I may not try it. The scars haven't really interfered with your life."

"Haven't interfered with my life? Are you kidding?"

"By that, I mean they haven't interfered with what you've chosen to do professionally, you seem very successful there. And you have long since adjusted to meeting people and being immune to what their response is to seeing your scars."

"But I've had no love in my life."

"No love in your life?"

"No."

"What do you call this?"

"This? I don't know what to call it, maybe friendship with some erotic teasing."

"And is this friendship and erotic teasing without love?"

"Do you love me?"

I hesitated, troubled at finding myself at the other end of the question.

"OK, my passionate erotic narrator," Leanda said slowly and deliberately "I'm sure you're telling a good story with all this rich material, and I know you pride yourself on being the detached observer (which incidentally is a big pain in the ass), but now I'm asking you to look inside and narrate to me what the hell's going on in there."

"Well, this is all pretty new and..."

"Give me a direct answer or give me no answer."

"Yes."

"Yes?"

"Yes."

"Yes what?"

"Yes, I love you."

Leanda was surprised to hear me say that. She studied me with a quizzical smile.

"OK, I believe you."

"Do you love me?" I said.

"I don't know. I haven't had much experience in this, at least not since loving Romain ended so disastrously."

"You insisted I answer your question with a yes or a no and then you answer my question with, 'I don't know,'" I laughed and said.

"It was an honest answer."

"Do you love my scar?" She asked.

I was surprised by the question, and disturbed by the question because I do love her scar and her question made me realize that her scar is fascinating for me and intrigued me far more than it should, in ways I have trouble defining even to myself. The question is too laden with implications to answer, so I skirt it.

"I would hate to be an attorney opposing you in a courtroom."

"I'd eat you for lunch."

"I'm sure you would."

"But right now I'll eat you for breakfast!"

Leanda dove under the covers, and began biting me here and there with ferocity just this side of pain. As I began reciprocating I thought, 'No cream puff this girl.'"

At one point with Leanda sitting on top of me pinning my hands down as she'd just won a schoolyard fight, she said, "I love you, Narrator." Then, as often happens in schoolyard fights, she leaned her face over mine, and with a bit of saliva between her lips she said, "Say you love my scar or I'll spit in your face."

I don't, and she does.

"That's the first time a woman has ever spit in my face, especially while being on top of me."

"Yes, well, these are all very animalistic activities, aren't they? Not to mention that I was only sitting on top of you."

"Meaning?"

"Meaning that we're not lovers anyway."

"So...?"

"So my point, in the beginning, was that the scar did interfere with my life because I've had no lovers since Romain."

"No, you said you've had no love in your life since the Forger."

"Well, you understand the kind of love I'm talking about. Passionate love."

"But Leanda, Isn't our love passionate love?"

"It's affectionately passionate, but it's not sexually passionate."

"You sound like a guy."

"Well, maybe that's the mentality my scar has turned me toward."

She continued, "Do my scars repulse you?"

I decided to be forthright. "Your scar not only doesn't repulse me, it attracts me intensely because they are such direct evidence of your physical presence, evidence of a physical event in your life which makes you so palpably Leanda. Plus it is an exquisite marking that expresses your own exquisiteness."

"That's easy for you to say."

"No, it's not easy for me to say because it seems peculiar to me to have that response to your scar, and I'm afraid you'll perceive me accordingly."

"So? You're not the first peculiar artist to walk the face of the earth."

To that, I can only answer, "True."

After a moment Leanda asks, "Then, why aren't we lovers?"

"We aren't lovers because I want us to be lovers, and that is not the contradiction it seems because what I mean is that if we were lovers it could be a connection that would eclipse every other intense relationship in my life."

"Such as?"

"Such as Ada and Blain."

"But it would be perfectly logical. You and I are mother and father to Ada and Blain."

"No, you are mother and Romain is father."

Leanda opened her mouth to challenge what I'd said but then thought twice about it, hopefully because she realized that it was not that simple. She took a lighter line.

"I see, it's your plan to honor the twins' wish that you marry one and have the other as your mistress."

"Precisely."

"Then they'll have a husband and a lover with teeth marks all over."

At this Leanda dove under the covers and attacked with sharp bites whatever body parts of mine I couldn't shield fast enough, mumbling, "I shouldn't be the only one privileged to have a scar from a scorned lover."

When she finally calmed down I did have a selection of if not scars, bright red imprints to match her teeth. We were silent and lay still for a few moments and then I said, "I was also reluctant to say I love your scar because I didn't want to influence your decision about letting Marconia try and erase it. But on the other hand, if she did erase it I couldn't continue my ritual of exorcising it with kisses that drives you so gratifyingly mad."

"You scar pervert. Good, then we both agree that Marconia and her pet leeches won't be allowed anywhere near my scars."

"If you say so."

When we returned to the pagan's convent (A term Marconia had begun to use because she liked the contradiction), we were met with the news that Romain had been spotted by the boy who had followed him to his lodgings. It turned out that he was in a rented villa just at the edge of Spoleto, within walking distance of the Duomo. He'd clearly begun to tap into the twins' bank account. Since Leanda and I weren't sure what move to make or when we decided to have him observed until we decided what came next. We wanted to avoid a premature action that would drive him away. And, because he was making no effort to conceal himself, we concluded that the twins were content for the time being and therefore Romain couldn't be accused of any kind of abduction. Unless, and this thought alarmed me, he had done something to them. Leanda and I decided that the immediate priority was to determine that the twins were OK, and that was going to involve some spying. We decided we should spy on all three of them. This was not our forte, but it needed to be done. I thought that it was as undesirable for the twins to see us as it was that Romain saw us. They had a way of getting enthusiastic about something and then resenting any interference. And who knows what power Romain may have over them by now. But we had to determine that the twins were unharmed.

We approached the villa from the back, up a steep slope, and through an overgrown garden so thick with foliage we couldn't see the wall of the villa until we were upon it. That was a good sign since we can't be seen prying our way through shrubs and hedges. The wall was ancient and in bad repair, with stones fallen away here and there. As we came close and slowly circled the wall looking for a way to see in, or climb up, we heard a stern male voice, "I warned you not to move, you're exactly where I want you." Then, "But it hurts!" It was Blain. Leanda and I looked at each other in alarm. Walking quickly further on we came to a heavy wood gate that looked like it hadn't been opened in a century. There were narrow gaps between boards and we bend down to peer in. The twins and the forger were under an extended roof from a tall shed so that they were all in the shade, but still in considerable light because the sun was so bright. This was apparently Romain's studio and his means of having enough light to work by because inside the villa there would be nowhere near the amount of light he needed. Blain was down on one knee with a hand out in front, her fingers in the prescribed gesture of Gabriel, the Annunciation angel, informing the Virgin that she had Christ inside of her. She was wearing a full pale rose robe of the Renaissance era, attached to which were a pair of large white gauzy wings. She repeated, "It hurts Damnit, I'm getting a cramp." Ada, in the role of the Virgin, was seated and leaning back as though in retreat from this news from Gabriel, her hand on her breast. She was also wearing a full robe, of pure white. Romain was dressed in a kind of mismatched Renaissance gear, a blousy top, and tights below. He seemed to be in a state of ecstasy, and I could see why. The twins were exquisite in the way that Lippi's people always were. Their precise features were perfect for Lippi, as was their red hair, which I noticed had grown out considerably, especially in Blain's case. Romain was standing before a triptych of stretched white canvases. There was the beginning of a preliminary drawing only in the left panel, and it was the scene we were observing. He was obviously going to be at work here for some time to come and that was a relief for Leanda and me. We need not worry about them suddenly disappearing into thin air.

Satisfied that the twins were safe, we decided to leave. The less we were here the less chance we have of being discovered. On our way back, Leanda said, "I wonder if he's made any kind of advances on them, sexual advances. He's a very sensual man.

"They wouldn't tolerate it."

"What if they wanted it?" Leanda said. "They are provocative."

"He's their father."

"So are you, and they both wanted you, and I suspect Blain actually succeeded in having her way"

I am silent.

"Did you?"

"Did I what?"

"Did you and Blain make love, have sex?"

"Yes"

"How would you characterize it? Was it because of the spell?"

"It went on for a period of time and it was intense. I don't believe it came from the spell."

"So, are you and Blain lovers?"

"It was confusing because I love Blain, just as I love Ada."

"But you didn't make love with Ada."

"Ada doesn't have the same feelings for me."

"Is this one of your qualified answers?"

"Sometimes the truth is complex, not just black or white or yes or no."

"By the way, over the years I've learned to keep my feelings to myself, but this news of yours is extremely distressing for me," Leanda said, with tears in her eyes.

"To begin with, I'll give you some history of the leeches here in our cauldron."

Marconia, Leanda, and I were sitting at the edge of the cauldron in the ancient stone circular building with the narrow vertical windows providing what little light there was. She had taken off her pointed hat and that reassured Leanda, who had agreed to at least listen with an open mind to what Marconia had to say.

"This building predates Christ and was used by pagans back then, back before the status and worth of pagans was so presumptuously judged and condemned by the Church. There were leeches in this water then and they were used for healing, medicinal and spiritual. Leeches, as you know, need blood to survive, and there was no natural source of blood in this cauldron. Of course, as people were submerged in the water for treatment the leeches had their fill of nourishment. But in between submersions there was nothing. So the pagans regularly offered various small animals to the leeches to keep them alive and healthy. Now it would seem that the water would become contaminated with bacteria as a result of this practice, but in time it was realized that the leeches had gradually become a higher form of life and had begun to take responsibility for their environment. No one knows how long this took, but it was centuries for certain and is still going on after two thousand years. So even in the fifth century AD, when Christianity was official and dominating, there were local pagans or descendants of pagans, who knew the healing value of the leeches and continued to keep them in blood so to speak. In those days everything was not so benign and occasionally accounts were settled by a person being judged guilty and condemned to the cauldron with the lid on, which kept the leeches supplied for months. So over the centuries, a small group of local people, some pagans, some not, assumed the responsibility to keep the leeches healthy because they were essential to the health and well-being of the local residents. Today, that is now our responsibility, mine and my pagan followers. I would also add that you are sworn to secrecy about this whole matter, because if word got out our way of life would be destroyed. You see these days even mainstream medicine uses leeches for certain treatments, and there are actually leech farms in various places that raise leeches and ship them to hospitals worldwide. But their leeches are nothing compared to ours, because ours, through inbreeding have developed powers far beyond any common leech."

Marconia silently watched Leanda. Then she said, "It would be one of the most gratifying experiences of my life as a pagan sorceress to employ our highly developed leeches to take your scar from you, Leanda. And I would add, nowhere else in the world would you be able to do this. Please give this serious thought. For you. Not for me. I mentioned how satisfying it would be for me to do it because you are such an exquisite creature."

The tough Leanda comes to life, "And with my scar, I am not exquisite?"

Marconia says, as she puts her pointed hat back on, "There are degrees and types of exquisiteness my dear."

Leanda embraced Marconia tightly and said, "Thank you for your knowledge and your concern and generous offer. You're an amazing person and I feel privileged to know you."

As we walked from the cauldron building, Leanda said, "You and Blain made love up here somewhere didn't you?"

"Yes."

"Where, exactly?"

"On the roof of that stone building down there." I point to Blain's and my roof garden.

"Let's go up there."

As we climbed the old wooden ladder to the roof, I looked back and saw Marconia watching us steadily from a distance.

Dusk was softening the hilltop as we lay back on the roof. The last rays of sun touched the roof of the round building up the hill.

Leanda took my hand and said, "I've never felt so at peace. Even the stars are beginning to show themselves, showing as they always do just how insignificant we all are in the end, just how insignificant a decision it is, whether to let leeches remove my scar or not.

It's no big deal is it?"

"Is what?" I said.

"That I may let Marconia's leeches elevate me to a higher degree of exquisiteness."

'No, it isn't."

"If I do it, will you do it with me, be at the cauldron with me?"

I began to think well, it's no big deal, and I love this woman. Then a different thought entered my mind, 'Marconia and her spells!'

In the morning we found Marconia and told her Leanda had agreed.

Marconia, of course, was not surprised and smiling just said, "Good." Then she explained the procedure, "It will involve you lying flat outside of the cauldron and leeches will be placed by hand over your face, shoulder to shoulder so to speak sucking away at the X.

"Will it hurt?" Leanda said.

"No it won't hurt, but it will be a sensation, unlike anything you've ever had before. Some have even described it as an erotic sensation."

"Erotic?" Leanda showed surprise.

"That's what I've been told, but I think it's different for different people."

Marconia continued with her plan description, "The first time we'll do just a couple of hours, and then we'll progress from there. The longer you have the leeches on your face each time the more effective it will be. We'll work it out so there will be no stress at all on your part."

Marconia smiled conspiratorially at me, knowing that I know that I am under a spell as well as Leanda. The unspoken agreement between us is that Leanda will never have this information.

Time has passed. How can I narrate with any kind of accuracy what Leanda and I have experienced? I'm afraid you would feel I've failed you. And since I hate failure, I'm not even going to try. But in the course of telling my story, you'll begin to glean certain things, that is if you're perceptive.

How much time? It's hard to tell. Leanda and I have been by the cauldron too many times to count. At first, it seemed no change was taking place but one day there was a quantum jump (Marconia said it sometimes happened that way) and we both noticed that both the color and height of the scar had diminished. When Leanda was certain the change had actually occurred, she cried. It was only the second time I'd seen her cry since we met.

Marconia said it was time for a recess in the treatment. She said the scar would continue to fade because the chemicals already injected into the tissue would continue to be effective. She said that the leeches had begun to become sated and had slowed down their work. This delay will cause them to return to work with their original zest.

"In three days we'll resume and then it won't be long before the work is completed. In the meantime, eat lots of protein, and get exercise. We want your circulation to be in top form for our finale."

Back at Signore Ponzza's villa, we took a careful look at Marconia's work (I should say Marconia and her busy little helpers). I'd noticed that the spell had resulted in some silly humor, probably necessary to offset the horror of it all. Leanda was standing before a mirror carefully scrutinizing her fading scars.

"I wonder if I'll miss it?" She said, "You have to admit it had character, or maybe gave me character. I wonder if I'll lose some toughness, which I can't afford to do in this world. I wonder if you'll love me less."

"Too many wonders. Next, you'll be asking Marconia if she can give you back your scar."

"I wonder how the twins and the forger are doing?" Leanda said.

One effect of the spell is that it led one to concentrate on immediate priorities at the expense of all else. We decided to go on a spy mission right away.

We were not prepared for what we saw when we looked through the cracks in the wood door. They were all at work on the second panel. The drawing for the first panel was complete and impressive. In the second panel of the triptych, the drawing was near completion and Gabriel and the Virgin were in position before Romain who was drawing obsessively. Blain as Virgin was pushed back in her large armless chair, her eyes wide either involuntarily or for effect or both. Her legs were apart and her gown had fallen back exposing bare thighs between which was Ada, as Gabriel, wings upright and her own gown hiked up exposing bare thighs.

Leanda gestured to me for us to leave. When we were out of hearing distance she said, "My God, what is that man up to?"

"I think he's making a contemporary Annunciation. Gabriel, as the messenger of God, is more than immaculately impregnating the Virgin. Our forger is making a literal version."

Leanda was silent a moment and then said, "I think you're right. But do you think Ada and Blain are doing this voluntarily, that they believe in what he's doing?"

"I don't know what they think about it, but they're clearly into it."

"What do you mean, into it?"

There was a lot I could tell Leanda to help her understand. Such as what Blain told me back in the beginning about the twins acting out the drama of St. Teresa and the angel penetrating her with his spear, but I decided it was too much information for here, right outside the forger's studio.

"It's too much to go into now, let's just say they want to make a convincing image," I said.

Leanda looked at me skeptically, and said, "OK, but promise me you'll tell me everything you know about this and their relationship in general. You're the one with all the information. You know more about the twins than anyone, even more than they know."

"Well, I am the..."

A glare from Leanda made it unwise to finish.

As prescribed by Marconia, Leanda and I ate lots of protein (easy to do with the meat-based cooking at Villa Ponzza) and we set out each day for a long hike in the hills of Umbria to keep our circulation healthy. I was sure Marconia had not let up on our spell because Leanda and I constantly examine the fading scars.

On the morning of our third day of reprieve, we returned to the pagan's compound to finish the job. Marconia was pleased to see Leanda and looked her over carefully and smiled at how the treatment had continued to progress even while we were away from the cauldron. This time around I was more relaxed and confident and was able to let my senses respond to the quality of the atmosphere in this ancient round structure. The fragrances were heady, a combination of dampness, stone, and human presence. I don't think I'd ever been in a building with such a strong sense of prior inhabitants, over two millennia worth, not to mention the ghosts of innumerable spells both kindly and not.

After some uncounted days, Marconia was satisfied with the total absence of scar tissue on Leanda's face and we all went outside for a look at her in the bright sun.

We were all in awe at the perfection of her skin. Leanda, could not help but dissolve into tears at the significance of this miracle. When I used the word, Marconia was quick to correct me. "Pagan miracle", she said, "Not to be confused with all the theatrical hype surrounding the staged dramas which the Church refers to as miracles." Leanda and I laughed, but Marconia was serious.

We thanked Marconia and the other pagans profusely. Marconia said, "We invite you to a dinner of celebration, some days hence. We will tell you when. Right now I'm sure you want to return to a more ordinary, drier world until you get used to your new exquisite exquisiteness."

Back at Signore Ponzza's, Leanda caused quite a scene. His housekeeper crossed herself repeatedly with her eyes perpetually raised to heaven. Even Signore Ponzza was moved to tears. He kept looking at Leanda and shaking his head in wonder. As a precaution, as Marconia instructed, I asked him not to say anything to anyone about where and how this happened, and I told him Marconia's reason. He swore to secrecy. When I nodded toward his housekeeper, he said, "Not to worry, she's terrified of even having this information. Her belief is that verbalizing it could bring a dark deed from God or the devil himself, or both."

After a few days of resting and drying out, it was time to check on Romain and the twins. When we were in place at the gate we saw no one. The three panels were leaning against a wall, and the drawings seemed to be finished, but they were difficult to see because of the angle. It was necessary to find another vantage point that would involve climbing the wall if we could. We walked around the wall until we found a place where stones had fallen away forming a kind of crude stairway up. When we were high enough to see over, we were overwhelmed by the intensity and elegance of the drawings. A twentieth-century Renaissance master indeed. Romain had begun to add color in the first panel and the pallet was pure Lippi, luminous and intense. We climbed down and circled the wall of the villa to reach the front gate which was unlocked. Inside, we circled the villa, which seemed unoccupied, looking into various windows. A window at the rear of the villa revealed Blain and Ada asleep in separate beds their faces turned away from the light of the window.

"What are they doing sleeping so soundly in the middle of the day? Do you think they're OK?" Leanda said.

"They're fine."

We turned to find Romain staring at us. It seemed to take him a minute to register everything, who we were, what we were doing here, and then most importantly, the absence of Leanda's scar. That fact seemed to stun him.

"What happened to you?" was all he managed to say.

When Leanda realized that he was referring to her missing scar, She said, "You mean, what unhappened to me. What happened to me was you, twenty years ago."

He reached out incredulously and ran a finger over the barely visible ex-scar on her face. "How did you do this?"

"You could at least say hello," Leanda laughed.

Romain was in no mood for pleasantries. He seemed enraged. He said with steely intensity, "I marked you." Then he turned to go back inside. "You're trespassing. There are guard dogs here."

After a moment, sure enough, two German shepherds loped around the back corner of the villa eyeing us hostilely. We were out the gate in seconds, pulling it closed behind us.

"Now I'm worried." Leanda said, "He seems to have reverted back to a mode I thought he'd grown out of. He was outraged that I'd erased his marks. He's dangerous and who knows what he might do with the twins now."

We returned to the Ponzza villa and explained the situation to Signore Ponzza. His immediate response was to call the Inspector in Rome who called the Spoleto police and there was much delay and hesitation about whether they should intervene since there was no sign of a crime committed. This went on for two days. On the third day, we received a call from a doctor's office in Spoleto asking us to come in. When we arrived, there were police there and they were questioning Blain. Ada was in with the doctor and after we had a confusing conversation with the police who spoke no English, Ada came out with the doctor. She had a loose white taped dressing covering about a three-inch line across her cheek. The doctor, who was white-haired said, "There is also a body at the villa."

The whole scenario was at once clear in my mind, and was confirmed by the Inspector who was walking into the doctor's waiting room.

"Aha, once again, the *Homicidal Theater Family.*"

As Narrator I must describe this family scene: Here was Ada with a dressing across her cheek. Here was Leanda whose absence of her X had compelled Romain to strike again, this time at her daughter and his. Here was Blain, who by her father's marking of her sister, was compelled to dispatch him with a bludgeoned cranium. And here was I, surviving 'father' of these twins and in a Marconian way almost 'husband' to their mother. A nuclear family if only because of an ongoing series of deadly explosions.

Ada was in shock and had not yet absorbed the heinous crime committed against her. She was sitting now with Leanda next to her embracing her.

Blain was, just plain furious at having once again been forced into the role of assassin. "I could see this coming and I just should have killed the bastard before he did what he did. But because of you (she looked angrily at the Inspector), I had to wait until he acted so I wouldn't go to prison for murder. *You're* responsible for Ada's wound!"

The Inspector could only raise his eyebrows and try to suppress his rueful smile. By now, I think he had trouble separating our lives from our theater. Too much art imitating life imitating art.

The doctor gave a prognosis on Ada's wound, and it was encouraging. "Sutures were not necessary because she was not cut deeply. The assailant seemed to have doubts about his action, because the cuts were superficial, and could be closed just with tape. What is amazing is that a man in such a state of compulsive rage was able to control his marks to such a degree."

"That's because the cut was a forgery, a forgery of my own cut which in his mind, was the original work of art," Leanda said.

We all silently considered what Leanda had said and knew that she was right.

Blain's rage continued. She walked to the Inspector and said, "So, super cop, now are you satisfied that this carnage had been carried out according to the requirements of the law? That it was necessary for me to act to keep my sister from being transformed into a platter of sliced prosciutto?"

"If I have more questions, I will contact you. Don't leave the country just yet," he said.

I sensed that he felt sympathy, but would never express it in this hostile environment. He graciously nods to all of us and leaves. Thinking about what this man sees in his life, makes our theater seem bland in comparison. The difference is that art seeks ineffable reasons why, and his work just involves the facts.

Further conversation with the doctor revealed that there would be a scar for Ada but a barely noticeable, superficial one.

It was Blain who was most affected by the whole thing. At one point she shrugged and said, "I killed my father. Bashed in his strange brain."

I sensed I needed to watch over her carefully. Because she's the most normal of all of us, she's the most vulnerable in our world of abnormality.

To further complicate matters, as we were all preparing to leave for the Ponzza villa, Blain said to me quietly, "I want you back." I looked at her eyes and saw that this was no idle, childish provocation. This was no longer a child.

"You will always have me." I squeezed her hand.

"You know what I mean," she said.

Part Seven

Well. Where to begin? So many events have occurred, initiating so many other events, I can barely keep track. And more significantly, I'm having increasing difficulty remaining the objective narrator because, well, because against my better judgment and preference, I am increasingly a subject of my own narration. Who can report on themselves in an unbiased manner?

"We will have you as smooth and perfect as a newborn baby."

Marconia had just had her first glimpse of Ada's cut. She had gingerly removed the bandage on her face and looked carefully at the forger's last attempted work of forgery. "Of course, healing has to occur before we have a scar to deal with," Marconia said. "I would say in a month we will be ready to perform our disappearing act." Blain was standing behind Marconia and Ada and looking vague and disoriented.

When Blain and I were alone, I asked her what was wrong.

"I can't tell you. I'm sworn to secrecy. You already have some information on the subject but you probably don't remember. It was all more subtle back then."

"Back when? What are you talking about?"

"I told you I can't tell you. In time you'll find out for yourself. Everyone will."

"Are all of our lives destined to be cloaked in mystery ad infinitum?"

"Don't get Latiny. Anyway, isn't mystery always more interesting?"

Signore Ponzza had, with predictable graciousness, invited all of us to stay at the villa while Ada healed enough to be the leeches' next culinary treat (of course he didn't put it that way). Leanda however needed to return to Zurich for pressing business. The twins would stay because the Inspector had not yet cleared them to leave the country. Leanda and I decided that I should stay with Ada because she was still dealing with the trauma of her-father-the-forger's attack. She wanted to start dancing again and I could help ease her back into a daily routine. And Blain? Blain was a total roll of the dice. She was outwardly calm but I knew that something was brewing inside.

"Blain, I won't interrogate you about what's going on inside your beautiful head, but I will offer to help you in any way I can."

"Yes, you can help me. Drive me out to see Marconia. I want to talk to her. But first, I want to go to the Duomo to look at the Lippi frescoes with you."

The next morning we left for the Duomo. Ada was left behind in the care of Signore Ponzza's housekeeper who insisted she sleep and eat to heal her wounds. Ada calmly agreed. She was exhausted from everything.

At the Duomo Blain and I walked the length of the nave to the apse to stand in front of and under the great Lippi frescoes on the subject of the life of the Virgin. The coronation of the young Virgin took place in the dome with God and the Virgin presiding over all the other chapters in her life seen below. Dominating everything was the image of the old and dying Virgin surrounded by witnesses, the most significant of whom was Lippi himself. He was standing to the side as one of many witnesses, and art historians all agreed that this figure was painted in the likeness of Lippi. But he was not looking at the dying Virgin, he was looking past her to a side niche where the Annunciation was taking place, and most significantly, with his hand against his chest he was slyly pointing with his finger at himself as though to say, 'I am responsible for the pregnancy of the Virgin.' And this was true. As Romain said in his note in Zurich, Lippi had absconded with the young nun whom he was using as a model for the Virgin in a fresco he was painting in the convent where she resided. He got away with this because he was himself a priest. And indeed, she became pregnant with his son, a Filipino who in time became a painter himself. And this young nun became his model for every Virgin he painted from then on.

I had been explaining bits of this story as Blain and I studied it.

"Look at the young Virgin and Gabriel, aren't they identical, complete with red/gold hair, and don't they look like..."

"Like you and Ada, yes."

"Exactly, and Romain was obsessed with this fact. He really believed that the three of us were reliving this event or to be more accurate, I think he believed it was happening for the first time, including fucking his young nun model for the Virgin."

Blain said this with such vehemence that I turned to look at her. She stared back, saying nothing until finally, she said, "Yes."

"Yes?"

"Yes, well, he tried to..."

"Tried to what...?"

"Tried to fuck me."

"And..."

"I fought him off viciously."

It was impossible to get more information from her. She was sobbing and couldn't get her breath. We left the church.

The next day, after we dropped Leanda off at the train station to travel to Rome for a plane to Zurich, Blain and I drove up to see Marconia and her pagan family. Marconia was always pleased to see any of us because we always brought her such interesting requests to test her powers. The nature of today's request was not revealed to me and Blain asked to talk privately with Marconia. In the meantime, I retreated to the roof of the stone shed that held so many pleasant memories. Lying on my back as audience for low moving cotton puff Umbrian clouds I was filled with the sense of reception that always accompanied any new creative phase in my life. When Ada is cleared of scars we all plan to return to our theater life in the beautiful Pacific Northwest, home of the Brewery awaiting us so we can start a new piece. I'd recently had word that some of the company were returning to Portland, ready to enter new dance/performance territory. Thinking of them all and of my new immediate family, I was filled with a sense of love for everyone, especially the twins, especially Blain, who suddenly and quietly appeared at the top of the ladder to stand facing me with the sun behind her creating an aura of light, halo-like, exuding passion and infusing me with passion, and a burning desire to hold onto her, to combine with her, and as she descended upon me, her dress lifted, the thought of the powers of Marconia entered my head, too late, too late. Pressing hard against me Blain urges, "I want you inside of me."

A perceptive reader has by now declared, "Of course, Blain brought you up here for Marconia to re-cast her spell on you. After all, she said she wanted you back. Don't play naive, or more to the point don't play dumb." To which, I could only say, You're right, it was a spell before a spell. And more to the point the first spell was cast by me. Cast by me on me. I wanted her. There, *mea culpa*. Just because I'm narrator doesn't mean I'm a saint.

When we are finally lying still, I studied Blain carefully. She had changed yet again. The combination of near sex with her biological father (I can't call it love-making because I know nothing of the nature of the encounter and Blain will tell me nothing) and the fact of her killing him, has added one more layer of veneer to her already guarded countenance. On an impulse, I asked, "Did you kill Romain because he was cutting Ada, or because he had tried to have sex with you.?"

She says, "Neither one."

"Then why?"

"Because I was obsessed with him. It was something like a familial Stockholm Syndrome."

"But why kill him?"

"Because I wanted him. Because I became obsessed with him. He was destroying me."

"So it was still self-defense, just not the usual legal version."

"Precisely."

"And what is the difference between you wanting Romain and you wanting me?"

"There's no difference."

"And you would kill me if you thought I was destroying you?"

"Yes."

"Do you think I'm destroying you?"

"I don't know. It depends on what happens between us now."

"What about Leanda? She is your mother."

"I have a hard time thinking of her as my mother. I'm more inclined to think of Marconia as my mother."

"Why Marconia?"

"Because she provided me with you again."

"But that was a spell."

"Only half a spell."

"What do you mean?"

"I mean you wanted me even before she did her spell thing."

"Why do you say that?"

"For two reasons, because I could tell, and because Marconia told me it was true."

I was silently troubled.

"It's true isn't it?" she said.

In the midst of Blain's forthrightness, I can't lie.

"Yes."

"Good for you, not hiding behind your narrator bullshit."

"How do you feel about having sex with me and almost sex with your father within forty-eight hours?"

"Well, the whole Oedipal thing was pretty well spent, wouldn't you say?"

I had to smile.

Blain and Ada and I settled into a month of calm, waiting for the cut to heal so Marconia could do her magic. Ada was anxious to begin dancing again and I carefully eased her into it. Once her stiffness was worked out she began to show her old inspiration in movement and was soon spinning around the Ponzza villa filling room after room with artistic grace. Signore Ponzza and his housekeeper and I were a rapt audience. Blain retreated to quietly observe.

Two months passed and one evening, I asked Blain how she felt about Ada being the center of attention.

"I'm used to it."

"When you and Ada were in the villa with Romain, was she the center of attention there?"

"No, I was."

"Why was that?"

"I was the Virgin. Romain was preoccupied with the Annunciation, with playing out his Filippo Lippi fantasy, you know, impregnating his model for the Virgin."

It was time to begin Marconia's treatment of Ada's scar, which even though there was only a slightly raised surface the color difference was noticeable. Ada was very cooperative. She hated the idea of leeches on her but she hated, even more, the idea of Romain having cut on her. She wanted no written history of that.

I left it to Blain to look after Ada while I flew to Zurich to see Leanda who had asked to talk to me about something important. I asked if we could just talk on the phone, but she insisted I come there. I assumed she had gotten some hint of what happened between Blain and me in letters from Blain, and I dreaded being confronted with it.

When Leanda opened her door, I was struck by how different she looked. She was radiantly attractive and dressed with flair. Her whole attitude imbued a quality of rebirth. It was the only appropriate term. I was surprisingly drawn to her so strongly that I wondered if my resistance to her previously was only self-protection against an impending intimacy that threatened me, and that perhaps she was potentially the love of my life. When I commented on the change in her she agreed.

"As you know, during all those years with the scar that I was determined to not let ruin my life, I actually began to believe it didn't matter. But now, we know it did. A lot. And everyone who'd been part of my life during that period agrees. I've never had such attention shown to me before, especially of course by men. But now I've found that men to whom I became close through my work have reassessed me, but not in any superficial way. It seems that part of my defense over the scar was to treat men as though the last thing in the world I wanted was a personal romantic relationship, which of course deep down I wanted more than anything. But I could not bear the thought of being rejected by a man to whom I was attracted, so I did all the rejecting, a priori. That's the general picture, my dear Stephen. Here is the specific picture: I am in love with a man with whom I've worked for a long time, and who it has turned out was in love with me right along, but felt he could not approach me. My scar stood between us."

Leanda studied me with sympathy. And while I love her and will miss her I realized that I also missed her scar. It gave her a quality of mystery and intrigue and challenge and even beauty. Without it she's too perfectly beautiful. This awareness underlines my conviction that the dark edge of life, of people, is not only necessary to my art, but it's also necessary to my capacity to love. Blain immediately came to mind, my homicidal adopted daughter/lover with enough darkness to last three lifetimes.

I was quiet. Leanda had tears in her eyes (a rarity). "I'm so sorry. Have I disappointed you by showing that I'm probably just an ordinary woman?"

"You couldn't be just an ordinary woman if you wanted. I'll miss you. But I'm also happy for you. If anyone ever deserved to have happiness in life it's you."

And that was that. I dreaded the idea of having to tell her about Blain and me and be the one delivering the hurtful news. It occurred to me that someday Blain would deliver hurtful news to me. Too much was going on in my mind. I decided to take the train back to Italy. Traversing the Alps by rail is a very effective way of dealing with life when space between one thing and another is called for. As the kilometers slid by, and the distance between Leanda and me increased, my anticipation of holding onto Blain filled me with passion.

Swiss trains were always punctual. But unnecessarily so today. When I returned to the Villa Ponzza I found no Blain, but a letter instead.

My dear 'father' / lover / provocateur:

I am gone because I couldn't stand the thought of murdering you. It was quite beyond my control, the image of you and Leanda (my mother) in a wild sexual embrace. The idea was destroying me just as my obsession with Romain was destroying me. The only conflict I had was choosing an appropriate object to smash your cranium. It had to be a significant object, because you are so above anyone else I ever disposed of. You were saved by my respect for your high standards. Another thought that saved you was my realization that the person at fault was someone else, not you and not even Romain. That person started it all. Maybe by eliminating him, I will exorcise the demon within.

Your damaged goods, Blain

As I reread the letter, it didn't take long to realize who Blain was talking about. It had to be Khalid, one more surrogate father, indeed the first. Now I have a huge dilemma. How to intervene. Not that I care whether Khalid is dead or alive. But I do care whether Blain goes to prison for attempting to even up the score. If I alert him, he'll set a trap for her. Catch her in an attempt to kill him, thwart it with the help of his nasty security people, and have her arrested and charged with attempted murder (aided by my having informed him that that was indeed her intention). He hated both twins and would have cherished ruining one of them.

I knew that Father Joseph and Sister Agnes had returned to Portland and I called them and asked that they keep an eye out for Blain and watch Khalid's apartment for any sign of her until I could get there. They readily agreed, one watching the apartment, and one Khalid's office downtown. I flew to Portland immediately.

When I arrived at the Portland airport, walking through the terminal I saw a television monitor with the local evening news. The announcer was saying, "The police have shot and killed a driver at a stop light." Our city is very civilized, very liberal, and very tolerant. It's one dark mark is that the police have a penchant for harassing dark-skinned motorists at stop lights late at night. I would have walked past if there wasn't also an interview with someone who had been at the scene. It was Blain. She told of being abducted by the man whose intention was to molest and kill her she said. The driver in question was of course Khalid. At a red light which he didn't stop for, he was quickly followed by a police car. This is what I have pieced together since: Having Blain tied up in the trunk, he decided not to stop. Since he was a wealthy man and driving a pricey Mercedes he assumed the police would be deferential. Bad assumption. When he was finally chased down by two additional squad cars, he was treated according to the color of his skin. They assumed he'd stolen the car. When they requested his driver's license and registration, Khalid became indignant and flustered. He'd left the apartment without his wallet and when he reached into the glove compartment to get the registration, a pistol belonging to one of his security thugs was in view of the police, one of whom gripped the back of his neck and pressed his face hard against the walnut dashboard. It must have been some combination of the pain and indignity of the policeman's act, with the thought that he was driving a luxury car and therefore should be immune to treatment like this, but something in Khalid snapped and in a blind fury he reached for the pistol and in return received enough bullets fired into his suspicious dark skin to kill an elephant.

As I said, all of this was pieced together later.

When I arrived at the Brewery, I was relieved to find Blain in the company of Joseph and Agnes. She seemed to be in a mild state of delirium. She was talking about God. When I finally understood her, I realized that it was not delirium at all but a mirthful account of her adventure.

"God saved me by doing the dirty work himself, saving me from a life in prison."

When she saw me she said, "While I was lying in the trunk of Khalid's car, listening to the gunshots, and it seemed like a hundred, with each one I felt one more degree of release from my demons."

We retreated to my room. Blain was exhausted, but she said, "Tell me about Leanda. What did she want of you? What's going to happen between you two?"

When I told her about the man in Leanda's life and her new attitude since the removal of her scars, Blain said:

"Good, I hated having to compete with my own mother for you. You seem very accepting of the end of the relationship. I think as soon as her scars were gone, she interested you less. I think perfection bores you and imperfection intrigues you."

"That does seem to be the case doesn't it?"

"Yes, and I'm about the most imperfect person you'll ever find, ex-assassin, no artistic gifts, and the murderer of my own father."

Now that the immediate crises were over, I felt a familiar mood arriving, torpor following terror. I was exhausted. What was next? Blain took care of that. She was wiggling out of her clothes with the efficiency of a snake, like old skin, useless now. Seeing her standing with late afternoon sun lighting her, as smooth and exquisite as one more marble sculpture, her red hair and her red hair luminous in the light, I felt the familiar nudge of idea taunting me, some vague vision of theater and movement. It took the form of a giant red-haired naked figure, large enough for others to emerge from, a huge papier mâché babe center stage.

Blain was in meltdown mode from fatigue. She was unwashed from days of pursuit of Khalid and confrontation with Khalid and physically fighting him off as he bound her to take her elsewhere to eliminate her permanently from his greedy existence. She was sticky and smelly and I said, "You're sticky and smelly."

Half unconscious from fatigue she muttered, "Good, stick to me forever and smell me. I have nothing to hide from you. Turn me inside out if you wish. I belong to you as much on the inside as outside. My brain and my body are so tied to you, that you could wear me like a second self. I'd complement all your artist's sensitivity with my pure blunt Blain animalism. I could stop speaking from now on and make only grunting guttural noises and you'd understand me perfectly. I've already said all I need to say to you."

Indeed, if what went on next was the soundtrack of a television nature special, one would think, "How courageous of this film crew to put themselves in such proximity to so dangerous an interaction of so ferocious a species. And Blain was right, there were no lines drawn between us. What is it that made this so desirable to me, so valuable, so steeped in sticky truth? Is it that I'm closer to her than I could ever be to myself because of the pretentious posturing of art? Do I find myself in her? If my art is a search for myself, and that search reveals less than this, what is art? What is this? How to even define it? Should I even try? The short answer is no. The long answer is a long way off. As I gave myself over more and more to this context of existence, I asked myself if I was capable of killing people as Blain had done so inevitably? Killing is killing and is not right, even if it was necessary and the other party deserved it. But if Blain is part me and I part her? Are Blain and I so connected I've absorbed her? No, she's still there before me. Has she absorbed me? Perhaps as narrator I could be absorbed, then she could finish the story. But that's wistful thinking.

In the morning, I woke to familiar voices. Rich voices and one was singing. It was Mojobe responding to Waldeebe One who had been lamenting at her for something She'd done. But the force and clarity and belief in Mojobe's voice showed that after all this time back in Niger, Mojobe had emerged as the force to be reckoned with in their little family. And family it was. I heard the voices of small children.

When Blain and I emerged from my room we were happily surprised to see not only the returnees from Niger but also Rasputin and Aimee. They all said the same thing, they sensed something important was about to happen and they wouldn't be left out. All this fit into my scheme for a production to acknowledge what had gone on among and between all of us since, well, since Ada mysteriously walked into our lives so many dozens of months ago. All we were missing now was Ada. And Vladimir. As if my thoughts had the power of Marconia's, that very evening we received word that Ada was on her way from San Francisco and Vladimir and Marconia were indeed also on route to Portland.

Ada had brought with her a fellow dancer, whose gender and ethnicity were not immediately clear, but what was clear was that Ada was enamored of this exquisite person. She, it turned out, was Latte, a name provided by Ada. Latte was androgynous in build, and as her name suggested, coffee-colored softened by a creamy tint. She was part Cherokee, part Jamaican, and part Swedish, the latter influence providing hair lighter than her skin color. Her eyes are a pale gray, too light to look into without feeling totally disarmed. Ada had met her match in cheekiness. By evening Latte had asked Blain if she'd spend the night in their bed with Ada.

"I don't mean for sex (unless of course, you would like that), but because Ada has said so much about you I wanted to be with you two together to experience what Ada has described as an ineffable ephemeral connection whose moment would affect the rest of my life."

Neither Blain nor I could decide if she was actually serious or had just picked up some of Ada's humor. Both, it turned out.

Blain, who was never about to be flummoxed (although Lucrezia came close) said in response, "Sure, if Stephen can be there. He's the narrator, and without him no one would know it happened."

Everyone was stunned to hear Blain refer to me by name, which no one in the company had ever done before. It was her declaration of the status of our relationship. Total silence prevailed, until Blain said, "Yes."

Latte registered a light-hearted puzzlement, "But surely, we'd all know it happened."

Blain, now sure of her terrain, said, "But that's less important than seeing it in the context of the story."

"The story?"

"When you've been with Ada for a while you'll understand."

So, it was Latte who was a little flummoxed, but in good humor, she just looked over at Ada and raised her eyebrows.

Later Blain told me, "If I'd accepted Latte's invitation, if I had gotten in bed with her and her exotic exquisiteness, I would have killed my sister, if necessary, to keep Latte to myself till the end of time. Can you imagine how she smells? Tastes? What kind of coloring there is in her intimate places? What kind of drama there is in her androgyny?"

I looked at her for some sign of levity, but there was none. I was reminded once again of how tentative life is.

Two months of obsessive work passed and the company was about to premier our magnum opus, God's Kettledrum. The dance movements most characteristic of each of the players were the prevailing choreography: Sister Agnes and Father Joseph, Rasputin and Aimee, Mojobe and Waldeebe One, Vladimir, Marconia and the pagan cult, and of course Ada and Blain.

On opening night, at the theater reserved for our performance, the stage was bare except for a large pink curvilinear form, the sensual form of Ada/Blain from top of thighs to belly button, with a bright red triangle surrounding a narrow vertical opening that a performer could emerge from with some spreading of the arms. From the beginning of the performance, each act ended with the players entering the Ada/Blain sculpture out of view of the audience so that the anatomical significance was saved for last. And in each act Ada or Blain or both had an obvious influence on the movements of the players and the meaning of the act. The finale brought players emerging one by one from the five-foot crimson vulva, each enclosed in a gauzy chrysalis glowing pink to red to pink from a neon tube within the fabric wrap.

The audience was wildly responsive with shouts of "Bravo", and the subsequent reviews were glowing.

We were invited to New York, to perform on Broadway. It was scheduled for the following spring. So we were taking a break for a few weeks.

Out of the blue one evening, Blain said, "I need to talk to you about Latte."

"Latte?"

"Yes, we've been together, casually, a few times and I said nothing to you. I can't get her out of my mind."

"Casually?"

"It's too complicated to explain."

"What about Ada?"

"Ada wants to marry you."

"What?"

"You remember, from the beginning, Ada said she wanted to marry you, and I said I wanted to be your mistress."

Determined to unravel this whole plot I said, "Why does Ada want to marry me?"

"Because she's in love with your choreography. She knows there are great choreographers out there who would love to work with her, but she believes you're the only choreographer for her. Something she couldn't admit until she came into her own as a world-class dancer. Now she believes the real creativity lies ahead. She trusts you totally, and wants you to concentrate only on her."

"Why hasn't she told me this?"

"She's been confused. We've all been confused, Ada, Latte, and me. Too confusing a mix of art, passion, and plot."

"Plot? What are you talking about?"

"Look, you're the one who's always talking about the "story" of all this, of all our lives."

"But that was when I was only the narrator."

"True, but you're still the narrator, you're just not only the narrator."

"And what about you?"

"I will be your mistress, your lover."

"And what about Latte?"

"She will be my lover."

"And what about Ada?"

"We all know that Ada's first and only love is dance."

"But why should I marry Ada?"

"Because it's a contract. Ada needs it to give herself over to you to form her dance for her, to form her. She knows she has genius, about that she is confident, but she has come to realize that she needs you to form the dark edge of her art that corresponds to the dark edge of her life, of our lives, hers and mine. It's that she needs to give expression to in her dance, her art."

Several times I opened my mouth to make an objection or ask a question, but I didn't. It was shaping into too incontrovertible an idea. But the thought that bothered me is whether Blain was telling the truth about Ada, or was just using the situation to fulfill her obsession with Latte, to have her to herself. Ada and I needed to have a talk. And I would confirm here to perceptive readers that, yes, I am indeed slipping back into my role as only narrator of what's happening around me. Just when I was beginning to think I was emerging as the architect of my own life.

"Ada dear, have you and Blain and Latte been choreographing musical partners behind my back?"

"What do you mean?"

"I mean, do you want to marry me?"

"Oh, how romantic, after all these years, my dream come true. Is this a proposal?"

I could feel irritation seeping in at the notion of being set up by Blain.

"No, it's not a proposal. It's a question about what you three have been plotting as the next chapter in all our lives."

"Oh that."

"Yes, that."

"Ok, I assume Blain has told you that I need you in order to fulfill my potential as a dancer, right?"

"Precisely."

"Can you really imagine me admitting that, even if it were true?"

"Is it true?"

"I just said I couldn't admit it even if it were true."

"Fine. So what about getting married?"

"What about it?"

"Blain mentioned marriage as a contract between you and me."

"What kind of contract?"

"One that commits us to each other as dancer/choreographer partners."

"That sounds good."

"Then why don't we just have a professional contract? Why get married?"

A flicker of seriousness appeared in Ada's expression. She was silent for a moment and then opened her mouth but no words came out. Finally, she made her statement, looking at me with her characteristic defiance.

"For two reasons, first because I've wanted to marry you since I was fifteen..."

"I thought that whimsy disappeared a long time ago."

"It never disappeared, I love you, it was just set aside for other things, my dancing mostly, which is my second reason for getting married. We both know that with the content we'll bring to the form of my dancing, we'll be saying important things to the world."

Listening to Ada, I knew that what she was saying was true, and as an artist, it excited me, but remembering my conversation with Blain I said, "And what about this business of Blain being my mistress after you and I are married?

"That's okay, I wouldn't be jealous."

"And Latte? Latte being Blain's lover?"

"That's Okay too, Latte's like tiramisu, you can't have too much at one sitting, too rich. Besides, everything she gives to me and takes from me contradicts my dancing which must be pure assertion."

"And if we get married, what about sex?"

"That's what married people do."

I was pleased to see the old playful Ada (or I should say the young playful Ada) revived, so I continued in the same vein.

"Yes, but we've never been together intimately. In fact, I've never even seen you naked."

"Oh, that's an omission we can correct easily enough. You've always admired my beautiful long red hair, right? Well, my pubic hair is as pretty, yes?"

Her easy transition into a playful Lucrezia alarmed me.

"Only caught a fleeting glimpse in Rome," I said lamely.

"Want to see? It can be part of my dowry."

Again, perceptive reader, you don't need my narration to picture what transpired during the charming and playful presentation of Ada's dowry. I'll only say that all the grace and sensuality of her dancing were put on stage to display my wife to be. In fact, not only did my narration seem unnecessary, I seemed unnecessary, as though life had gone full circle and was once again pulling me randomly with irreverent currents across an arbitrary sea, a sea wherein I could only float and observe and narrate what appears and disappears, in a life it seemed, with no dearth of events worthy of my observations.

HISTRIA
BOOKS

Addison & Highsmith

Other fine works of fiction available from Addison & Highsmith Publishers:

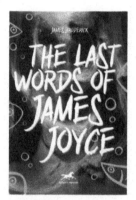

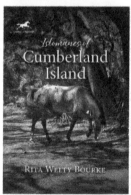

For these and many other great books visit
HistriaBooks.com